GRAVE TRADE

STEVEN LEWIS

To Edward
Ste

GRAVE TRADE

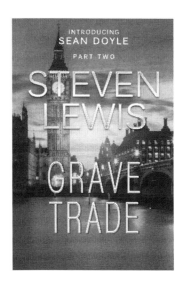

GRAVE TRADE

BOOK TWO
OF THE DUET
THE HOMECOMING
by
Steven Lewis
A Sean Doyle novel

RIGHTS

CONCLUSION

Homeless Bones conclusion.

It took him a minute to get down, sitting for a moment, he slipped into the water – it was cold and it took his breath away on entry, but somehow it eased the pain. Five minutes it took him to doggy paddle with the one hand across the canal, two rats and an otter overtook him. Thirty minutes later after the explosion Sean was back in the makeshift container that he called home.

'Fuck! I knew it'd be a shiner, and it's probably one of the best I've ever had,' he said out loud while looking in the mirror, delicately pressing his left swollen cheek. Still in the half-completed container, he slowly undid the crisp plastic wrapping on the crepe bandage. Couple of bits of surgical tape stuck ready on the back of hand. He rolled the clean material around his torso, covering up the purple and yellow markings. He thanked the gods he hadn't punctured a lung.

The explosion had severely winded him, plus set back the hip repair a couple of months. The phone rang.

'Sean Doyle,' he answered, still examining the cuts and bruises in the mirror.

'Sean, we're waiting, are you coming for tea, like we arranged? It's all ready.'

'Ann, I r ... real...' He gulped stopping himself, coming back into "normal" society, remembering the invite, and memories of the regiment, you come out of action; no excuses to be a civilian, that's what made you a soldier and not a gangster.

'I've prepared your favorite, lad. Ten minutes, Seany, spag bol – like Mary used to make it, with extra sauce and thinly sliced real Italian salami.'

'I'm coming o...' Sean realised he was no longer talking to anyone.

Bandage off, a quick painful shower then the bandage was back on and hidden with a clean shirt, courtesy of Ann, when she had ambushed him going to the launderette.

An hour and I'll be out there, he reassured himself, resigned to visiting Ann, either that or days of ... well, he knew what, and to be fair he was hungry.

The two-hundred-metre walk again and Sean was close enough to the flat to hear voices, and not just Ann's and her husband's, several, over a dozen at least.

'Shush, he'll be here in a minute,' whispered Ann.

At first he decided to decline the offer and actually turned away, but curiosity got the better of him. And he was in some pain, a rest would be a good idea, and Ann was right, spag bol was his favourite. *Knock! Knock!* his hand was on the handle. 'Ann, you in, it's Sean?'

The hallway was dark.

'For he's a jolly good fellow, for he's a jolly good fellow, and so say all of us... ...'

The flat was rammed. Ann and Danny met him at the door. 'Happy birthday, Sean.' She leaned forward, kissing his cheek, a wet sloppy one, an old aunt's kiss. He raised his eyebrows, and she gave a smile back, aware he was not annoyed but secretly happy.

'All the best, Sean, get this down yah,' said Danny, offering him a cold bottle of Becks. 'Sean!' was shouted from somewhere.

']ohn!' He acknowledged with a short wave.

People started rallying around the birthday boy. He was shocked. He hadn't celebrated a birthday for well over ten years, not even in the army. He didn't even remember today was his birthday, there had been so much going on.

He hadn't really moved anywhere yet, but somehow had ended up in the kitchen, people still greeting him.

'Hey, birthday boy, I can't stay, I'm flying out tonight.' Sean spun around just as Nash was finishing his story. 'I wanted to come and say welcome back properly and drop off these finished drawings for your tin can, and for your birthday, I'll chuck in an air conditioning unit, like I said the other day.' Nash gave Sean a one-armed man hug, not too close, but meaningful. He slipped a small box into Doyle's pocket, then gave a small slap on his shoulder. Sean looked him up and down. 'Where the fuck you going? Some good gear you're wearing.'

'Dress to impress, that's me,' replied Nash.

'Who, you trying to impress then? The fucking Queen?'

'The Prime Minister actually, and a lord, the old council are putting on a bit of a show. This lord, he wants to get into property "water front" and expensive.' replied Nash.

'You're shitting me?' Sean was openly gobsmacked. He

threw his arms around his mate again. 'Tell me all when you get back. Thanks for coming. And we need a real catch-up,' farewell over, Sean turned again.

'I didn't know it was your birthday.' The sweet voice came from his left, but he saw no lips moving. Ann forced her way through, bringing along the sweet voice.

'Lisa,' said Sean.

'Hello again, Mr Doyle, how old are you then?' she knowingly teased him, and then she leaned in to kiss his cheek. Her hand slid along his ribs as she fell into him. 'Arrr,' he muttered, creasing slightly.

'Sorry, someone bumped me,' apologised Lisa.

'Not your doing, something I did earlier, don't worry about it.' His face showed the pain.

He smiled but had to think: how had she got here? Why was she invited to his surprise party, he remembered what Ken had said? But he was also glad she had come.

'Sean, catch,' shouted Danny. He was going to approach but he noticed Lisa and mingled instead.

'Thanks,' came out of his mouth, his head went back as his hands came up, catching another bottle of Becks.

'You're very popular, judging by the number of guests, but not liked by everyone it seems.' Lisa relieved him of the bottle he had just saved. She ran it under the cold tap then opened it. He looked at her a little puzzled. 'Your face.' She touched the swelling.

He felt her fingers and they seemed to heal him temporarily. 'HAH, got yah, you mean this.' His hand pointed to the black eye. 'Nothing just a ...'

She stopped him short by raising her eyebrows. Her calf muscles came into play increasing her 5ft 4 to 5ft 7, allowing her to peck him on the cheek, right below the bruise.

'Goodnight Mr Doyle, I must go on my rounds, no rest for the wicked,' she poked her tongue out at him, 'Enjoy the rest of your party. I really have to go.' Slipping away into the many hot sweaty bodies, her tiny frame was soon out of his sight.

'I didn't know you knew Lisa,' remarked Ann.

'Just met her the other day, she does something with the homeless people. She was in cardboard city,' Sean was talking to Ann but still looking for Lisa.

'She's caught your eye, I see ... you like her, don't you? Your mother would have approved. She's a lovely girl with a big heart.' Ann's hand went up and gently pinched Sean's cheek.

'My mother, Ann, what do you know of my mother?'

1

MY DAUGHTER - MY WORLD

'Please ... brigadier, please, could you wait out here, sir, just let us do our jobs, please? I understand what she means to you...' The nurse had her palms pushed flat against Charles's chest pushing him back with both hands and also using half her body weight to ensure his compliance. He stopped when the words finally registered with him. She let go and didn't hang around; she followed the trolley catching up with the rest of the crash team. The pair of swinging black rubber doors settled, kissing each other in the middle.

Charles reluctantly did what was asked of him and remained still as he watched her catch up to his world, his square face covering the small round window. The hospital was busy and loud, full of voices and machines orchestrating strange high pitched noises, but all the brigadier heard was the voice of his little Tanya at six years old, refusing to be carried on his shoulders as they crossed China. The nurse had been correct and he knew that he would be nothing but a hindrance inside the theatre, but unlike the doors he didn't settle.

A small boy and his mother stared at him as he punched the wall twice. His knuckles started bleeding yet there was no acknowledgement of pain verbally or written on his face. The mother quickly turned the boy's head away. Charles wasn't in uniform he was dressed in civilian clothes but immaculately presented. He wanted to punch the wall again, but no, he stopped himself. The mother turned her head again her son was now two feet away from Charles, she was up off the chair and rushing over.

'Well, thank you my little man.' Charles relieved the tin of Cola from the young boy. 'You looked like you were sad mister and when I'm sad a drink of Cola always makes me happy. Does your hand hurt, mister?'

'I was sil...'

'Come on, Lance.' Her hand grabbed her son's hand and cupped it, now locked like a magnet. 'Let's leave the nice man alone, he's busy. Come on son let's sit down again.' Her second hand was now on the lad's shoulders already turning him away.

'He's okay... a sweet kid, and well mannered,' said Charles, offering the tin up.

'No, we must go. Sorry to have troubled you sir,' nervously replied the young mother. Charles may have not been in uniform but the clothes he wore clearly informed people of his status and stature.

'Your mother knows best and get yourself another Cola.' Charles passed over a two-pound coin; the lad ran off. 'You have a great boy there, you must be really proud,' added Charles. The boy was at the vending machine. The mother started crying in front of the brigadier. 'Are you okay?'

'Sorry, really I am, and you clearly have your own

concerns, excuse me.' She turned away, her fingers wiping the rolling tears.

'I have things under control,' said Charles. The mother turned back and looked at his bleeding knuckles.

He quickly covered one hand with the other. 'Nearly under control.' He gently laughed. She cried again and at the same time tried to acknowledge his comment. Charles offered a cotton handkerchief.

'Thank you.'

'What is wrong with him and why does he have the pipes up his nostrils?' enquired Charles. A moment of silence as she attempted to gather herself. With a couple of sniffles her nose was blown on the cotton. She pulled her blouse straight and her hand brushed through her hair with some determination, like somehow, if her hair was put right, she would be put right.

'He has a chest infection, but he was born with a rare condition which makes his immune system faulty, and it works at less than eighty per cent.' She had to swallow a lump. 'So, when he gets ill, I...' She cried again when the lad returned, she quickly sniffled followed by wipes across her eyes and another blow on the cotton, the handkerchief was offered back.

'Please... keep it I have plenty.' Charles hands were out with the palms down.

'Thank you.' She pocketed the material.

'Are you peeling onions again, Mum? I will be alright, you'll see.' The lad looked up, all the way into the brigadier's eyes. 'My mum cries a lot, sir, and she worries about me, but she shouldn't, I have everything I want.' He took hold of her hand; she swallowed another lump.

'It's a mother's job to worry about her children and a

very important one. You will understand one day when you're a dad with your own children.'

This set the mother off crying again. He watched the young lad squeeze his mum's fingers.

'What must you be thinking of me, sir?' She pulled out the handkerchief again.

'I'm thinking what a wonderful mum you must be to have raised a fine young man like this one here.' And he ruffled the lad's hair.

'Come on Lance that's us they're calling,' informed the mother. She had spotted the receptionist waving over to her.

'Nice to have met you, mister.' Lance followed his mum, then broke away from her and ran back to Charles, 'Your change.' And he slid the fifty pence into the brigadier's hand. Charles opened his fingers the silver coin lay there as the boy ran back; the brigadiers hand closed again. Amazed he had been given the change.

The crash team had completed their initial assessments; Tanya was stable for the moment – hospital stable – not regular life.

'What do we have here then, Sister?' confidently enquired the consultant, the doors closing behind him.

'A 30-year-old female, usually healthy and very fit with no past medical history and no recent trauma, well none we are aware of. She is on no regular medication or taken any recreational drugs, yet a relative, her father in fact, states she is having a lupus attack.' The nurse stopped reading the file and looked to the consultant.

'Let's see then shall we team?' The consultant walked over to the bed where Tanya was wired and tubed up.

The brigadier remained outside. He was speaking into his phone after composing himself now the lad had gone. 'Tom, sorry to have had you pulled out of a meeting, but it's happened... Tanya is in hospital now and I fear it may kill her like you warned us.'

'Brigadier, Charles my friend, listen to me. If you remember at the time I gave you that prognosis it was only as an outside possibility, a worst event if you like, and that possible outcome decreased with every month she didn't have a flare up. Charles, it has been close to two years with no signs of this cursed disease! Never mind a flare up. If you also recall I stated that the blood transfusions had worked exceptionally well.' His words rested with the brigadier.

Tom was one of the leading consultants in the world who specialised in blood disorders. After Tanya was told that all her siblings had died from lupus, Charles stopped at nothing to ensure she received the best treatment.

She may not have been his child by blood – but by God she was his daughter. After the discovery that she may have some form of lupus, she spent three days at the clinic in New York. A full check-up was carried out and she underwent full body blood cleaning and transfusions. Tom and his team had discovered an underlying condition which did indeed present as lupus. Yet when it was examined closely in the laboratory it appeared as a stand-alone strain of the disease. One that was not known to the medical world. So, to correctly treat or determine the required course of action would be virtually impossible.

However, with every cloud comes a silver lining and

sometimes a golden one. Because the mechanics of this new strain were larger than the other variants it allowed scientists to produce an up to date, and much stronger, medication for the regular strain of lupus which could aid thousands of sufferers. This in return gave funding for clinical trials in which Tanya's blood would play a major part with the development. However, while the medications that were to be produced would be a fresh resource for many, they were not guaranteed to work on Tanya!

'Which hospital have you attended, Charles?'

'Kings, Tom, and I'm here ... waiting. She has just been taken through into the theatre.'

'Ah, ah, right ... that will be our Mr Williams then. He is a very good surgeon, one of the best, but he will not have a clue as to what he is up against. Even if you have told them she has lupus it won't present as the standard. I will contact him right away and have Tanya made ready for transfer to me via helicopter.'

'Thank you, Tom, thank you, and I will always be in your debt for this.' His words were soft and filled with sincerity.

'Don't think anything about it. Oh, and Charles, ... in the meantime please don't be worrying. Listen to me I am greatly confident Tanya will be back on her feet in no time. We have done a lot of research with the blood she has been donating. The most recent vaccines for the regular strain have shown positive effects on her blood to.' The call ended.

'Theatre room Nurse Hems.' The female spoke into the intercom phone fixed on the wall.

'Could I speak to Mr Williams, please, and as a matter of urgency?'

'Mr Williams, you're required and it's urgent.' She pulled out and held the receiver toward the consultant.'

'Hello, this is Mr Williams. Who is this?' He asked, immediately followed by saying thank you by mime to the nurse.

'Rufus – Tom Lockland, I apologise for the interruption of your theatre, but I have been informed that you have a Miss Tanya Howlett as your guest. Am I correct with this assumption?'

'Yes, I do indeed, Tom, how d...'

'No time to explain at the moment, I am afraid. Could I possibly be a pest and ask you to prep the patient and please would you have her ready for air transfer in a maximum of... well could we say ... twenty minutes, and if you could, be ready and waiting on the helipad, this would be a great help to us.' Tom put his thumb up through the glass, sending a message to a pilot on standby.

'Of course, we can dear chap and it will be my pleasure. Just one question though: is it a lupus attack as reported?' he asked with professional curiosity.

'Yes, it is, that's correct and a very rare strain, the first to be discovered. She is the only one in the world that we know of. I will copy you into the completed paper before publication if you would like.'

'Much appreciated, Tom, I look forward to reading it.' He moved away from the phone, the nurse turned replacing the receiver.

Mr Williams clapped his hands together three times. 'Team could I have your attention for a moment. There has been a change in plans. We will need to stabilise our patient and prep her, ready for a transfer via helicopter. We have fifteen minutes and counting, ensure the ice is close to her body, but please, at least two layers of insulation in between. We don't want any burning.' His finger tapped his wrist then pointed to the large clock on the wall.

Eighteen minutes later, a freshly washed black Lynx helicopter collected its pretty cargo and flew twelve miles. This would have been triple the distance if travelling by road in London, but this was as the crow flies. The steel bird eventually landed on a hard standing somewhere in Surrey. The landscape around the big letter H was cultivated gardens; 200 metres and you were at the rear of a grand house.

'Can you sign this, please?' asked the co-pilot, the visor on his helmet raised.

'There you are and thanks, we'll take her from here.' The paperwork was handed back.

'Here are all the clinical sheets you asked for. Her stats have remained virtually the same since we collected the patient. Temperature is still high, 39.9, even though she is well packed in ice.' The core pilot stepped away and climbed into the Lynx. He waited and watched untill the stretcher was 20 metres away; the bird was airborne again.

'No time at all to waste, let's move her straight inside people. I want her in theatre in less than twenty minutes.' Tom looked at each of the medics. His voice picked up a little, 'I cannot emphasise this enough, this is a life-or-death situation and time is of the utmost. Alan, could you get a temperature probe inserted and monitor it every minute,' said the small man in perfect English.

'Roger that,' answered the ex-military medic. Tom left the crew with their orders and made his way to the surgical prep station, he wanted Tanya in theatre ASAP, more for the monitoring ability and cooling system.

Two minutes later...

'Mr Lockland we have your patient on the ward if you would like to come and clerk her in at your earliest convenience, please.' The male nurse left a message on the doctor's answering machine.

Tom arrived at the nurses' station twenty-five minutes later. 'Peter, I am expecting a female patient and she is to be taken immediately to theatre. I will complete the paperwork later, here are her details could you register as arrived, please.'

'I left you a message on your machine. We have her here, sir, she's in room four waiting to be clerked in, she arrived five minutes ago. This is her file and here are the administration papers.'

'Thank you, Peter. I am unsure as to why sh...' he cut his own speel short and changed tact. 'Would you instigate prepping theatre room three please, and for immediate use and more so now! I want the fans on her. NOW! She was to be taken straight to the theatre from the helicopter, not brought onto the ward. Every second without cooling treatment will be an added risk to her life.' Peter was on the phone, his urgency fostered by Tom speaking like that, the nurse had never in five years heard him raise his voice. Mr Lockland walked off in the direction of the theatre.

On Tom's mind was the fateful day, just shy of two years ago when he was first introduced to Tanya.

He and a colleague were perplexed by the gene they had discovered in her blood cultures. The pair between them had over fifty years of experience in this field but neither had seen a case of lupus like Tanya's. Their hope was that they would never have to see it again. The gene that had been discovered had been altered or deformed in

9

a lab by some very clever person indeed. The prognosis was that if the altered segment of the gene became active the result would be a catastrophic lupus attack. One resulting in not only the death of its carrier, but it would also degrade the individual's DNA. In effect – It would wipe out any trace of this person at the biological level. Their building blocks of life would be diluted in hours and washed back into the face of the Earth.

Tom had decided at the time not to pass on the inevitable outcome to Charles, knowing full well Tanya was his world, plus he and his counterpart from Germany both strongly believed they would have a cure within the timeframe allowed, although they both acknowledged the wistfulness of their thoughts.

Their initial intention was to discover a way in which the gene could be stabilised or even temporarily walled off at least at cellular level, giving the experts more time to eventually eradicate it completely from her body by ensuring permanent reduction.

Tom pulled out his phone.

'Brigadier Howlett speaking.'

'Hello, Charles we have your daughter with us at the manor. Have you time to come over?'

'Of course, I can be with you in thirty minutes. How is she doing? Sorry, forgive my nerves Tom. I didn't mean to place you on the spot.' He looked at his watch.

'I can't say too much at present Charles, but I will be operating on her in less than twenty minutes, but I am telling you, both as a friend and a surgeon we are ahead of this. Our main priority is to prevent her temperature increasing which I believe we have achieved, please take a deep breath. I know how resilient a woman Tanya is, and we should be in theatre for a couple of hours at least, maybe longer depending on the number and location of the active genes.

My intent today is to simply isolate the flare up; basically, I will be buying us some much-needed time. After that I will have some news for you, and we will also have a way to go forward – and one of which I am confident will ensure a full recovery for her. So, like I said earlier there's no need for excessive worry.' Tom was speaking and reading at the same time.

'I will be waiting outside the room when you finish.' Charles was at ease after Tom's words. 'While you're on the phone could I impose and ask another question?'

'Of course,' replied Tom, looking at his watch. 'But make it quick.'

'I don't have that much in the way of, shall we say, medical information; however, I met a small boy when I was waiting for Tanya at Kings. He was wearing an oxygen pipe and a small bottle tied to his side. His mum says he had some type of low tract infection in his chest, but his immune system wasn't functioning at more than twenty percent.'

'A lower respiratory tract infection or LRTI, most likely pneumonia, not promising I'm afraid, not if his immune system is faulty and that will be most likely down to PIDDs.' Tom looked at his watch again.

'I was wondering if there was anything you could do for the lad. Such a well-mannered child and there was something about him?'

'Ask the mother to bring the patient here with his notes – we must have his notes. I will of course endeavour to alleviate his infection then look at the underlying disorder.' Tom looked again at his watch. 'I must go Charles.' And he ended the call.

Phones off Charles pressed the intercom. 'Could you contact Rupert, please Helen. Ask him if he could attend the C.O.R.B.R.A meeting in place of myself, 6 am in the morning. I will be out of communication for most of today and we better cover all of tomorrow's appointments as well... In fact, cancel my week's dairy.'

'You are to have lunch with the P.M. and his wife on Thursday, sir.'

'I'm not in the right frame of mind for that I'm afraid.'

'I will sort it all out, sir, reschedule where I can, don't give it another thought. And please give my love to Tanya, sir.'

'Of course, and thank you, Helen.' The brigadier's phone rang. 'Sir, how can I help you?' answered Charles. He knew to whom he was speaking as only one person called the ivory phone.

'I'm calling as Tony, Charles, not the P.M. I know how, damn stubborn you can be. BUT on this occasion let us all help? And plenty will rally, you mark my words, if you need anything, anything – please call me – anything my friend?'

'Thank you, Tony, and much appreciated.' A small silence then the call was over.

Charles redialled on his office phone. 'Oscar, I haven't marked any flight time, but I need to be in Surrey within the hour.' His words were passed over in general form yet translated in Oscar's head, it was an order for the helicopter, and it was confirmed and obeyed willingly as news of Tanya's illness had expanded through the organisation in which she was loved and respected by all she came into contact with. The pilot made ready.

Charles redialled.

'Mrs Barrow?' asked Charles as soon as it was answered.

'Yes, who is this?'

'I met you at the hospital earlier today you were there with your son, Lance, I recall.'

'I know who you are, the man who punches walls.'

A chuckle. 'Yes, and that's why I'm calling to apologise for my behaviour.'

'No need, Lance wasn't frightened. He said you were upset and that's why you were hitting the wall. For a young lad he has a strong ability to assess people and situations, it's frightening sometimes how accurate he is. After we came home, I heard him on the phone to his grandma telling her he had met with an army officer, telling her that he wanted to go in the army.' She slowed her voice holding back the emotions, but still they came even without invite.

Charles heard what she said, thinking, *how could he know this*? Then he spoke, 'Nevertheless your son actually did me a good turn. So, I feel the need to repay him.' Charles waited a moment as it sounded as if she was peeling onions again, as Lance had put it.

'How so?' asked the mother.

'I took the liberty of enquiring into the health of your son.'

'What? ... You did what? I'm not fully understanding, a strange man who we met for, f ... what – five minutes – who has now called me up. AND ... AND! Where did you get my number from? How did you get my number? Is this some sort of pick-up line? You trying to get in my knickers? Because...'

'Good God no w...' Charles rose, the heavy chair

scraped the floor, making the young PA outside turn to look through the office window.

Lance's mum questioned again, 'Then what? This seems a lot of effort to go to. Just to say thank you for a can of bloody Coke. I will pass on your regards to Lan...'

'This isn't going as planned. I have spoken to a consultant regarding your son, and he would like you to attend, with your son, at the private hospital in Surrey.' He beckoned the young PA to enter the office. He continued, 'It's a research hospital in Surrey one of the finest in the world.'

'Even if I wanted to go to some *posh* research centre.' her eyebrows raised along with her voice, 'How the hell would I get there? I'm a single bloody mum on benefits, living on a council estate who can't work because of the care my Lance requires.' Her angry and sarcastic but also intrigued tone wasn't interpreted by the brigadier. She started again, 'Thank you for the offer but I must decline.' She hung up and was gone. Once more peeling onions, her gaze through the bedroom door, it rested on her son, asleep laying on a bed piped up with oxygen.

'That's strange she's just hung up on me. I was trying t....' The brigadier still had the phone in his hand. 'I don't understand ... I was trying to help her son.'

'Could I interject, sir?' asked the assistant. Charles agreed with his eyes and a nod, remaining perplexed from the phone call. 'I overheard the conversation, sir; please remember she would have been worried regarding how you were able to get hold of her details.' She went quiet.

'What's your point? Speak freely.'

'Sir, she lives on one of the largest and roughest council estates in the city. She is a single mum who works two jobs and takes in ironing. And all this around looking after her poorly boy, whose father left them three years ago when the small boy received his diagnosis. No disrespect intended, sir, but your world is far from hers and if a strange man contacts you talking about, "I got your details, and do you want to go to a research centre"? Its walls up for her, survival mode or she would have thought it was a come-on line.' The conversation muted. The PA glanced to the mobile still in his hand.. 'Would you like me to try, sir? Speak to her, that is?'

'She said she didn't work. You said she worked two jobs? And yes, call her I will be out of communication so I will leave it all to you as you seem to have a handle on it. And please use my name to arrange transport for them, also if you feel it appropriate sign a hundred pounds off the book for her, again, reference the draw to my name?'

'Consider it done, sir, and please give my best to Tan... Miss Howlett.' The young assistant left after placing a folder on his desk. She was new to the department after recently completing an admin apprenticeship, one which had been designed especially for the needs of the clandestine world; the main ability was to keep a secret. Keep it as well as the Bletchley Park lot.

And the council estate to which she had referred to was also the place she was raised. Thanks to both Tanya and Sarah, Danielle had followed a path leading to a career and not prison after the death of her father, a hero who had jumped in front of a bullet to protect the brigadier.

Danielle didn't need the brigadier to give her the telephone number, she tapped - I, in her contacts for "ironing lady".

Ten minutes later. 'So you see Debbie, Charles is actually a real pukka brigadier, and a very close friend to the Prime Minister. Your Lance helped when he was in a complicated place. The brigadier was moved by his strength of mind and the fact he appeared more concerned for him, than himself, given his illness... hence the brigadier would like to help, and this is genuine he has got your little boy into one of the top hospitals in the country. His daughter is there now; sadly, she's very ill.'

'His daughter's ill? Well, I guess that explains why the colonel was punching the wall then.'

'Brigadier, he's not a colonel and he was punching the wall? Are you sure about that? I've never seen him lose his temper or even get frustrated.'

'Yes I am, he did it a few times, that's what caught our attention in the first place.'

'He's the coolest person I know but that explains the bandage on his hand, I guess.'

'Well, if his daughter had just been taken ill and if she's like you say, very ill, I guess it's understandable. We'll be ready for the car and thank you again, Danielle, hope your mum is better?'

'She is on the mend. Thank you.'

'Good, oh, your ironing's ready I'll leave it with Ruby next door.'

2

SICKNESS TABLETS

'Hello, this is your captain speaking. I would like to inform you that we will be touching down shortly in the exciting city of New York, the greatest city in the world where the lights are never turned off and the music doesn't stop. I hope you have all have enjoyed your flight and will not hesitate to fly with us again. Enjoy your stay in the big apple.' The speaker was switched off and the pilot flicked a couple of switches. 'Leave her on auto for another 200 miles JP.'

'Roger that.' The core pilot adjusted the computer before checking the weather in New York.

None of the passengers had heard a single word of the captain's descent speech. He welcomed them to New York. But none of them would see the tall lady with a lamp. All of them were dead or deep into an unconscious state. The hostess with a blonde bob and perfect cheeks walked amongst the passengers. She struggled to read the names from the planes manifest then began checking these against the seat numbers and name tags of the passengers. On sixteen of the people, she had earlier pinned a small badge in the shape of a triangle, made from brass and displaying three green bent arrows. Each one pointing to each other, top to tail. Bending over she wafted the cloud of smoke away as she felt for a pulse on the neck of one of her colleagues, then another and another.

Thirty seconds passed

No pulse felt, next her fingers pressed a small button in the middle of a cable. Her muted words didn't leave the rubber gas mask, yet the captain heard them perfectly in his earpiece. He acknowledged her confirmation with "Roger that". His next words were spoken to the co-pilot. 'Jean Paul, Caroline has reported an issue with the oxygen masks during the test. Could you go and assist her, please? Apparently, she's struggling to manually release the bottles.'

'With pleasure, Simon,' replied JP, unclipping and climbing out of the chair.

Nine seconds it took him to open and close the cockpit door. After walking for three more seconds, he smelt the toxic fumes, then he saw tiny almost transparent clouds of smoke. Only a couple of feet away from the cockpit with the aid of his vision his brain put two and two together quickly. The slumped and motionless bodies then the powerful smell persuaded him to turn back and retreat to the safety of the cockpit. On his turn the only thing offered to him was the handsome face of the captain; it appeared to be a caricature and was laughing on the other side of the small egg-shaped window. As the bottom of his fists banged hard against the sealed door the pace of the thumping slowed as the gas entered JP's throat and nostrils. It began burning upon on contact, the coughing came, then he vomited, and with each breath his lung capacity halved. Giving up his attempt at getting back into the cockpit, "get to the toilet" his brain told him, with his heart racing he about-turned as panic set in. Standing in front of him was Caroline, the five-feet-two, sexy – drop-dead gorgeous female who Jean Paul had always had a crush on. She did not move. He ran to her screaming in her face for assistance, staring at the rubberised gas mask. His lovesick puppy eyes diluted with anger and surprise.

He grabbed at her throat, but his weak and pathetic attempt made her giggle. His last living thought was *how could such a beautiful person be full of so much evil?*

She moved back one full step.

J P fell to his knees, his limp upper body had no power, his head fell leaning against her legs. Her hand pushed him aside. Keeping walking she knocked on the door of the cockpit. 'Quickly get in,' coughed the pilot, then pushed the door hard automatically re-engaging all four powered locks.

The pilot started to cough into his arm. Caroline pulled at her face to remove the mask followed by her uniform. Stepping out of her navy skirt and white blouse she rammed them into the plastic bag then drew tight the seal trapping in the nauseous gas. She looked at the pilot who was holding open another bag, this one bright yellow and twice as thick as the first with a clinical seal zip.

'Simon, we've done it. We've pulled it off. I'm so happy.'

He passed her a bundle of fresh clothes as she dropped the plastic contaminated bag and he zipped up the yellow liner now full of her uniform. He looked up and she was stood in front of him scantily dressed in her underwear. Her body so perfectly curved the feline figure was too much for him. His pupils expanded.

'Do you really want me to get dressed?' she teased, and stood knowingly like a virgin, her hands in front moving slightly, shoulders forward and rounded one knee bent, her body slowly moving side to side, her stunning eyes looking up to him. His left hand went behind her head his fingers travelling through the short, soft blond hair – his right hand down the back of her French knickers pulling her towards him.

'You drive me crazy Caroline, you're so s...'

'I'm all yours. And will be forever when we get married.' She gently nibbled at the lobe of his ear, her tongue venturing inside.

He groaned pulling her into him – tighter and tighter, the fingers of his right hand exploring between the perfectly formed cheeks. The foreplay was well underway the temperature rising – the planes radio totally ignored as he came as close to eating someone as you could get.

'FLIGHT 47 47 5 - ARE YOU RECEIVING, OVER?'

'FLIGHT 47 47 5 - ARE YOU RECEIVING, OVER? OVER???'

Simon spun Caroline around. She firmly pushed backwards into his groin. He pulled at Caroline's hair telling her how excited he was his...

'Flight 47 47 5 - are you receiving us, over? We have received a distress call. Please respond before we instruct further action, over, over.' On the ground the well-formed voice was becoming anxious.

'Fuck me! Fuck me, Simon! I love your cock, your big cock,' loudly begged the blonde hostess, her words morphing into moans as her bottom pressed harder against him.

'FLIGHT 47 47 5 - THIS IS THE JFK CONTROL CENTRE. We will not try again to contact you, please reply immediately ... ... or we will hand control over to the air force authorities. They will bring down your plane – respond – respond immediately, over!' All in the control centre held their breath in unison as they waited, half in prayer and the other half in denial, or disbelief, of the events. Yet they were desperate for a response trying hard to fight back the thoughts of – 9 / 11 as the thoughts were still fresh.

Simon penetrated Caroline and fucked her hard over the control panels.

'Flight 47 47 5 – receiving, over.' came from the plane's radio, JFK had to try one last time.

'At last, Simon, we were becoming worried down here... another five minutes and you'd have been staring through the windscreen of an F22. What's happening up there? Where have you been? Over.'

He fucked her hard again and as he shot his load, he wrapped his hand around and over Caroline's mouth, his finger and thumb pinched her nostrils.

'It looks like I am the only survivor left on board. We must have had an exhaust leak or something. I don't know what's happened, I think I must have passed out myself for a moment, which is why I didn't respond earlier, sorry.'

Caroline heard the words of the pilot, realising this wasn't part of their PLAN she began to fight and for her life.

'That's right baby, fucking squirm as much as you want, I like it rough, and marry you, ha, ha, a joke, your nowt but a slapper.' He towered over the hostess and nearly twice as broad, she had no chance of escaping his grip. His cock still in her – he felt God-like power. Simon had groomed this pretty little doll over the last six months. Using romance, his all American looks, and a promise of marriage based around a new life in the United States, and along with this came the pleasure of spending the millions of dollars this escapade would yield them both.

'FLIGHT 47 47 5 - TO CONTROL I AM UNABLE TO ASSESS ANY DAMAGE, OVER.'

'RECEIVING. FLIGHT 47 47 5. Simon, will you have enough control of the craft to land her safely and alone, over?' eagerly enquired the flight controller.

'I will, I have to ... Please clear a runway for us. Seventeen minutes to hitting the tarmac, and here goes, over.'

'Roger, wilco... and good luck my friend – JFK out.' The radio went silent, but the channel remained open.

As the auto pilot was rapidly engaged Simon pressed the silver stopwatch entering the time of two minutes. He picked up Caroline's gas mask. After extending the elastic it fitted him perfectly. Cockpit door open, he dragged the unconscious hostess into the main area. As her lifeless, left foot crossed over the threshold the door automatically closed.

The pilot dropped her in front of the emergency exit. Resting on her tummy was the yellow bag. He bent over and pulled out a full body harness hidden in the meal trolley. His legs in, his arms quickly followed, and last the chest strap was pulled tight across and clipped securing him. The lanyard was secured to the steel seat legs. He drew a pistol and shot the window out. The two atmospheres attempted to equalise in seconds the yellow bag was gone. Caroline was vacuum packed into the twelve-inch square.

The wind was no longer shouting, but only for a split second before she was fired out like a circus act followed by anything not secured down. Simon had taped a towel in a square on the side of the food trolley. Knife out he cut the rope; it flew to the window staying in place aided by the suction. The pilot steadied himself before he clipped out of the harness. Oxygen masks dropped and were dangling down above every seat. He sniggered to himself thinking "*bit late*".

There were bodies all over, but all he cared about was that all the toxic gas had been completely dispersed. Fishing in his pocket, out came an oblong shaped plastic meter, complete with LED lights; these flashed intermittently, red, and amber then they both turned light green and flashed faster. He stared at the sensor: the flashing stopped and both lights were now green. He pulled the mask away from his face waiting a few seconds longer before he dared breathe, not trusting the gizmo a hundred percent, even with a green light.

Full mask off and he was now breathing naturally he returned to the cockpit door, thumb on the sensor, then came the two bleeps followed by his name and he pulled the door free the window showed his reflection, it was one of winning. As he pressed the stopwatch, there remained just two seconds. His personal best from weeks of training.

'47 47 5, to control you receiving me, over?' Simon strapped himself back in the seat.

'Control receiving, is all okay up there? Our radar has just shown you dropped drastically in altitude, nearly 6000 feet in seconds. Confirm your status, over.'

'The exit window blew out; Caroline has been lost. I found her on the floor with a pulse I was about to start first aid when the window suddenly blew, I can't explain what's happened.' Simon's voice instantly became mellow. A short silence was observed by control.

'How are you, Simon?' No "over". Personalising the communication.

'I'm good. I grabbed hold of the hostess seats and managed to keep a grip. I've fixed the window temporarily, so let us get this flying machine on the ground, over.' His tone came back from "sad" to "I'm in charge". And he felt good as the stopwatch told him Caroline's body and evidence would now be sinking in the ocean – shark food.

'Roger that, Simon. Flight 47 47 5 - you are cleared for landing. The comms will remain open until I shake your hand on the ground. All the other airborne traffic is queueing or has been diverted – you know the protocol. The show is all yours and good luck, over.' The atmosphere in the control tower became soup as the people looked at each other and prayed.

'Get that kettle on.' Simon rallied, as he took back the plane from the autopilot.

'Better than that I'll take you in the bar, my shout,' gave back Lee. The heads in the room nodded and faces smiled – adrenalin rose.

Everything became quiet, no more friendly banter, as the larger than life Boeing descended and finally reached an altitude low enough that the meal trolley fell away from the window. This was no longer a problem; in fact, it was a plus as it would ensure any remaining gas would be removed.

Simon had clear visuals of the runway. The last few hundred feet, "ground rush", came towards him so fast. Pulling up on the controls drained him. A dozen vehicles drove at speed to meet the incoming aircraft. Four fire engines shot from the sides towards where the plane had stopped and the tarmac smoked. The only damage visible from the outside was the window Caroline had previously exited by.

'All clear!' shouted the lead fire-fighter, at the same time as his hand flew up giving permission to a small powerful tug-like truck to tow the temporary stairs over to the Boeing.

Simon emerged to the applause of everyone gathered below on the tarmac.

'STOP! STOP! GET THE MEDICS UP HERE. HELP MY TEAM, PLEASE!'

'You heard the man get up there. Come on?'

Simon walked down on the right as the fluorescent jackets rushed by him on the left.

'Simon, Simon, this way mate. Come on, let's get you checked out and I owe you a drink remember.' The bear-like Lee threw his arm around the neurotic pilot who had begun to physically shake.

Simon walked to one of the many waiting ambulances stationed 150 metres away from the aircraft. Parked in the designated safety zone in case the plane burst into flames. The rear doors of the emergency vehicle were open and welcoming.

'I don't know what happened – It was w... wa... all so fast. Just not sure ... what went wrong. All was well one minute, it was, everything was standard, checks completed and everyone had been served their meals, I gave the descent speech, the next thing I knew all hell was upon us, I can't explain it any other way. The co-pilot and th... an... she was g...' Simon shook, producing tears whilst sitting on the edge of the stretcher. He rambled on, his years in drama class as a young man, in college, were at last paying off for him. While he played the unworthy hero, his hand slipped into his pocket, fingers gripped the round tube, his thumb pressed down on the top.

The cockpit exploded. The Boeing cracked in two at the neck. The main body separated from the plane, some of the outer shell and window cases fell, smouldering, onto the ground. The cockpit immediately became an inferno, powerful flames shooting into the air. Everyone hunched over covering their heads as the flames roared into the semi-dark night. Even at the safety zone the vehicles shook. Black smoke filled the area. Lee the controller looked at the paramedic then at Simon.

The whole scene changed in seconds as the firemen reacted in an instant. A six-inch ridged hose aimed at the aircraft started pumping thousands and thousands of litres of foam. The flames were extinguished in less than a minute; it took longer for the foam to stop flowing. Thankfully, none of the medics had been hurt – stunned, grazed, bruised, but not really injured.

'Do you want to sit back and put your feet up? Relax, you're a hero.' The female medic rubbed Simon's shoulder.

'No, no, let me out. I need to get to my plane, see if the rest of my crew are okay. Let me out, please, I need to help. I can't just sit here, get off me!' His abdominals crunched bringing his torso forward; feet on the floor, he was off.

'Stop him, someone grab him!' she shouted.

The bear-man spun quickly and caught the pilot with his arm outstretched like a prop-forward.

'Come on, Simon, let the medics do their job. It's a lot to take in, I know. We'll inform you the moment we have any news. It's going to take a while longer after that explosion.' Lee, slowly turned the upset man around and began walking him back to the ambulance, still talking away as two police officers approached them both.

'We will need to have a word with you, sir. Could you come with us, please?' The officer spoke politely, but with authority, his arm out towards Simon.

'Are you mad, man? Can't you see he needs to be checked out. He's just brought a plane down single-handed – lost his crew – and now just watched as his plane was torched,' defended Lee, his arm out towards the burning cockpit – as if it needed pointing out.

'He's going nowhere, not until I give the, all clear,' stated the paramedic.

Simon was back on the stretcher still very agitated. His hands came away from his face. The tears started to flow, his college drama again paying off perfectly. He pushed the bits of onion further under his thumb nails. His external façade was broken – tired and away from reality. Internally he patted himself on the back for such a great performance. Both the officers retreated ten feet, they spoke to each other as they guarded the back door of the emergency vehicle.

3

THE DE PEN COURT ESTATE

Continuous water fell from the dull, two-tone sky. It hadn't stopped for three days and three nights. But that's just Scotland, so beautiful a place, but always being washed.

The De Pen Court estate was quiet. The native birds ran from the cover of the shrubbery seizing the opportunity of a meal as the earth worms appeared through the soft ground.

'Get a shift on woman, we have ten for breakfast.'

'Ten, ten ... why ten?' She turned from the oven.

'Builders have been rained off from working on the stables, its coming down faster and it's not gunna stop today. They're just pulling sheets over the roof as we speak. You wanna see the state of the walls with the cement being washed from the joints. Lady De Pen court has asked if we can feed and water them, dry 'em off. And in return John said they'll bring all the clobber down from the loft rooms, ready for the annual charity auction at the hall this Saturday. That'll save us a lot of back-break luv. I'm still hurting from last year.' The 6 foot 7 man walked over and bent and kissed Alice on the top of her head. 'You smell nice,' he told her, sniffing at her hair.

'It's medicated dandruff shampoo.' Her head shook but she was happy, especially as of late he hadn't been so keen, but they had recently adopted a teenager. Her lips formed again, 'Geraway wit' ya, ya big oaf.'

He slapped her bottom, saying nothing, and turned away. He walked a couple of feet then bent right over, half his right size fifteen shoe was on the first step – It began the climb of the 13th century narrow stairs, fifteen in total taking him back into the main residence.

At the back of the kitchen Alice walked through the solid wooden door to the walk-in larder with thick stone walls and floor, with the tiniest window at the back and rummaged through the stores.

'Six builders for breakfast... and at this short notice. Plus, our four. What am I, a magician?' she muttered as if this were a chore, but she loved the fuss. And with the builders came the joy and plenty of banter and they filled up the swear jar. She grabbed another bacon back and moved over to the slicer.

Upstairs in the main residence the fire roared, forcing the heat into the large drawing room. In the far corner Lady De Pen Court dropped small live fish into the glass tank. Nessie, her hybrid croc swallowed them whole. She smiled as her unique creature splashed the water with its tail thanking her for the food or at least that is what she believed.

A gold and porcelain art-deco telephone rang on the desk. 'Lady De Pen Court.'

'I, I, I've some g ... g ... good news ... for ... regards your child.' Dr Moe failed to pull off confidence.

'Speak to me, man, do not mumble. I cannot abide

weak people, and especially males. Pull yourself together and then address me again.' She shaped her fingers one by one around the crystal glass waiting for the caller's second attempt.

'The American team have been ma'am.' He took in a good breath. 'And the transfusion has taken place like promised.' Another breath and a small pause, 'Monitoring has taken place through the night which has convinced me that the implant was very successful and will remain this way. I am so excited to tell you that you now have a child who is carrying your bloodline. And b...'

Emma didn't wait for him to finish she ended the call, smiled, finished the malt, and spoke loudly. 'Alaskin!'

'Yes, Lady De Pen Court,' said the giant, standing next to the door.

'I will be leaving immediately for London. I will require the car to take me to the airport.' She didn't look at him.

'Right away, Lady De Pen Court.' Alaskin left. She dialled a number.

'The Plaza Hotel, Kelly Carr speaking – how can I help you?'

'Kelly, what a lovely surprise to hear your voice, I wasn't aware you took a turn on the desk.'

'Lady De Pen Court. I fill in for breaks, ma'am. I am trying to become a permanent account holder and establish my own list.' Kelly had subconsciously straightened her posture whilst speaking to her idol.

'I will be in need of two night's stay as from this evening, Kelly. I do appreciate the short notice therefore a different room would be acceptable on this occasion.'

'Of course, ma'am but I will have your Chatsworth Suite ready for you.'

'Perfect, just perfect. And if you succeed in retaining my room, I may have a word with Mr Lockington regards moving my account.' Call ended. She made a second call whilst holding a photograph of a teenage girl, short, with hundreds of freckles and two red pigtails.

'We will be leaving in five minutes be ready I want it done today!' Receiver replaced, the photo was put back in a file then locked away.

Alaskin was sitting in the car, around the front of the house, waiting with the engine running to warm-up the Bentley.

Her ladyship had settled in the rear of the vehicle. She pressed the diamond encrusted button, and the centre divider came down.

'I will be away for two nights, Alaskin. Will you make sure Nessie is fed, and maybe a water change? That's if you have the time, of course.' She looked into the rear-view mirror.

'Yes, ma'am,' he answered with his negative monotone words. His brain wanted to say "NO". He looked at his hand – his left hand: it was minus two fingers from the knuckles down and the skin had yet to fully heal.

Emma's unique Nessie had been created in lab a year previously by Dr Moe. He had altered the genetics of two types of crocodile and a Komodo dragon. The offspring of these reptiles were then subsequently bred several times with seals. The stem cells from this reptile / mammal's dead babies were used to alter a young Kaman's DNA sequence. It took six months and fifty attempts before this was successfully spliced with a giraffe giving the world a real Loch Ness monster.

Alaskin altered the rear-view mirror. Catching her gaze, he grunted a reply. His frightening stare re-appeared and locked in the mirror as he drove down the quiet country lane.

'What are you looking at?' she questioned.

'There's a van behind us, ma'am. And I don't recognise it as a local vehicle or the driver.'

He slowed the Bentley.

'And?' She was about to turn around.

'Hold tight ma'am, hold on. Now, hold on ma...' The Bentley was rammed from the rear. He regained control of the wheel. It was hit again this time from the side and just as the car left the lane going up the grass bank.

'Are you okay ma'am – ma'am?'

There was no come back from the rear seat.

Alaskin was forced to grab the wheel as the Bentley took another hit again on the driver's side. His knee was up and back down squeezing the brake pedal to the floor. The Bentley's near side was up the bank, the van in front slowed down and stopped for less than ten seconds before screeching out of sight.

'Ma'am, Lady De Pen Court, ma'am! ... answer me.' Alaskin was out the car pulling at the back door, he could see blood running down from her head.

Crack, crack, crack.

It was his knees that hit the mud first then his square over-formed chin smacked the top of the car. Like a freshly felled tree, over to the side the giant went. Three bits of lead travelling at twice the speed of sound had ripped through his back, in the area of his left shoulder blade and one round came straight through entering Lady De Pen Court.

The rifle was quickly disassembled into six pieces and fixed to the motorbike. The driver was on and sped away from the cover of the trees, the rear wheel spinning tearing the turf up.

Ten minutes later.

'Officer 34 79 to control. Are you receiving?' The copper was bent down on one knee two of his fingers on the neck of the fallen giant. His search for a pulse was unsuccessful. His senses heightened after receiving a call to respond to gun shots fired.

'Control receiving, over.'

'Sally is the inspector about?' asked officer 34 79.

'Somewhere, John, why? You can't finish early again he's getting annoyed with your efforts, or lack of them – son in law or not.'

'No, I'm not leaving early, just ask him to call me on my mobile, please and urgently. Go and find him Sally, now! Please.'

'Okay, hold yah horses John, control out.' Sally did as she was asked because of the scared voice she had just spoken with that wasn't the usual playboy John.

He clipped the radio back onto his vest, standing up with his police issue torch, his arm up high, the beam aimed down he looked through the back window. *Smash*! John's night stick went through the driver's glass. Arm in, the door open, in he went through the driver's door, his knees on the seat and arms over into the back, his shaking fingers placed on the second person's neck. He attempted to calm his own breathing.

'Yes!' he said out loud as the mobile rang and the pulse tapped back.

'John what's so urgent, it better not b…?'

'Car crash boss, just off Horse Water Lane. We have

one dead, I think, and a female with a very weak pulse. Blood everywhere and his chest has been ripped out at the front.' John suddenly felt sick as he looked from the rear of the car at parts of Alaskin's lungs stuck to the window.

'Have you called for the medics?'

'No boss not yet, I called you straightaway. Only one vehicle here and the man's been shot, that's what I responded to... the female has also been hit, and, and boss...'

'What John? Cut the suspense.'

'Lady De Pen Court and her driver Alaskin, boss, these are the victims.'

'Close off the lane. I'm on route and I'll sort the medics. No one to be near the car until we have it secured, I don't want anyone discovering their identities! And John...'

'Boss.'

'Be careful we don't know if the shooter is still around.' The inspector closed his phone.

'Will do sir,' said John into the dead phone. He then positioned his car across the north end of Horse Water Lane just as instructed.

At the station, the inspector walked into the open office. 'Sally, will you get the armed response coordinator on the line ASAP. Sam, can you get ambulance control on the phone. And do we know who's out in the area car and their current location? Update me as we walk.' He left the comms room Sam following.

'Luke and Amy are both in the big van, sir.'

'Get the pair of them over to the "T" junction at the west end of Horse Water Lane and fast. I want the road closed off, no one's to enter or leave, and inform them that they may be facing armed offenders, they're to be cautious at all times. And no bloody heroics I want everyone to be going home tonight?' rallied the inspector, at the same time as opening the wall safe in his office. 'Sally could you also call Kev, get him and his dog back to the station yesterday,' he said, pulling out two Glock 17s.

'He's back already, sir, he's having his break now. I'll go fetch him right away.' The sleepy small town cop station had been woken up. About to leave when the phone rang; she leaned over the desk. 'Sir, the armed coordinator.' She passed over the landline receiver and left quickly heading for the station's canteen.

'Inspector Shaw.'

'Chris, what's happening – you wanted a call back?' spoke the coordinator, his location 49 miles away.

'Yes, we have an incident, a shooting if you can believe it – one dead and one injured I've been informed. I'm on my way to the scene right now. We'll need to keep this quiet at present as the female involved is Lady De Pen Court, and her driver whom we believe to be dead.' The inspector slid one of the Glocks into a holster.

'Got yah, Chris, the press would love this. Text me the address, don't do a call on the computer, we'll be mobile in five and I'm with Alan, he's ok, so we can talk freely. I'll coordinate by radio keep one with you on channel six. The last thing we need is the press getting wind of this. Like I said they'll love it, and it'll fetch 'em down from the city, this will.' The armed officer was walking towards a black four-by-four vehicle, wearing overalls, body armour, and a machine gun attached to his chest with a sling.

'Thanks, Dave for your speed and understanding, speak soon,' replied the inspector.

Several hours and a lot of stress later the moon was full giving plenty of natural light. Forensics had added to the celestial illumination by installing several tripod lights, set at a height of seven feet pointing downwards in a large circle. The generator played its loud music whilst pumping gas into the atmosphere. Blades of grass were being flicked through by the many blue gloved fingers. Liquid plaster was mixed then poured out of plastic jugs and into the fresh tyre tracks and footprints around the large tree. The plaster was allowed to dry then dug out and placed in trays next to the half dozen cigarette butts and single piece of gum.

A couple of hours had passed, and the inspector had just sat back in his Range Rover. Window down. 'Call it a night, lads, we'll resume at first light tomorrow. Two men to remain here, I want no trespassers,' shouted the inspector before answering his phone.

'Inspector Shaw,' he answered, whilst looking at the scene?

'Boss, Alaskin has been confirmed "no life". Lady De Pen Court has just come out of surgery … I've been informed she will be fine. She's recovering on the ITU ward.'

'Thanks John could you stay on duty until I have a chance to relieve you? But it may be a few hours.'

'Will do, sir.' Call ended. John lifted his hand to relieve the pretty nurse of the cup. 'Thank you.' She increased his testosterone with a smile.

Four days Later – GLASGOW HOSPITAL.

'Tanya!' Was shouted from a distance of at least 20 feet. She easily heard it as the tone was deep, and it carried through the crowd.

'Sean! What are you doing here?' she was surprised to see Doyle approaching her in the hospital and so far away from London.

'Visiting a friend, you?' He nodded as the bottle of orange juice went to his mouth.

'Same.' The awkward encounter moved on; both of them made their way to the reception desk. 'Emma De ...' said Tanya.

'Lady De ...' said Sean. Both questions coming out at the same time.

4

CONTAINER HOUSE

T he train had just vacated Peterborough station when Sean's mobile rang,
'Are you at home?'

'No, ... I'll be back in about an hour, why? You, okay?'

'I have a couple of days off the rigs, so I was going to make a start on your house designs ... that's if you still want me to? With you not showing up the other day – wasn't sure if you... d ... changed yah mind. I mean its ok if you have ... I understand.' Kev was clearly hoping the answer would be "yes".

'Cheers, appreciate it and yes I want it building, but I haven't a lot of money at the moment. And I forgot last time something came up, sorry.'

'Oh ... ok, I understand. Let's see what we're up against first. I'm looking forward to doing it, this work is something different and who knows it may take off and get me off the rigs for good.'

'Sounds great. See you at eleven.'

'If you're sure you won't forget.' Kev hung up in

humour, but then started to worry in case his comment had offended Sean.

The train continued on its journey, and it wasn't long before Sean heard – "Waterloo Central" as it was announced over the train's intercom. Tanya had offered him a lift back to London; he had declined and used his return ticket within the hour. It had been awkward enough when they both asked to see Emma at the reception desk in the hospital.

But at least he was now aware of the secret source from where Emma had got his name and references. He declined to see Lady De Pen Court and left: a little bit too strange a situation. But given the fact the lady was in hospital recovering from an attempt on her life, he decided to not push it – not today. He just hoped it wasn't Tanya he was working for; because if that was the case, it could complicate things with another person, one that Doyle had too much respect for to keep in the dark. Doyle's first stop after vacating the train was the funeral parlour. The mention of the word "Mother" by Ann at his surprise birthday party had yet to leave his head; in fact, the thought of what was said was only just taking seed.

Emma had sent information about his family origins, a bonus she called it, and it was pretty clear his family originated from Ireland. But exactly where and in what decade or century even? The information had come laid out on an A3 sheet of paper in the form of a family tree. Not particularly that personalised. Sean at first had his suspicions that she was just tracing his surname then dressing it up a bit, apart from the mention of one small village, he couldn't remember why or how? But the name of the place rang a bell. Add to the fact, he knew nothing about his past, so he digested everything given to him. Then the contents of the file were wallpapered over one wall in the slender closet room he'd seconded in the parlour, and this was the start of the search for DOYLE.

The Parlour was quiet on Sean's return, he heard a door opened on the second floor, 'Ann have you a moment?'

'Bit busy Seannnny, can we catch up a little later?' She knew what the conversation was going to be about, and she didn't relish getting into it. Unwittingly she had accidently slipped out with the elusive "M" word after a couple too many shandies at Sean's birthday party. Unfortunately for her, to Doyle the "M" word was more valuable than gold itself. It wasn't from wickedness that she withheld the information it was more from a strange loyalty she still held to Mary. And if truth be-known, Ann didn't know that much about Mary before she came to London.

She spoke again, 'I have Lisa coming over soon, she needs an office and asked if there is anything available here, somewhere she could base herself. I thought maybe at the back of the soup kitchen, you know the old safe room, its empty now, I thought w....'

'Lisa!'

'No need to be so loud,' Ann said, realising she was off the hook, at least for the moment.

And just like when you mention the devil's name, she appeared in doorway.

'Hello again, Mr Doyle.'

'Oh, you have arrived Lisa, good timing, Sean has just walked in, luv.' Ann smiled with relief.

'I am really sorry to hear about your friend, Mr Doyle.'

'Sean, call me Sean, I keep thinking you're addressing

someone else. And thanks, but she's more of an employer than a friend, and I was told she'll pull through.'

'Would you like to take Sean down to the soup kitchen and walk him through your idea, luv? It makes sense to me but he's the boss, so the final decision will rest with him.' She side nodded her head to Doyle. She was very happy for the distraction Lisa had brought.

'If you have the time, Sean. I presume you're a busy man and I wouldn't want to be a nuisance.'

'He'll make the time for you, Lisa. You couldn't be a nuisance,' Ann muttered quietly.

'Sorry, Ann? Did you say something?' Sean had heard her fine, but he wanted her to know he had. She replied only with a courteous smile and left them alone in the office.

'Of course, I don't expect you to provide the space for free. I'll pay the going rate for the room, and whatever else we use, Mr ... sorry, Sean. That goes without saying. Just in case you thought I was after a freebie.'

'Let's have a look first see what you have in mind. We may be able to help each other out without swapping any money. That'll be ok with me, lead on.' His hand waved towards the stairs.

At the soup kitchen

'Hello.'

'Are you eating with us?'

'Hi, Lisa.'

'Lisa.'

Four or five people all spoke to her at once as she walked in.

'How is the food here?' was her blanket answer.

'Good.'

'Are you joining us?' replied at least two of them.

'No, not right now, I'm here to speak with Mr Doyle.' Her head turned towards Sean. 'He started this café.'

Sean hadn't even opened his mouth when the applause began which was led by Lisa, all the people eating, and the ones serving were clapping, staring straight at him. His introverted inner-self wanted out; he never had enjoyed receiving accolades from people in his presence.

'Not really me, a few others had a lot of input into this place and without them it wouldn't have happened. I just front it. So please no need to thank me.' Sean didn't want to be there. He didn't start this cafe or the gym next door to be cheered, but to simply plug a hole, and give a bit of payback. This was all Ann's suggestion originally and he saw it as a duty and naming it "Marys" was the icing on the cake. And just like his time in the regiment when he flew all over the world carrying out life or death missions; that wasn't for the applause, it was because he could – and someone had to.

The applause hadn't stopped, in fact it was getting louder.

Lisa sensed Sean wasn't feeling comfortable with the attention. 'I'll see you all in a while. This way, Mr Doyle.' She led him away from his audience. 'Sorry about that but I do believe people should be praised for what they have done for others! Don't you?' Her arm was touching his, softly resting on his bicep, just below the winged tattoo.

'If I'm honest, I'm not one for praise and if we could keep it that way, it would be appreciated.' They were both alone at the back of the kitchen, the darkness of the windowless room transforming them into shadows.

'You're a very interesting man Sean Doyle. A lot of people would have loved that attention back there, they would have used it to big themselves up. Yet I do believe you really aren't interested in the self-promotion or showmanship that many enter charity work for.'

She waited for his answer, but it didn't come.

'So, what is it you need from this place?' He deflected, switching the torch on from his phone.

'A base really, an office, at the moment I use my bedsit above the off-licence and then there's the library if I need a computer or to do some printing. But it is becoming a bit cramped as I am trying to expand my work and centralise the admin.'

'What actually is it you do? I see you're always around the homeless but ...' His phone started vibrating; he looked down at the screen. 'Shit I forgot,' he blurted out. 'Kev, you here yet?' he answered.

Lisa smiled as the yellow glow from the phone's screen lit up his face.

'Yes, I'm here, where are you? Is it another no show?' Kev tried to be funny but was still worried.

'A couple minutes mate, I'm only around at the front – bit of business. Don't leave, you hear me.' He looked to Lisa. 'Sorry forgot I had a friend coming.'

'So, you're not a loner then. And I'm a bit of business, am I? Mr Doyle?' Her eyes twinkled in the dim light.

'I guess. You are after an office, and that's business. And Kev's an old school friend, just got back in touch with him for a building project, more than friendship, and I like to keep business as business. Simpler that way. So, will this room do for you? Give me a week and we'll have a window put in and the electrics sorted.'

'We all need someone, Mr Doyle – Sean? And this will

be perfect just the right size.' She smiled and held it there not at all embarrassed about her brace.

'From what Ann told me we don't use these two rooms at the moment, so, if these suit your needs, please feel free. I must go, so if you're interested liaise with Ann, let her know what you need. If we can help, we will.'

'What about – rent, Mr Doyle.'

'Put in what you can to the utilities at least for the next couple of months. Let's get you on your feet. It's a good thing you're doing here. And Ann runs this herself, so she may need some assistance with admin and stuff. We'll call that rent, shall we?' He walked off towards the building's back exit not wanting to do an encore in the cafe.

'Sean.' She spoke as if her tiny voice box was unable to shout.

He turned.

'Thank you.' Her smile was still being held for him but inside the smile was for her as well. She had used her looks to achieve her wants. How proud her sister would have been.

5

SAY NOTHING

A sprint – his arms up – pull up – leg over the tin clad wall. 'Kev! Kev!' shouted Sean on landing, not seeing anyone around he was about to reach for his phone.

'Sean,' Kev was unable to look his old friend in the eye. It had been a decade since he'd seen him.

'Thanks for coming. Not putting you out, am I?' Sean offered out his hand. Kev wiped his hand on his trousers and gave a limp shake.

'Nah... not at all, I'm really looking forward to doing this and like I said I've had enough of working away. Been taking a look around the yard while you weren't here ... hope that was, okay?' Kev was fidgeting from nerves, still unable to hold a look Sean's way. He was also thinking is this Sean? As the kid that left at fifteen, was half this man's size and at least nine-inches smaller.

'Not a problem. What do you think of the old place?'

'It's big, bigger than what I remembered. You don't realise from the front do yah? Is all this yours then?' Kev panned around the yard.

'Yeah, ... guess so. Not much in the way of accommodation but it's quiet and I like quiet. There's a mooring on the canal for this place as well. It would be nice to get "Big M" afloat again.'

Kev's eyes widened as he looked at the 50ft barge sat on stilts in the corner.

'Wow is she still here? I remember us playing in there when we were kids. Do yah remember when we slept on her?' He looked away from the barge not sure if Sean was interested in reminiscing. 'I thought you said you were strapped for cash, Sean.' Kev changed the subject.

'At the moment yeah, we've set up a community café and the boxing club is being refurbed and started up again. This place, well, according to the bank, is worth over three million quid, at least. Yet the business is cashless but with no real debts and that's how I want it to stay.' He looked again at the boat. Then at Kev.

'No, I didn't mean sell Big M and didn't mean to pry. When I was looking about, I pulled some canvas off the stacks in the shed.' Both their heads looked at the partially derelict building with its well patinaed sides and old asbestos roof.

'What did you find, anything we can use in the container build?' Sean set off walking towards the shed.

'It's better than that mate, timber and lots of it,' replied Kev, trying to keep up with his friend's pace.

'I want to build the house using containers, not timber.' They entered the 250 by 50ft shed. 'Fuck, looks like no one's been in here for years,' said Sean, his hand up brushing away cobwebs.

'Over here, look - look.' Kev shone his torch on the dozens of stacks of timber.

'See what you mean. I'll have it cleared out. We can use this place as a workshop.'

'You're missing the point, Sean,' Kev had started walking closer to the ten feet high stacks of wood. 'This is as good as CASH and lots of it too.'

Sean looked puzzled.

Kev caressed the timber whilst talking, the dust causing him to sneeze twice then cough. 'I'm a welder and steel man but I come from a family of cabinet makers. What you have here is English oak, walnut, and a few other hardwoods. A quick calculation: I'd say this lot is worth well over seventy grand.' He pointed the torch at Sean.

'You having a fucking laugh. Come on tell me you're taking the piss.' Sean then started to caress the timber to.

'No ... not kidding ... and that's a conservative estimate. My dad could give you a much better idea and help sell it if that's what you want.'

'If you're right about this you'll be working "On-shore" before you know it. Where would it have all come from, do you think?' Sean looked down and seemed to disengage for a good few seconds. This was noticed by Kev. 'You okay, ... Sean?' As sensitive as ever.

'Yeah, I am, sorry, just that if this lot has been here all this time I was thinking about Mary and how she struggled to keep this place from going to the banks.'

'Yes, I heard about Mary from my mam; very sad. Did you find out what happened to her?' Kev then quickly retracted the statement, realising it might have been a shit subject for Sean to talk about.

'Forget what I just said, Sean, this is about your new home and the future.'

'This is a great day and I owe you, mate. I haven't seen

you for years then you make me thousands of pounds in less than an hour.' Sean continued to shine the phone at the stacks of timber.

'Do you really want to stop working on the rigs?'

Kev nodded, yet still fidgeted from nerves, neurotic even.

'How much do you earn while you're out there?'

'Thirty-two K, a year but ...'

'Can't match that, fuck, that's a good salary. Why do you wanna, leave?'

'No ... no, a grand a month will be enough to start but I also get to do some of my own shit in the workshop. I can soon make up the difference and I have savings,' insisted Kev, not letting the chance of leaving his job get away.

'Deal.' Sean's hand was held out for the second time.

'Come here.' Kev grabbed him and gave his old friend a big hug.

A surprised Doyle didn't know what to do, so he tossed out the question again, 'How did it all get here and when? What do you think?'

Kev stepped back. 'Judging by the gauge of the wood and it's all been planked by hand so, I'd take a guess it's at least a couple of centuries old, maybe even towards three. They would have brought it here via boats from out there on the canal, well, it would have been the old river back then, before the canal was officially dug. It was still being used commercially as a river, bringing goods into London. And don't forget back in the day undertakers were also joiners. It wasn't 'til around eighty years ago, it really separated and became a solo business. So, your great, great, great, great family probably bought the timber in bulk planning for the future.'

'Yeah, bulk for sure. You know your stuff.'

'I just like history and spend a lot of time reading.'

'What's all that shit over there?' Sean pointed to the far corner.

'Machines, saws and old tea chests full of stuff completely covered in dust.'

'Ask your old man to come and take a look, ASAP. Let's get it all sold get started on the build. I've already sort of moved into one of the containers, but I guess it's just a camp. We'll build a workshop first. Can I leave the details to you?' Sean questioned.

'I'll willingly sort and build the workshop, my pleasure, but I'll give you his number, my dad that is, you'll have to call him yourself we don't talk anymore,' replied Kev, looking away and down again, unable to look his old friend in the eye.

'And you still want to help him. Why?'

'I guess, but I'm helping you as well, and then you're helping me. It's a win, win.' Kev sounded genuine.

'These issues with your dad are they because you're gay?' asked Sean outright, without a blink of the eye.

'You know I'm gay? How, how, when, who said?' Kev was gobsmacked and the question knocked him back, his nervousness trebled bordering on a panic attack, he was completely embarrassed. Sean was such a macho man, and he always was including when they were at school together, yet he didn't seem bothered about his sexuality. It appeared to be just "matter of fact".

'All the issues relate to me and my sexual orientation, but he'll never admit to that. He called me "A sick creation", "An abomination", and after that according to him, I was just "Attention seeking", "A fad", he called it.

'I still see my mum, but she has to visit me, and she stays over at mine more than she goes home, she hates him, wouldn't admit it, and still goes and does his washing and meals, I guess it's that generation.'

After a small silence, 'Who told yah - Sean ... that I, I, I... wa...?' Kev was upset and lost his words, wondering if this fact would now come between two old friends.

'No one told me, I've always known.' Sean was still looking around the storage space.

'What?' asked Kev, his panic on standby.

'Remember when we all went to that Halloween disco at the old golf club. I think it was the year before we left school.'

'How could I ever forget? You were drunk and then spewed up on the bins then turned and threw up all over Speck's shoes when she tried to help you.'

'Thanks. You do remember.' Sean laughed. 'You kissed that boy, and do you remember what Specks did?' Sean asked.

Kev couldn't continue the conversation; he didn't know where to look or what to say. He desperately wanted to talk about the past, but he didn't know if him and Sean had a future. Was this the reason Sean hadn't contacted him for years?

All he could think about was the names his dad called him and the pure hatred from some others.

'And that's why Gary stopped hanging around with you. He saw you kiss him as well. We were sat on the wall above the bin area.' Sean had now climbed up the stack of timber to see how far it all went back.

'But ... b ... ya ... you never stopped hanging around with me. Why not?' bashfully asked Kev. He was on tenterhooks as so many of his wishes had come true in a day; he was paranoid they would now vanish.

'Why? Should I have? Is that what you wanted?

There's tons of wood here, fuck can't believe how far it goes back.' Sean was crawling across the stacks. He dropped off at the far end and continued talking as Kev didn't reply.

'Remember when Tony died. I nearly went off with Gary to steal that builder's van. He was going to sell it to Ahmid's brother. You stood in front of us both and told me I was a fucking idiot. That was the only time I heard you swear. Gary pushed you away you got up and smacked him across the face. That was the night Gary got nicked and went down the road, sentenced to borstal four years for theft of a vehicle and carrying a knife without legitimate purpose. If I'd gone with him, I'd have got done as well, it would have killed Mary and devastated Danny. I had the ABAs coming up. Not to mention I'd probably be in and out of jail with Spanner now.' Sean had taken to shouting from behind the timber to ensure he was still being heard.

'I don't know what to say. You were my friend. I didn't want you in trouble. You weren't a bad person like Gary. Just not sure why you didn't say anything. Sorry I'm gay.'

'I said nothing. Why have I got to say something? You're a good guy, great guy, and a good friend. You need to start believing that, but let's remember I'm straight.' Sean laughed. Kev joined in; his fidgeting was less visible. 'Oh, and Kev, one more thing?'

'Yeah.'

'You ever apologise for being YOU, again and I'll slap you myself and that's the end of it. Come over here and look at these I've found.'

Kev struggled but managed to get up to where Sean was. 'What's in there?' he asked, the previous conversation now a sweet memory. A true friend was back in his life, and he had done more for him in an hour, than the Zopiclone and Prozac had done in two years.

∮

The gorgeous smell of warm soup hit Lisa as she came from the back and re-entered the dining room of the cafe. 'Do you want to try some?'

'I would love to,' replied Lisa grabbing hold of a dish.

'He seems a nice guy that Mr Doyle,' she told the elderly lady delicately holding the ladle.

'He is from what my sister says, and she should know.' She up-turned the ladle above the plain white dish, the warm, orangey and red coloured, aromatic liquid, levelled. Then the same server tilted a small white jug; an erratic circle of cream was added. 'Would you like a bread roll with that? They're made fresh daily, here on site.' The server smiled proud of her endeavour, as it was, she who did the daily baking.

Lisa nodded appreciating the fresh bread smell. 'Can I ask how your sister knows Mr Doyle?'

'Ann's my sister. She's known Sean since he arrived here about twenty years ago now,' replied the server, as she placed the mis-shaped tiny bread roll on the side of the dish, a wrapped butter cube next to it. 'Tesco donates them. I don't make those.'

'Oh, Ann's lovely, I'm only here because of her invitation. She is very caring.' Lisa pushed the roll further onto the plate.

'You've never played bridge with her then, she can be ruthless, a proper bitch sometimes.' The server laughed but Lisa picked up on a sadness she smiled on the turn, but she wasn't comfortable with that "B" word and for good reason. Her gaze enjoyed the brightly decorated walls and fresh laid tiles covering the uneven floor.

No corners had been cut in the decorating. "*A job well done on this place*" she thought to herself. Keeping walking she joined a couple of men and one woman sitting at the window table. Her first impressions of the café were what a great place it was, but she also knew what these set ups cost to both run and maintain and that wasn't cheap. People were always generous at the start of these types of projects, but time made them forget and continuously prompting of the public was a fine art, especially in today's world. You turned on the TV and some charity was asking you for three pounds a month for an exotic animal or to save or sponsor a donkey. It wasn't so much the topics of the charities that offended people, it was more the large salaries attached to the executives who forced the ads down their throats. Against the law to ask for a pound in the street, but they could ask for any amount in your living room.

The young, pretty lady pondered as she saw here a wonderful operation and wanted to get involved and she would. 'Tea?' asked the disabled man pushing a four wheeled trolley. He couldn't look her in the eyes.

'Please.' The mug was filled to the brim. 'Can I ask how do you find it working here?' she enquired.

He placed the stainless-steel teapot back on the trolley and the mug went to her lips. 'Shit, bloody shit, and for a pittance. I can't live on the money these people pay me.' And he walked away.

Lisa's mouth fell open, her moment of "heaven" changed. 'Don't listen to him he's waiting for Doomsday when the world will end.' The server pointed with her head to the wall near the door. Lisa looked and there for all to see leaning against the wall was a dual-body sign:

The end of the world is nigh.

❧

'Bloody hell that hurt. Shine the torch this way, Sean, I can't see the floor.' Kev had fallen trying to climb down to see what was inside the box Sean had found. Well, a coffin, not a box.

'You, okay?' Sean shone the beam of light down to him.

'Wow! How many in there? I'm okay, grazed and bruised,' said Kev, rubbing his elbow and leg whilst looking inside the coffin full of old, really old, flint-lock rifles.

'Looks like it wasn't only wood your ancestors were dealing in.'

Sean put his hand out to grab one of the antique weapons; each was in immaculate condition. They must have laid there undiscovered for at least 150 years, but the coffin had been lined out with lead and the weapons themselves lightly oiled then wrapped in hessian rags, without a doubt helping the preservation.

'Here, hold this.' Sean passed the torch to Kev.

'Shine it over here, there's some words.' Sean tipped the barrel.

"Derby 1838" was just readable as Doyle rocked the barrel side to side. It had been engraved on the brass work.

'Give us a hand we'll get this lot back to the container.'

The pair dragged the heavy coffin around to the front.

'I know someone who could value these,' said Kev, hands placed where his kidneys were, stretching his back.

'Not your dad.' Laughed Sean.

'No, Sophie.'

'Sophie?' Sean repeated.

'Sophie Cellest.'

'Specks – our Specks! – little, short ass,' replied Sean.

'Yes, our Specks, and you wouldn't say that if you saw her today. She has a great job, works for Christies and she's also one of the curators at the museum in the high street. Done very well for herself and she's been to university and everything.' Kev's tone was so full of pride when talking about Soph, the total opposite to talking about himself.

They'd managed to get the full coffin to the bottom of the steps. Rifles out and carried up, the coffin was then brought upstairs, and the rifles laid back in their home. 'Fancy a beer?' asked Sean, holding two in his hand.

'Yeah.' Kev took the bottle. 'Right, now down to your house, Sean. I'll take some measurements then do some sketch drawings and get back to you with ideas then I can get a feel for what you want. Plus, I'll need to test the strength of the structure because these are old containers, and we need to have a strong shell before we start.' His knuckles tapped the side. 'Once we have the basics on paper, we can work out what you want as an internal design.' Kev was in his element. With this new start and with an old friend.

'Good, because I need to be completely out the big flat. Ann wants to move in, and Danny needs to get in her old apartment. I have him in a little tourer at the back of the stables.' Sean threw back the lager.

'Looks like you've already moved in,' replied Kev,

looking at the army camp bed and curtained-off makeshift bathroom.

'You know what I mean. Take one of the rifles with you and let Specks take a good look see what she thinks. We might get a few more thousand get us started properly.'

'No, leave them all here. I'll take a couple of photos and message her. I don't want the responsibility of any of them going missing.

I'll pass your number on, she can call you when she has a minute. Better if she comes here, there's a lot more stuff down in the shed, and one thing is for sure ... you're no longer skint.' Kev was already measuring and writing notes whilst chatting. 'Is there anything you want in the layout?'

'Not really thought that through yet.'

'I'll need to know certain things for the fabrication, like any heavy or stress creating appliances so I can combat vibration and counter-balance.'

'I'll leave it all to you, that's over my head, oh ... a gym in one of the bottom containers with a small sauna.'

'Bottom containers, what?' Kev stopped writing and looked to Sean who had bent over to reopen the small fridge.

'Didn't I say? I want four joined together, two up, two down. You know, in a box.' His grin was there; Kev screwed up the sheet of paper. But inside his interest level moved up a notch and he was loving the challenge.

'Arrange to get Specks over here to look at the rifles. I've gotta be somewhere.' Sean walked away to find his Mac, leaving Kev still measuring everything in sight then multiplying it by four. His last hour was spent outside taking photos. His final act was taking measurements of gates and driveway.

6

HARVEST

J FK Airport

The pilot had been sedated, all part of his plan. Asleep on the carry cot the ambulance remained stationary.

'They're all dead?' repeated the chief controller.

A nod from the paramedic's head confirmed his unbelievable words.

'How? What could have done this? Everyone is dead.' The controller shook his head from side to side; the small group stood in silence as a smartly dressed man approached them.

'Stop right there, sir, you can't go any further,' advised the police officer guarding the aircraft.

'I am responsible for the plane and all of the English passengers aboard, so I have to go in there.' The man's tone was smooth, calm and collected. His eye contact full.

The officer stepped aside without saying a word as if he'd been hypnotised. Mr Smooth walked past him and took the first step onto the stairs not in the slightest bit fazed by the cockpit being separated from the fuselage. Underneath the Boeing was a team of men busy erecting a scaffold frame at speed to support the burnt-out neck of the aircraft. As he reached the summit, the scaffolders punched through a handrail. Mr smooth turned the only way possible, into the fuselage.

'Who are you? You can't be in here. Please leave sir.' Followed by 'The police are stopping everybody. How did you get past?'

'I am here representing Anuar-Lucas, the people who are responsible for the passengers aboard this Boeing. I am here to officially inform you gentlemen that Anuar-Lucas, are to take control of this aircraft and retrieve all of the bodies and with immediate effect. I would appreciate your cooperation in vacating all your staff from the vicinity. I will subsequently inform you when we have completed our task.' He passed over the sheet of paper he had just read from and a branded pen. The controller read the sheet and looked up.

'I've never seen anything like this document. Do you really expect me just to sign this and walk away? And what makes you think you can just swan in here and take over the plane? This is an airport matter and we will be handing the plane over to the police after our initial investigation.' His voice became louder as he spoke, most of the emotion related to the devastating loss of life that surrounded him. 'I'm signing nothing 'til we get out of this area. Have you no respect, sir?' It was clear the controller meant what he said.

They all left the plane in silence, stopping at the bottom of the stairs. The scaffolders had finished their work and were being escorted back to their vehicle. 'That won't go anywhere now, sir, its safe,' said one of the hard hats.

The controller nodded. 'Thank you and your men for your promptness and hard work.'

'Not a problem,' replied the scaffolder then ran to catch up with his buddies.

'Read this.' The man passed over a second sheet of paper at the same time as he raised his arm in the air.

Two dozen black vans approached the plane; the first two stopped and reversed up to the bottom of the steps leading up to the fuselage.

Ten men all armed with automatic rifles were out the vehicles and guarding the plane, rifles up at chest height. The police came over to the group stood talking to the man.

'What's happening?' asked the officer.

'We're taking it from here, son. You can leave now,' answered the man. 'Who are you ordering about?'

'He's right, officer, I have your boss on the phone, you are to stand down immediately,' added the controller as perplexed as the young cop.

The smartly dressed man walked away from the astounded group heading over to the parked vans. After a few words were spoken through the driver's window all the doors on all the vehicles opened together.

Men in white paper suits, black gloves and goggles walked up the temporary steps, they were carrying several stretchers and bags. Thirty bodies were brought back down. Two at a time and loaded into the waiting vans, each stacked neatly onto the specially designed stainless-steel shelving. Only three dead bodies remained up in the fuselage. The smart man from Anuar-Lucas organising the event was the only one alive who remained on-board.

After speaking with the police chief, the controller and the police officers were ordered to vacate the area until informed otherwise. Aboard the plane the man from Anuar-Lucas began injecting a substance into the bodies of the staff left behind, he stared at his watch.

One minute lapsed, he began lifting the limbs of the three dead staff. These were no longer rigid. Next he placed a see-through mask on each of them – this complete he unzipped a holdall. One large canister with three nipples for the hose connections. He stared again at his watch. Two minutes lapsed, hoses disconnected masks off the dead bodies, the carbon dioxide canister and masks were placed back in the holdall. His hand remaining in the bag he pressed a digital screen five times; it began flashing. The brass teeth connected slowly all the way up. He let go of the pull now that the zip was closed. Bag on the floor, he slid it with his foot over into the cockpit and looked at his watch.

The running stopwatch said, "four minutes". As the bag rested in the remains of the cockpit, he approached the passenger side of the van.

The running stopwatch said, "two minutes".

The driver looked at him uttering no words.

The running stopwatch said, "one minute".

The driver passed over a pair of bright yellow sponge ear defenders.

Four ears were blocked as the watch stated, "Ten seconds".

The driver squeezed the wheel; the smart man held the door tight. One, two, *boom!* The scaffold collapsed as the flames shot from the cockpit into the fuselage the heat was immense the steel scaffold tubes glowed red.

Less than forty minutes since their arrival and the black vans were full and began pulling away, one by one they formed a straight convoy. The last one slowed its speed; the passenger's window came down opposite the group, who'd amassed near to the exit gate.

'Your three members of staff are still onboard. Thank you for your co-operation.'

Window closed; the van caught up with the rest of the convoy.

The firefighters raced to the plane.

One hour twenty minutes later the first of the black vehicles drove under the solid concrete beam arriving at the underground car park. Awaiting in the artificially illuminated space were two large pickups, each full of ice. The confident man was out the lead vehicle and giving out minimal orders, yet so much took place.

'Quickly, the subjects with a recycle tag on them need packing in ice,' said one operative. The remaining sixteen bodies were placed in black body bags, zipped up and put into temperature-controlled steel coffins. The man in charge clapped his hands and the car park became a hive of activity.

Looking to the entrance, he nodded and got the same mirrored from two large men standing next to the lowered barrier. Each was the epitome of a white supremacist. He removed his phone.

'Complete, sir, the first two will be in the elevators in ...' He looked at the workforce. 'One minute.' He continued talking into the iPhone as the silver doors slid open.

'Good work, Renee. And what about the garbage?' asked the voice.

'I have Evergreen Crematorium on standby, sir. I will start the deliveries there as soon as the last fresh product enters the elevator. I don't want the meat spoiling, sir.'

'Good man, and excellent work as per usual.' The phone conversation ceased.

Four homeless bodies were in each van, they had left England less than twelve hours ago. Their expectations set so high. By the time this day would be at an end, each would be burned, and their homeless bones incinerated and turned into ash, spread on an exclusive golf course as feed for the greens.

'The first two are here, nurse. Have you the inventory there for a ... John Peterson?'

'Peterson ... Peterson ... ah, yes, here it is, doctor.' She passed over the plastic envelope containing two checklists.

'Liver, eyes, kidney, heart, lungs and his left arm, sorry hand. His blood group as well is a rare fluid, a good chap this one.' He smiled as he read the numbers: $184,000. 'Let's get this donor into theatre, nurse.'

'Yes, sir, right away, doctor.' She clicked her fingers and two porters appeared.

The doctor walked off and dialled a number on his phone.

'The delivery has arrived. You will be receiving at least a million dollars for the full crop. It's set to be a great harvest. We will put in place our systems in the London clinic. They will be the same as we have working over here, much more efficient this way and less noticeable if we transport parts and not full bodies.

'In the coming months, you will be prepped to provide individual donations on request. These are the bread and butter of our organisation, bringing in at least $1000 dollars at a time, and that's just blood, the rarer the group, the more the zeros attached. I will be in touch.' He was gone.

7

MISSING PERSON

L ondon - Cardboard City
    'Molly Malone – you seen her about?' Sean
    asked the first person he saw.

'No, sir, not since Thursday night. I think it was ... Thursday ... it's easy to lose track of time and days in my world.' The girl of around twenty-five waited patiently for the blue note Sean was now famous for parting with. 'Thank you, sir, thank you.' She placed a quick kiss on Sean's cheek, only a peck then she was off.

Sean took another blue note from the Mac pocket and passed it over to a short guy waiting quietly to his left. Doyle for some reason began to think he must be a dwarf, a small person, of small stature. What do you say today? There was no malice behind his thinking, just curiosity and a blindness to political correctness.

He didn't even ask him if he had seen Molly, but the short guy heard the question posed to the girl.

'I've seen her, sir, Molly that is. Yeah, I have.'

'Where? Today? Here?'

'No, not here, down at the old fish market but she

looked different today, but it was her, the eyes.' His lips curled upwards, head moving back and forth slowly; the lips turned to a big smile. 'Yes, the eyes gave her away and she leans to the left when walking, with her fingers clicking on her left hand. After ten paces she's nearly wobbling she has to slow down to reset her gait.' The short guy started to recite poetry all based around Molly's eyes and the limp, summarising her as an imperfect clown from the courts of old.

'Why was she different, just her eyes?'

'Her clothes, sir, a smart suit she wore, and she carried an attaché case, brown beigey leather. Good gear it all was too, sir, expensive. She pulled out a folder which remained in her hand.'

'What time was all this?'

'Two-ish. I work between twelve and two on the crab stall, yah see, then Jimmy takes over again. It's like an extended lunch for him, he's not a young man anymore. I dress them and the punters give me a tip for that, it's not as easy as y...' Shorty was about to embark on the life and tales of the North Sea crab, but as bad as Sean felt, he was in a hurry. 'Tell me the facts about Molly. Was she with anyone? Did she acknowledge you? Do you know where she was going?'

'Talking to a ladder man she was. He was also in a suit, but his shoes didn't match, and they weren't clean. He wasn't a regular whistle and flute man, and white socks! Please.' the short guy's hands went in the air.

'Focus, come on focus,' encouraged Sean.

'She didn't move for ten minutes then her and the younger ladder man gave chase. The male had pointed to a guy coming out of the fish supply office. She looked inside the folder. He was in his mid-50s, bearded and wearing white wellingtons and a three-quarter matching overall. Clean, so he must have been management.' Shorty stopped the conversation and waved at a young lady. Sean raised his hands upwards, palms going out. 'And?'

'OH yeah, they didn't catch him. Both Molly and the male came back and got into a nice car, dark grey Mercedes then drove off.' Shorty gave the biggest grin possible and thrust his hand out.

Doyle didn't know if he'd been spun a yarn or told the truth, but still he passed over a second fiver.

He was about to ask if that was it, but he couldn't put up with another story leading nowhere so instead he said, 'Thanks,' and turned away.

'Don't you want to know the rest?'

'The rest? What do you mean? They left in a car.' Doyle had used up the day's ration of patience.

'She's a copper! I followed them. I have an electric bike you see, it's brilliant, I can go anywhe… and I charge it at the BP garage for nothing. I just sweep up twice a week for the owner an…' Sean stared at the short storyteller who was excited talking about his bike, in fact excited talking about anything!

'Where did you follow them to?'

'To the police station, where else? But she didn't go in, no, two uniformed cops came out and met her next to the side gate. She took out her ID card as did the ladder man, then a small notebook, listened to the young cop and wrote stuff in the book. I was close enough that I could clearly hear their conversation. I'd pretended the bike was broke.' Shorty's head started nodding, his eyes wide.

'And?'

'Oh yeah, the conversation.'

"It's all in here, ma'am, everything we have on the

Bitch" is what the uniformed cop said and then they left, passing over an envelope of some type.' Shorty waved again to another young girl. 'It's frustrating they all just see me as a friend and other people don't even notice me, it's like I'm invisible.' This was a lightbulb moment for Sean. It was clear that Shorty had a fantastic memory, and by his own labelling he was invisible.

'What's your name? I keep wanting to call you Shorty.'

'People do call me Shorty, but Christen Luke Alexandra Day, is what my parents put on the bit of paper before they dropped me at the orphanage, a couple of weeks after they signed the birth register.'

'How would you like to earn a bit more cash, Chris? Can I call you Chris? Don't like Shorty, don't feel right,' said Doyle.

Shorty's massive grin was back.

'Which station did this happen at?' asked Sean.

'Pebble Mill, the old one not the new flashy glass building and yes, I like Chris.' This was said with the smile intact.

'Here, call this number, ask for Kev. Tell him Sean has offered you some work on the build, carrying and fetching that sort of thing. You okay with that?'

The smile widened and he nodded.

'There's also a café on site so you can eat there. Set up a tab ... just for dinners! And I'll clear it once a week.' Sean gave Chris a couple more fives and left looking for a taxi. Virtually on the boundary of Cardboard City, he had just offered a man labouring work, but he had other things in mind for him. There were no taxies around so a walk it would be.

'Three pounds ninety, please. Sugar, sweeteners and

milk are just behind you,' said the man, wearing a unisex uniform and silly red cap. *Ballsy*, thought Sean.

'Thanks.' Sean took the coffee, thumbed the lid off. Two brown sugars in, the thin bit of wood stirred three times and he left the store.

'Sorry, shit, I didn't see you there. I'm so clumsy. Sorry.'

'Don't worry about it. Here, you may as well finish the coffee,' said Sean as the woman was clearly upset.

'Okay, thanks. You're that man, Mr Doyle... You're the man giving money away.' Sean was puzzled, then the person who had bumped into him showed him a handful of blue notes. Sean's hand dived into the mac's pocket; it was empty.

'Hey!' he shouted. The figure didn't reply, just kept going.

'I want to talk, that's all!' shouted Sean. The figure increased their speed then turned as they got to the end of the row of shops.

'Mind... sorry, out the way,' shouted Sean, practically running through people trying to get to the corner. 'Fuck!' he spat. The figure had disappeared; an old woman had just won him in a sprint. His fingers travelled through his hair.

'Are you the man giving money away to homeless people, mister?' asked a young girl and boy.

'Why do you ask?' Sean was still partially looking for the magician who he had followed. He turned and shock hit him. 'How old are you two?'

'Eighteen,' was their joint reply.

'Yeah, and I am as well. How old?'

'We just need some money for food. We ain't ate for a couple of days, mister. Hungry we are, please?' said the girl with those eyes only a girl has.

'Fuck off! Go on, fuck off now, you're scum,' shouted an older woman.

The pair turned and saw the scruffy figure; they ran. Sean's magician had re-appeared, but now he was angry with her. 'They were kids. What's your problem? Anyway, I've nothing left to give away, have I?' he said pointing to his pocket.

'Yes, kids you're right about that, but rich kids from the posh estate up on the hill.

They come down here and earn hundreds a day then buy drugs with the money. Go to the rear of the arcade and you'll see them getting changed into rags, then they put their good gear in one of the lockers at the train station. They aggressively beg then we get the reputation as being greedy.'

'Why did you run earlier? And is pickpocketing how you earn a living?' enquired Doyle.

'I thought you were someone else. I owe money you see. Need to be careful who I talk with, and no, well yes and no. I used to, but I need to get some cash together quick, so the temptation won through. Sorry.' The old woman was out of breath, panting whilst looking both ways as she talked to Sean.

'How old are you?'

'Didn't your mam tell you never to ask that of a lady? But I'm 62, today as it happens.' She started drinking the coffee.

He looked at it, realising she hadn't even spilt the coffee during the getaway. 'Plausible, I guess. Who do you owe money to?'

'The bitch. And this is black! What's wrong with you?'

she responded, her face comically contorting. 'What did you want to talk about?' She laughed and took the twenty blue notes from her bra. 'I'll split them with you. No hard feelings I hope.' She began counting.

Sean put his hand out. She slapped ten of the divers in his palm.

'Looking for Molly, Molly Malone. Do you know her?' A second opinion wouldn't go amiss before he went on a wild goose chase to Pebble Lane, he thought.

'Yeah, course, everyone down here knows our Molly, she's like the Mother Teresa of the place. Why do you seek her?'

'Have you seen her around lately?' Sean replaced the fives into his Mac pocket.

'Now you mention it, I haven't, not for a couple of days anyway, maybe longer. But she does often go missing for a day or two, now and then. I think she has a problem.'

'Problem?'

'Problem. You know?' The old woman was shaking her hand going back and forth near to her mouth.

'She likes a drink you mean.'

'That's your opinion ... not mine. I didn't say that so don't be gossiping, lad, I want no trouble, do you hear me, not with Molly!'

'Call me if you see her around.' Sean passed over a card with nothing on it apart from his number typed in the centre. 'Will do,' she replied. Becoming anxious, she passed over the other half of the money and was off again at speed. Two men passed Sean in a hurry.

He watched them, then followed he couldn't allow two big guys to chase an old woman. As he walked back towards Cardboard City, newspapers, empty *Costa* cups and the odd pizza box flipped over, the wind aiding their escape.

'Tell her I'll have it all with interest on Tuesday, every penny. It's only a couple of days away, she knows I'm good for it,' expressed the old woman.

'She's had enough of your empty promises,' said the lanky man.

Sean was twenty feet away as he watched the small guy snatch the woman's bag, at the same time knocking the coffee out of her hand. She looked scared, really scared.

'I bet your mam's really proud of you, son.' Sean interrupted.

'What? Who the fuck is you?' said the tall guy.

A page from a travelling newspaper wrapped itself around Doyle's leg.

'How much does she owe?' he asked.

'This isn't Gotham City, and you haven't got your boxers on the outside of your trousers, so jog on, Batman.' The pair laughed.

'I'm not going anywhere, so we can either talk and sort this out, or ...'

The short, bearded man ran at Sean, a blade visible in his left hand. With the newspaper still attached his leg was up, kicking the blade away. Going off balance, Sean punched the guy's head. 'How much does she owe?' he asked again, not fazed by the futile attempt at scaring him off.

'Just tell him, Lofty,' Squeaked the short man from under Sean's foot.

'Forty quid, not that it's owt to do with you, Batman, let him up and fuck off, go on now?'

'Forty pounds! What was you going to do to her if she

couldn't pay it back?' Nothing was instantly said, but the homeless woman held up her right hand. The end two fingers had been bandaged and a wooden lolly stick taped to the dressing. 'They would break the rest, and maybe start on the left,' she said.

Sean's foot started to subconsciously twist down into the back of the short guy underneath it. 'Is this how second-rate psychos get their kicks today?'

'You don't know who you're messing with, prick. You best fuck off, home now and we won't say owt about this little episode again,' said the tall man.

'Stop it, you're scaring me,' grinned Sean. His heel began to twist even deeper, this time consciously.

His hand fished in the mac's deep pocket. 'Here's your 40 quid, with ten percent interest for your trouble Take it and fuck off while I'm feeling generous.' He dropped the fives on top of the shit under his foot. 'Come over here, luv,' he told the woman; she obeyed. The pair left walking backwards for at least ten feet.

'You shouldn't have got involved; they won't forget you. She's a real bitch and runs this area. They won't let people think that someone is protecting us, she'll hurt you to make a point. Watch your back, are you listening? I mean it, she'll hurt you. Everyone owes her money down here or depending on who you are the bitch asks for a favour of some type, or something instead of the cash back. It's just how you get by with no roof over your head. But thank you, that took a lot of guts. Here, take this back, I feel bad now.' Her hand disappeared into her bra again to retrieve one five-pound note.

'Keep it, please, it's your birthday remember. Who is this bitch you're all so scared of? Tell me her name and where I can find her,' asked Sean very confidently.

'No, sorry, I can't say. Sorry, I must go now. Soup kitchen is on soon, got to get in the queue.' And with that she was gone.

Sean watched her blend into the crowd of homeless, once again becoming invisible. He scanned the area.

"How could a place like this exist for the hours of darkness alone and then daylight wash it all away?" A glance at his watch. Maybe time to get some kip. He was still covered with bruises from the building blowing up. Tomato and cheese omelette then bed, his version of comfort food. Reaching the front of the funeral parlour he saw a light still on in the back of the café. He was tempted to nip in and see how Lisa was settling into the place, but it might have come across wrong, creepy even, at this hour.

Give it a miss he decided. Eleven o'clock and the heavy steel door on the container was pulled open and closed.

The inviting mattress lying on the floor won him over, the omelette would now become his breakfast. He pulled around the curtain. He was out cold in a few moments, dreamland in seconds as the container's dark room induced his brain to produce melatonin.

8

PEEPING TOM

7:oo am the next morning

'Hello, Sean? Hello... anyone in?' She had knocked on the container door, but it hurt her hand so there was no second attempt. The four-foot-wide door with a rubber seal around its perimeter was a couple of inches ajar, Sean had neglected to slide the bar across. Her intrigue persuaded her to enter; pulling using both arms it still took her more than one attempt. The inside was sparse, with the same blue on the walls as outside with patches of rust and stickers galore from every country a geography teacher would know and more. One old pine chair, a folding table with one leaf up, and an off-cut of a kitchen worktop that was sat on a door-less white unit, which was home to the bottled gas stove and plastic washing up bowl. Light entered through two circular bucket size holes cut into the side wall, clear Perspex glued over these to waterproof them.

'Hello! Anyone in here? Sean, Sean are you home?' Specks felt strange saying the word "home". It looked more like the canteen found on a builder's yard. Feeling wrong for being inside, she stopped herself from going any further.

Her and Doyle knew each other very well, but that was over ten years ago. A full decade of growing up had separated them, a different world, one where the smile from a friend could change the path of your day. She remembered Sean as a lanky schoolboy with ears that his body had not yet grown into. A kid with a good heart, but troubled spirit, always walking a tightrope along the path of right or wrong.

Fate however, had a funny way of nudging him along and keeping him on the right side of life, or at least that's what she believed.

She stared at the heavy curtain pulled across the rear of the container.

It hung from a yellow washing line, kept in place with steel crocodile clips, the ones you see on market stalls holding the waterproof sheets in place.

Still frozen to the spot she heard the sound of breathing on the other side of this flimsy wall.

'Sean, Sean, you there? It's me Specks, Kev asked me to pop by. Sean?' Still no verbal answer apart from a low toned snore.

Like a stupid teenager in an American horror film, she pulled aside the curtain even though she knew it was wrong. Her features changed from the solemn, tightly screwed expression caused by the fear and anticipation of the unknown situation, to a warm smile appearing in its place. Curtain still in her well-manicured hand she stared at the virtually naked body of a mature muscular man. A far cry from the lanky teenager with big feet and head to match that she had gone to school with. Never had she had a thought romantically regarding her mate.

Lying in front of her on the mattress, and only wearing his boxers, was a real man. Doyle wasn't your pretty designer type, nor was he a devilishly dark Mediterranean type. Above average in the looks department, yes, a couple of scars in the right place on his face, but physique wise he was a clear winner. Her face felt warm as the blushing started. Her eyes not concentrating on his face, she no longer wanted him to wake up. Not for a few more moments anyway. Specks was secretly enjoying the voyeurism. 'No!' Her conscience stopped her. She knew it was wrong, so she allowed the curtain to fall. It was only back in place for seconds.

'Who the fuck are you?' demanded Sean, in a tone that under no circumstances could be mistaken as friendly.

Specks cowered, not really from fear of Sean, more from the shock that he had just appeared as she hadn't seen or heard him wake.

The eighteen stone, 6 ft 4 man towered over the petite 5 ft 4 female.

'Sophie Cellest, it's me Specks, Sean. Kev said to come by. You and him found some old rifles for me to appraise,' she explained as fast as possible then waited.

Taking a minute to come around, Sean remained quiet; the silence that floated between them was vanquished by Specks. 'The rifles, the flintlocks, very old weapons. In a coffin apparently, strangely.' She had gained her confidence back; she knew deep in her heart he would never hurt her.

'Specks, you look different.' The curtain fell behind him as he came closer.

'I could say the same, and I see you're still fighting.' She looked at the black eye and bandages.

'Actually, this was from an explosion.' He grinned as if that somehow normalised all the bruises. And yes, to him "explosion" was normal in a sentence.

'Explosion? Were you at that old pumping station?' Her voice speeded up.

'Yeah, how did you know that?' He yawned still coming around from the deep sleep.

'It's all over the TV and papers. Some people were killed, weren't they? I'm glad you are okay. But why was y...'

'I should put some clothes on,' said Sean, not wanting that particular conversation to continue. He had smiled out of respect for the nursery rhyme teller, he went quiet and took a secret moment of remembrance for a person he wanted to know more about but wouldn't now have the chance. She, to him was fuel; he would stop at nothing to ensure he got answers for her.

'Do you really live here?' Specks asked looking around the inside of the shipping container.

'I do, why? What's wrong with it? You aren't one of them people that better themselves, and turn all judgmental? Two minutes, put the kettle on while you're waiting.'

The next sound she heard was the falling water from the make-shift shower. The swan box was opened. She struck the match. Gas knob turned; the blue flames warmed the bottom of the kettle.

'Where do you keep the cups?' she asked but received no reply. There were only two cupboards and three plastic boxes with lids. With the water boiling on the camping stove, she searched for the cups to take her mind off the urge to become a voyeur once more. The second box did contain the cups, tea, and coffee.

'Two sugars, please,' said Sean, pulling the navy-blue T-shirt over his abs. 'You found everything then.' He spoke softly this time, using his Sunday voice.

'I did. How are you, Sean?' Specks walked to him and grabbed a hold, hugging him tight; nothing sexual, despite her earlier thoughts. Sean had been there for her when Specks's stepdad did the unthinkable to her. The topic was never discussed between them, as they were only young teenagers and didn't in all honesty understand. But he ensured that everything was normal between them, which was all Sophie needed at that awful time in her life.

The image of her, Kev, and Sean on a crisp evening, all of them sat with their feet swinging, heels tapping against the wall of the railway embankment. Laughing whilst sharing one bag of chips steaming with the scent of vinegar and taking turns drinking from a can of Shandy Bass, one mouthful each. That's what she remembered as she squeezed the big man even harder. 'Lovely to see you, Sean, I've really, really missed you.' She held on even tighter for at least another four Mississippi's.

He broke the embrace and took the cups out of her hands.

'Good to see you, and from what Kev has told me you're doing well for yourself, I'm proud of you.' He was out of her grip and walked the few feet to the worktop. The kettle began whistling louder. He turned the knob and the whistling slowed.

'I guess I am, yes. I finished university and was lucky really, I walked into a job at the museum and then I got noticed there and a second job opened up at *Christies*, just the right time and right place. And I owe a lot of it to your Mary.'

'My Mary, why?' asked Sean, turning to pick up both coffees.

'After you left, my mam went back to HIM. I was taken immediately into foster care for the last year of college. Mary found out and got custody of me. She remembered what you had told her about my stepfather. I was so happy to see her face when she picked me up from college on that Thursday afternoon, telling me I was going to be staying with her for a while, if I wanted to that was. The social worker who was with her asked if this arrangement would be okay, which of course it was. I dropped my bag and books then threw my arms around Mary. That evening we went out to the shops; she spent a small fortune on me. I stayed here, well over there.' She pointed across the yard and the steel fence that Sean had erected.

'I never knew. Mary didn't say. What about your mam, do you see her now?'

'No, and to make things worse my brother moved back home when he was released from prison. I presume Mary never informed you of any of this because you told her when you were bigger you would sort him out if he hurt me again.' She took one of the coffees from him, quickly moving it from one hand to the other.

'I remember, and I should have come back and sorted the scum out for you, sorry.' He silenced himself for a moment. 'I could so...'

'No, stop, I didn't mean it like that, and that wouldn't help anyone would it? I've got over it, it's part of my past which is what's made me who I am today.

'And like I said, Mary was my saviour she taught me that by becoming successful and happy I could then ensure I was well rid of them forever. And she was correct. She also helped me discover the name of my biological dad.' She took a drink of the coffee, a bit hot, she blew on the cup, it was swapped in her hands again.

'Did you get anywhere with that? Your dad?'

'Somewhere, but nothing was confirmed. Then life got busy as I studied harder.' Her expression made it clear that the subject was to end right there regarding the identity of her real father.

'Bad news your Todd, the worst type. A fucking thug with a chip on his shoulder. Thinks he's one of the Krays and using them as an aim in life.'

'Tell me about it, he's running the Mockingbird crew with that racist psychopath Ahmid.' Her voice was full of hate and more so with the mention of the name, Ahmid.

'Set of wasters, always made me laugh. Ahmid thought he was white. Do you remember? When we were at school he would pick on the other Asians as if this would somehow assimilate him to the whites. It's amazing that you came from the same blood as your Todd.' Sean passed Specks a towel. 'Warning, it may need a wash.'

'Only half the blood of Todd,' she reminded him. 'And Ahmid still thinks he's white, and hate's the Asian community, he's nastier than ever, he really hurts people now. I can't understand why he's not in prison. Last year a reporter was looking into a story about him. To this day they've never found the reporter's body, just a lot of blood in his flat. At the inquiry it was surmised that with the amount of blood discovered, he could not still be alive. I think it said in the paper that the coroner estimated 3.5 litres had been lost. You knew him at school, Sean,' said Specks re-attempting the hot drink.

'Did I?'

'Alex Warren, the ginger-haired kid. He gave one of his kidneys to the girl in the year below us. You remember, we had that assembly for him, and you did his paper-round for a couple of months while he was getting back on his feet,' she told him.

'I remember it was Christmas time I got all the tips, I thought he'd joined the cops though. Alex was a nice guy he'd 'ave made a good copper.'

'He did, but left a couple of years later because of the corruption. Disillusioned, he went back into education and got his degree in journalism, and from Oxford, no less. He was a very clever lad, yet very modest. I helped him on his final paper. It was brilliant, and so insightful, he really wanted to make a change. He had ambitions to enter politics, but he had a run in with a minister.' She passed back the towel. 'Thanks, and I agree, that could do with being washed.' She smiled.

'What was the story Alex had got his teeth into?' Sean poured the fluid caffeine down his neck.

'Ahmid, he torched his uncle's fish shop killing both his auntie, uncle and two cousins and he never went down for it. He wasn't even questioned over it by the police. Everyone knows it was him, his uncle called him a thief in public and Ahmid threatened him.' Specks was mad and upset repeating the topic, but she continued. 'The word going around is that he passes information to the police, and in return he receives immunity for his "world", allowing him to be free to do what he pleases, as long as he passes stuff on.' Specks held the mug with both hands, sipping the drink.

'Let's change the subject. Tell me whether or not I have a fortune in antique rifles. You are the resident expert.'

'I am indeed an expert, but not in armoury I'm afraid, so don't get your hopes up, but from the description Kev gave me the type you have found are ever so rare. I only know of six in the country, and one is in our museum.'

Sean handed her his coffee. 'Hold this.' He turned and pulled an old quilt off the coffin.

'Jesus, Sean, how many are in there?' Her eyes were wide with disbelief.

'Sixteen, plus these two sets of pistols. Kev ain't seen these yet. I found them after he left, I did another recce of the shed. Oh, there's a couple of suits of armour, looks like they're full ones, but in pieces and stored in old whisky barrels. Can you believe it?' Before he'd finished speaking, she was down, kneeling in front of the coffin gobsmacked. Sean watched sipping his coffee. 'Well tell me, am I going to be rich?' He laughed. It wasn't riches he wanted but the funds to complete the house of steel and ensure the forthcoming future of the parlour and all the add-ons.

Still no reply. Polished wooden box in her hands covered in dust, she blew and revealed a small brass plaque inlayed perfectly into the rosewood. "John Slough of London". Her head started to move from side to side, re-reading the maker's name her pupils showing the excitement. Then she licked her finger and wiped the name. 'You've won the lottery, Sean Doyle ... the ... lottery, well, ... that's if these are authentic, and I believe that they are.' She spoke to Sean without looking, as she was engaged with the duelling sets.

She turned holding the box open. Sean laughed.

'What's so funny? You're rich, I said. Didn't you hear me? ... I mean RICH!'

'Your face, Soph, its covered in dust.' He laughed some more back as a child for a rare moment.

'Sean, did you hear what I just said?' She pushed the box towards him.

'Something about the lottery. Winning. And I'm rich.' He took hold of one of the pistols, feeling the balance in his hand. 'Beautifully crafted, but no good in a firefight, I imagine.' He placed it back in the case, it fitted perfectly into the green felt.

'They will have to be appraised by an expert in weaponry of course, but like I said, I do believe that they are all authentic, especially where and how you found them. I would put a value of at least £5,000 for each rifle and £10,000 upwards for the duelling sets, if not more in the right auction house. I'll be honest with you I've never seen such a set in this condition come up for sale. These are literally in pristine condition, so they may go as high as a hundred thousand.' She was much more excited than Sean.

'Have you always kept in touch with Kev?'

'Yes, we're really close. Why? And Sean, did you hear what I just said?' She answered his unrelated question.

'May go as high as hundred K, I'm not deaf, just selective.'

Specks nodded her head; realising he may not be that bothered about the money.

'I know that you're excited about the find, but to me the money is only another resource. A good one I admit. Would you be able to take over the sale? All I want is the final sum after whatever has to be taken.'

'It's going to be a lot of money. Do you trust me with thi...?'

'Of course, why shouldn't I?' Sean opened the small fridge and pulled out two bottles of beer. 'Celebration in order.' He offered her one of the bottles.

'You should be looking at ... at least £100,000 for everything, Sean, if the suits are in as good a condition as these, it's hard to be precise because of the pristine condition. That is what I call a celebration, and yes, you can trust me, of course you can.' Her hand went out to take the bottle.

'We're not celebrating the weapons find, I'm celebrating seeing you again Specks, and how well you've done for yourself.' Sean offered up the bottom of the bottle to her.

'I really have missed you, Doyle, and your reassurance.' She hugged him once more; even he couldn't get out of this grip. They broke the embrace; the bottoms of the bottles tapped.

Specks looked around for a resting place then sat on the coffin.

'I will arrange transport to the auction house, they will be much safer there, and then I will ensure that all the necessary paperwork is completed that will provide these with authentication. But like I said, if you can find any proof, any paper trail whatsoever, as to how long they have been here at the parlour and how they came to be here in the first place, who brought them and such. All this will give them a solid provenance, that's what we really need. The sky could be the limit with a watertight backstory as all serious collectors thrive on the provenances that are attached to antiques like these.' She took a drink and her eyes became brighter. 'Especially where weapons are concerned, the intrigue is never ending, pirates, terrorists or civil war, it's all there.'

'Will do, boss.' Sean grinned, as did Sophie. She was conscious of the fact she had slipped into work mode. 'Sorry, Sean, I get excited over things like this, and it's my job too.' She blushed.

'Don't apologise, I like it, shows real passion for what

you do. There was one story that Tony told me a couple of times, back when I first arrived here. I was playing pirates and he said that one of his great grandads was a real pirate, a smuggler, over 200 years ago.' A small silence followed as Sean reminisced. It was broken by Specks.

'Work on that if you can. It's the exact backstory that will bring the sale some genuine mystery and with that we will have them eating out the palm of our, sorry, your hand.' She moved to make a second coffee. 'And what's this, are you looking up your family tree?' she continued picking up the blue folder sat on the leaf of the table. 'This folder has Mary's name written on the front.'

Specks read the name innocently and opened it with prying eyes.

'What about her?' He heard what she said but didn't see as he was too busy pulling the cover back over the coffin.

Her hands slapped against her face, the folder fell to the ground, all the papers and photos spread everywhere.

What she saw in the folder was the first crime scene photo. This horrific picture was face up and displaying sweet Mary in the open coffin. A close up picture of her body with a couple of bullet holes in the centre of her chest. She started screaming, becoming inconsolable, yet she still gazed at one of the pictures.

'Hey, hey, shush.' Sean pulled her into his chest. The screaming became crying, then reduced again to heavy sobbing. Sean held his friend. Looking over her head he began reassessing the information scattered on the floor. The folder was empty. The embrace was quickly ended. He pushed Specks aside, dropping down to the floor as his brain ran faster, processing all the data newly presented in a different format.

Three of the gruesome pictures were practically the same, identical in pose, that's what he'd thought up to now. Looking at each of them individually, comparing them close at hand, it was like staring at triplets. Separated, and laying in different positions, but all still in view. His brain could re-analyse the data and because he was now forced to spend more time on each image, he kept on analysing every microscopic dot, then he was over again to pick up the last image.

'Look! You can see in this one that she has something gripped in her hand, here.' His finger tapped the glossy paper. 'But not in these two. The photographer must have shifted a bit.' Sean continued to stare at the pictures. To him they were no longer horrendous moments of Mary's death, that had been caught and locked in a slice of time, these had become a map. He grabbed a notebook off the table, flicked open the cover and began scribbling.

'Sean, Sean, what's going on? I thought Mary had died from natural causes, but this, all this,' sobbed Specks.

He didn't answer her, not at first, he just kept on scribbling away in the book, sheet after sheet, flick after flick, muttering to himself and re-arranging the images hyper focused on the details.

"Persons of interest" he scribbled as the title, then listed people: crime scene photographer, investigating police, staff member who discovered the body. Under each of these names he wrote three question marks, each one on its own line.

'Sorry, Soph, you shouldn't have had to see all that, but it'll teach you to be nosy.'

'Sean, please tell me what's going on? Why do you have that folder? It has police, confidentiality and evidence stamped all over it – and in red as well. Should you even have it in your possession? And all that stuff on the table, is that all related to this lot?' She was questioning but more so out of shock than interest. Her arm pointing at the table, but her eyes weren't there. She trembled with nerves.

'It's a long story, one that I really don't feel the time is right to tell you. One day maybe.' He replaced the contents back in the folder.

'Give me it all, here, come on. Give it to me.' Her hand went out towards him. 'I'll take the folder with me and destroy it, shred the lot. Sean, you must leave this to the police, let them deal with it. Sean! Sean! Are you even listening to me? You don't know who's involved... they may come after you?' She tried to grab the folder from him.

'I'll drop it at the police station if you prefer. I will tell them I found it in the street.' She grabbed at it again.

He pulled it back. 'Leave it, Soph, you're here for the weapons, remember.' He tossed the folder on the mattress. 'Time you left, Specks.'

A month previous – Sean's homecoming

The rain had made the same journey to London as Doyle had that night. He exited the vehicle, but this time there was no beret to deflect the downpour.

His big hand ploughed through his semi short hair, pushing out the water. His now wet hand tried the handle of the main entrance to the funeral parlour, as he pressed down, he looked up at the sign, "Barchards and Ward". His shoulder was virtually touching the window as he leaned in, staring through the large glass panes, a flashback to his arrival all those years ago.

Tony standing there holding him tight in his arms, gripped in a cradle-like position. That was the first time Sean had ever felt safe. He remembered pretending to be asleep as he listened to Tony and the dream lady, their voices were raised yet no aggression was sensed by him. He couldn't recall what was actually said.

He muttered to the image of Tony. 'I'll find out who killed her, and they will pay for what they did! That I promise you.' The door was secure; it was way too early to knock, so he returned to the Audi.

The street was quiet as it should be early doors. Back in the car he reclined the seat a little and lay back, his jacket pulled up and over him. A couple of hours kip was his intention. Still in darkness his eyes opened an hour later. His ears had pricked up to the tintinnabulate of the milk bottles and the milkman singing along. He didn't move a body part.

His eyes followed the Hi Vis jacket as it ran back and forth, jumping on and off the silent vehicle; this happened four times down the road before the milk float turned left and went out of sight. Sean sat up just as the front of the parlour illuminated. At the door, undoing the many locks, stood a strange creature, with hair tightly wound around plastic rollers, wearing a nylon padded dressing gown, half a fag glowing bright red, in the centre of its lips.

'Hello!' shouted Sean from the half drawn down window. The creature was caught off guard. The fag lit up even brighter before it was removed from the lips. The creature lent out from the building looking both ways and then across at the Audi. But its poor vision still didn't identify where the voice had originated from.

'Hello!' he called again this time more for Sean's pleasure than to give a location. He laughed to himself as he pushed open the car door.

'Ann, over here – It's me, Sean.' He shouted again closing the door automatically by pressing the fob.

She didn't know where to put herself. It was around five fifteen in the morning, and she was unrecognisable as a human and here was Sean, someone she hadn't seen for at least ten years. The cigarette was dropped, the milk nearly followed, rescued by Doyle as he reached the door.

'You startled me, Sean.' Ann was flustered. Sean was back home; it was a lovely surprise but his return clearly understandable.

'Sorry, that wasn't the intention, but it was funny.' He laughed offering to hold the other milk bottle.

'Have you slept all night in the car?' She nodded over to the Audi.

'Only an hour, don't worry. What about some tea to go with this?' He shook the milk.

She gave him the once over. 'You look really well.'

'And you, Ann, you l...' He shut his mouth.

Her eyebrows raised high, very high, she turned and slapped him on the chest. 'I see you haven't got rid of your cheek, my lad.' Then she leant forward to kiss him.

'Really nice to see you, Sean, I just wish ... I ... well, it wasn't under such horrible circumstances.' Eyebrows fell with the emotion.

Her expression was the perfect pose of a grieving friend. Sean didn't reply, instead closed the glass door behind them, dropping only one lock. The strange, comforting but not very nice smell of the place was exactly the same.

He recognised it instantly. Even though he hadn't been

home for a decade, if not longer. Sean remembered commenting on the strange smell once to Tony.

'It's not just a smell, son, it's the scent of all the souls that have been released here for over two centuries.' Tony told him. It freaked him out then, but not so much today, it somehow comforted him. His eyes closed giving a moment to Tony and Mary. Maybe their souls were once more united, although not religious the thought of that was okay.

Over the years Doyle had kept meaning to return home – catch up, but that wasn't him and things happened, well that was his excuse. He had flown Mary out to Gibraltar three times in two years whilst he was stationed out there; the last time had only been six maybe seven months ago.

'Come on, I'll rustle you up some breakfast to go with the tea. Full English do yah, lad?' Ann had started on the old stairs, one leg up and her hand pulled on the rail to aid the second.

'I don't wanna be any trouble, Ann, I'll just grab a sandwich.' He waited for her to be at least six rungs up before he began.

'I don't bloody think so young Doyle. Mary would kill me if I fed you with just a sandwich on your return home. You know what she believed in ...' At the top of the stairs she was forced to take a deep breath, 'Start the day on a big meal – face whatever was coming on a full belly.'

'I remember, then after that she'd tell Tony he was on a diet.' Sean smiled as they entered the kitchen. She went straight over to the old stove, then left a touch, and bent down to open the fridge, in went the milk. The conversation continued over breakfast, but nothing of substance was mentioned.

'That was great, Ann, biggest breakfast I've had in years, thanks.' He splashed down the last bit of gypsy toast with the remaining sweet tea. 'There's plenty more,' she said, frying pan in hand.

'No, no, thanks, really, I'm stuffed, I couldn't eat anything else,' said Sean, placing the mug on the table. Again, another flashback as he picked up the tea cosy to cover the pot. It was the same pot he and Tony would drink from. Sean loved it on a Sunday morning because it would be just him and Tony, Mary would be at church. Tony would supervise, Sean would do their breakfast and he would serve. He felt so grown up and so humble to look after the big man he saw as a god.

'I don't know what to say.' Ann placed the pan heavily back on the gas ring and burst into tears. Sean remained in his seat, but her tears kept coming. 'Come sit down.' he told her; she didn't move. 'Come on, Ann, it's only to be expected it's the grief.' He was up and over to the stove. Sean's hand was on her back gently persuading her to sit at the table he pulled the Union Jack tea cosy back off the tea pot and poured her out a cup.

'Sorry, Sean, I'm so sorry, lad, you shouldn't have to come home to this?' several sniffles before more words came, 'It's just I haven't been able to let it out, you know ... ... what with keeping this place running – and the staff and – customers.

I've just concentrated on the parlour, day comes, the day goes. Nights are the same. I hardly sleep because there's no Mary. I miss her so, I sometimes feel like she has gone away to visit with you, 'more sniffles, 'And she'll walk through the door at any moment, drop her bags and ask me for a catch up. Then all I'd get for the next week was how well you were doing, which is all I want. We were planning a holiday together, just five days, we were gunna surprise you in Gibraltar, we should have left today.

Then we'd talk about when you first arrived, we'd sup all the tea, then by eight we'd be at the brandy.' Ann started to cry again, spitting out more words as the tears rolled and her breathing whistled as the air went in, the words didn't make a lot of sense, some joyful, but most dark.

'She was my best friend and like a big sis. I miss her so bloody much it frigging hurts, here.' Ann pointed to her heart. 'Who could have killed her, and like that, and why – why Sean, why? No one had a bad word for her, did they? No one, Sean. Who would do such a thing to a kind woman? I don't understand.' Ann had become inconsolable with the grief finally being allowed out, although she hadn't told Sean everything, partly through fear, and partly because of Mary's memory in his eyes. He hadn't known fully what occurred and she wasn't going to tell him and tarnish her memory.

Sean's hand patted Ann's shoulder, it rested there then softly squeezed.

'I don't know either, Ann, but I can promise you one thing, I will find out, if it's the last thing I do. Anyone who had a part in her death will die.' He squeezed her shoulder again.

'Kill them, hurt them. I want you to make them suffer. Do you hear me?' Ann sounded loud and hateful, and there was good reason, but she was also scared. She continued. 'Promise me, ... that you'll kill them all, won't you? Don't listen to what they say, no excuses, no telling stories. Sean! I want them dead.' The crying had stopped, the middle aged, normally quiet and caring woman had so much hate inside that her eyes burrowed into Sean's.

The words she came out with were not of her character or usual vocabulary.

He responded with a nod. Words to Sean meant nothing, to him actions determined an outcome and a person's worth.

The kitchen was in silence for the following ten minutes. Ann cleared away the table, while Sean contemplated what was ahead of him as he looked around a room that had been locked in a time-capsule.

An external door clattered down below them. 'Don't worry, that'll be my John. He leaves early on a Monday morning. It's his turn to open the workshop. He hates the place since it was privatised but a job is a job today, but knocking pallets together is a waste of his skills.' The thought of her husband helped calm her.

'He's a good man your John, I remember him from being a kid. I thought he did kitchens?'

Sean looked across at Ann as she washed the pots in the same kitchen where he had too, it had been one of his chores every other night, he either washed or dried. Some great memories in a kitchen that was stuck somewhere between the late '50s and early '60s.

"Why change it, its functional"? He could remember hearing Mary telling Tony as she was baking. *'I thought you'd like a modern one like the Lloyd's have just had fitted."* *"Waste of good, hard-earned money. They may have it to waste but we certainly don't, and I'll hear no more on the subject, yah hear me?'*

Mary had this way of sort of shouting, but her Irish passion made it acceptable, then came the look. She'd then polish the tops even harder. In later years after Tony had died, Mary told Sean that she had really wanted a new kitchen back then but discovered that Tony's dad had built this kitchen from scratch and with his own hands, whilst Tony's mum was visiting her dad in Scotland. The kitchen never changed especially after Tony's passing. It became a memory box.

'How's the place running?' Sean asked.

'It's ticking over, we're getting enough custom to get by, but we really need to get some longer-term plans sorted.

I know Mary was concerned because the whole industry is changing so much and quickly. There are a lot of death hunters in the business now, offering these pre-plan offers. We have a lot of regulars but if I'm honest, less, and less. I remember Mary once saying that she hoped we'd still be open when it comes time to bury ourselves.' Ann silenced herself after realising what she had just said.

'Let's not get into "can I say this or that". You speak any way you want around me, Ann, we both loved her, remember?'

'Thank you, Sean, and she loved us in her way, and so, so proud of you she was. Mary used to do all that, you see. The planning, the bills, she was our Steve Jobs. Most of the regular bills go out of the bank these days, but contractors, supplies, this, and that, some of the bank payments ... I'm not sure what they're even for, but they've been running that long – I don't know if I should stop them? Then there's the mail ... just been piling it up,' she replied in shame, then took a deep breath, she was still washing the same plate. 'They need to be checked. I'm getting more anxious every day. What if the place is in debt? Oh my god what have I done!'

Sean just listened. It was giving him some information and allowing Ann to vent.

'What do you intend to do with this place, Sean, now you're back?' she asked in hope but with no eye contact.

'I think a visit to the bank first, don't you? Then can we meet up we'll have a sit-down for a couple of hours, sort that growing pile of mail out? I think that would be a good start, and then, well, let's pretend I'm invisible for a week, that way I'll get a good look at the place and how it runs.' Sean and Ann both looked at the stack of envelopes growing nicely on the side. 'It's only paper, Ann, don't lose anymore sleep, we'll sort it. I promise.'

'You're just like Mary, want to get to the bottom of things to see how they tick, then make your mind up. So glad you're back. I've been losing sleep, I 'ave and don't mind admitting it.' Her tears came again but these were from relief and a bit of joy maybe.

Three weeks soon passed, and things were pretty quiet, at least for Sean anyway. He had begun to look at the place with a view to its future, both short and long term.

The following morning at seven-fifteen he returned from a road run. Entering the parlour door he bent down to retrieve more mail. Six more envelopes, but at least there was no more pile. Four of them were addressed to Mary, one to Ann and a beige one to him. His eyebrows raised then his finger slipped through the edge to reveal the white, quality paper. Sgt Doyle, it was addressed to, it contained orders, the initial line instructing him to "complete a welfare check".

Sean read the official letter with some intrigue. "Report to desk 16, third floor, Chatsworth building, 0900 hours November 6th".

The orders were being issued by serving Brigadier

Howlett. After re-folding the letter and placing it back in its envelope, he slipped it into his pocket.

He had no idea what this welfare check was about. His memory's eye flashed quickly back to the date. *Shit, that's tomorrow* he realised. He also semi-recalled his Commanding officer from the regiment telling him he may have to report to somewhere, for something. So, he guessed this would be the first of many.

'Seany, is that you? I'm cooking, would you like some breakfast?'

'No thanks, Ann, going for a workout, I'll grab something after that. There's some mail here. Open it, don't start another pile.' His voiced dropped to indoor volume with some humour added as Ann appeared from the kitchen, standing at the top of the stairs. Four wide strides for Sean, and the post was passed over.

He made his way out to the yard. Surrounding him were at least half a dozen old sheds. He remembered being banned from going in them as a child.

They'll collapse on top of you, Mary used to say. But Tony went down the ghost story path and told him of the legend of the black thing, which was a shadowy ghost of a pirate ancestor. It lived in the sheds looking after treasure, and if disturbed, it would materialise and kill you.

The following morning, he returned from his run, twenty minutes earlier than the day before. A quick workout, a quick shower, two buttons left to fasten on the shirt, his ring and wallet secured, he was out the door.

'Have you a taxi right away,' was said into the mobile.

'Where from, where to?' the female asked.

'Mary's Parlour, going to Whitehall.'

'Is that you, Sean?'

'Who's asking?'

'Sonya.' There was a short silence. 'Sonya George.' She extended the name for clarification.

'How are yah, and how's your Beverley?' he asked, enquiring after his first love, a crush at the tender age of 15, she was an older girl at 17.

'I'm good, really good and our Bev's just married Karren Jopling, you know the chubby with albino eyes, the one from your year. You must remember half the school watched you beat up Ahmid, because he wouldn't stop picking on her, and her dad had just died.'

'Didn't see that coming.'

'You and the family. I'll tell her you're back home. She'll be over the moon. Your car is on the way, Sean, five minutes, please be waiting outside, and I look forward to seeing you soon. ... Wait. Can I take your number down?'

'Course, yeah, 07987...'

'I have it here on the system, speak soon,' she said, blowing the biggest exaggerated kiss through the phone.

She was spot on with her estimate on the arrival of the car. It wasn't a long journey, not distance wise but it was a quiet one. Sean looked over at the middle-aged driver and by the size of the suitcases she carried under her eyes she was finishing the night shift. 'Been a busy night?' He tried to be polite.

'Wouldn't know, lad, you're my first pick-up. I only work the days, can't do with the shite the clubs bring.' She indicated, and never said another word, which to be fair suited Doyle.

Although not a lot of tarmac to cover, the amount of traffic on the roads ensured he didn't have too much time to spare on arrival.

'Thanks, keep the change.' Sean was out the cab, instantly walking amongst the suited, booted, and uniformed workers. Dozens if not hundreds of them he thought then began feeling uncomfortable amongst so many people, they were so close to him. Londoners and New Yorkers are a different breed, was his next thought.

After all that he'd been through, his senses were heightened. But the saving grace was that it was only a short journey into the building, which was sparse of people.

'Hi, I've been ordered to report here, by a Brigadier Ho...' he was cut off once more.

'Yes, that's correct; we are expecting you, Sergeant Doyle. Welcome,' said the smooth, quiet, female voice. She was looking down at a computer screen from behind a desk. A uniformed man appeared and stood in silence close to Doyle. A touch too close for his liking.

Sean sensed he was there and he didn't appreciate being watched, still on alert from the herds of people outside. He turned from glancing at the security officer to be greeted by Tanya Howlett, her hand held out in his direction.

'Thank you for being prompt, Sergeant Doyle, I can assure you it is appreciated as we are quite busy at the moment. I hope you found us okay,' she said, shaking his hand. To him, she came across well-mannered, polite, but with no airs and graces.

'Taxi and came straight here. So, can you tell me why I've been ordered to attend today. It's a strange place for a squaddie on leave to be brought to, don't you agree?' He wasn't as amicable as most and not as much as his host. Sometimes it wasn't his choice, it was a shell, his steel coating that just appeared, usually when he was in stressful situations, mainly the falseness of people allowing them to function. He understood it and why, but sometimes he wouldn't play along.

'Nothing to worry yourself over, sergeant, again I can assure you of that. We merely have a few questions for you and later a general medical and some exercises regarding your leg injury. Also, the brigadier may request to speak with you.' Tanya turned.

'I'm not worried, more intrigued. After all, to be ordered by a brigadier to attend Whitehall is not an everyday event. Well not for me anyhow. All the brigadiers I've had contact with have been up their own a...' Sean remembered where he was and re-joined the game, reluctantly.

'Please, follow me, sergeant, and we can make a start. Shall we?' She instructed.

Two flights of stairs later. 'Please take a seat.'

'Was that the medical?' joked Sean looking back to the stairs. He tapped his leg. Tanya smiled, acknowledging his attempt at humour then asked, 'Are you okay with completing forms, sergeant?' She offered him a blue clipboard complete with a pen attached by a chain. Tanya left him alone sitting on a well-worn brown leather sofa which was at least ten feet in length with a high back and thousands of stud-like buttons all pulled in tight. He filled out the date and signed the sheet; twelve questions followed:

"1. How do you feel when you are surrounded by crowds"? *Here we go*, he thought, *they want to label me with PTSD again, pension me off*. He quickly lied, as did the majority of his regiment and he did the same with the rest of the questions. He looked at the back of the sheet when a door opposite him opened halfway. The solid wood, tall door remained semi open for a couple of minutes.

'Do I get a second chance? Can I retake it? Would you at least give me some feedback?'

He heard a voice ask, a voice that was pissed off with the person it was talking to.

'No!' was the stern reply to all the questions. The security officer that Sean had seen earlier at the desk made his way closer to the tall door. Sean watched as the uniformed man stopped four feet clear of the pissed-off voice.

'But bu... you know what, ... fuck yah, ... SIR.' The voice spoke again then the door fully opened.

The first figure was a soldier in uniform and with Sean's regimental beret. The naysayer was a tall, immaculately dressed officer, wearing no head dress.

'Thank you for coming in. Have a nice day, soldier,' said the brigadier then he looked at the security officer standing by before he returned into the room. The massive door closed.

'Carl! Carl!'

The soldier looked over to where Doyle was sitting.

'What's going on?' asked Sean, at the same time giving the security officer a look that stopped him in his tracks.

'I'm out the regiment in eight weeks. Was put forward for this Whitehall outfit, yet apparently I've fucking failed to score high enough on the chart, or like the brigadier put it, "I did not quite make their selection".' Carl looked down, the words cutting sharper than any knife that had ever cut into him.

'You pass everything, Carl. What was this one about? It must have been hard.'

'No. That's just it, I don't know what tests I've fucking

supposed to have taken. Set of freaks if you ask me. Watch yourself here, Doyle, this lot aren't what they seem. Maybe that's it.' Carl's voice was as loud as you'd expect.

'Sounds a bit cloak and dagger.' Sean wasn't sure what else to say.

'What you here for then?' asked Carl, becoming agitated with the guard stood right behind him.

'Been summoned for a monthly welfare check and a medical, I think. Not sure why I'm here though, well, here in Whitehall, I mean bit posh for the likes of us this place,' answered Doyle, then he side-stepped in front of Carl. He spoke again. 'Can you back off a bit, mate – we're having a personal chat here. What's yah mam say about being rude?' Doyle's stare was fixed.

The security officer obeyed, taking four or five steps back.

Carl screwed up his face then spoke. 'Good luck, mate, your gunna need it with these lot.'

He patted Sean on the shoulder and left with the guard following but at a good distance. 'Don't get too close to him,' Doyle warned the uniform.

'Sergeant Doyle.' A skinny female wearing a tight grey pencil skirt and white blouse pronounced his name perfectly, as good as a newsreader.

Tanya appeared and escorted Carl out of the building, not saying much. She shook his hand at the door and said farewell. He simply smiled, trying not to hold a grudge. The security officer winked at him and gave a sarcastic smile. Carl shot at him, three blows and a knee. The guard was laid out cold. Several more uniforms arrived and got Carl out of the building.

'I warned him to stay back, you just can't help some

people,' said Sean to the skinny woman as she wondered what was going on in the foyer.

'Please, take a seat, sir,' said the skinny secretary. The only chair in the room was a hard wooden circular one. It had been set six feet back from the officer's large desk. Sean clocked that the chair was particularly low.

'I'll stand if that's okay, sir?'

'Please be seated, Sergeant Doyle, I don't have time to see which one of us has the biggest dick,' answered the brigadier without looking up from completing his paperwork. Sean followed the order, finding the language different for an officer.

Sitting on the small wooden chair, it rocked, and he couldn't keep still on it. One of the legs had been intentionally shortened, only by a couple of millimetres, an old trick to put someone in an awkward position.

He had done it before himself during interrogation. The secretary approached the desk and relieved the officer of a few sheets of paper, an open envelope waiting in her hand.

'By secure courier and it must arrive there today, Miss Crown,' said the brigadier, sitting upright with good posture. He removed his silver rimmed glasses.

'I'm afraid we have no secure slots available until this evening, sir, I believe 1830 hours will be the first one I would be able to book,' replied the secretary.

'No, that's no good, they will be closed, and I require an answer today. Sergeant Doyle, could I be forward and ask a favour of you?' The brigadier looked at him.

'Yes, sir,' he replied, slightly surprised by the sudden request.

'Would you deliver these for us today, before 1600 hours?' He pointed to the papers held by the female.

'Give me the address, sir, and consider them delivered. I'll do it straight after this meeting.' Doyle's shell had somewhat fallen as he found this particular brigadier to be or seemed to be "a good guy". Never before had he been told to stop dick fighting; well not by an officer, he was still laughing to himself. But then he remembered what had happened to Carl and the warning his friend gave as he left.

'Excellent, sergeant, good man. Miss Crown,' directed the brigadier, and he waved his hand for her to pass the sheets over to Doyle. 'I will secure them first in an envelope, sir, confidentiality!' Her eyebrow talking as she sealed the envelope.

Doyle got a quick glimpse of the top sheet whilst they talked, several boxes containing ticks and some crosses; certain lines had been highlighted in red.

'Excellent idea, Miss Crown, we're not to pass on feedback regarding failed candidates after all.' The brigadier sat forward again in the large chair, glasses still off.

For a few seconds all motion had stopped, then the glasses were back on.

'Please follow me, Sergeant Doyle,' said the secretary, adjusting her skirt. Sean stood but remained there looking towards the brigadier, who had glanced back down to some paperwork. A few more seconds ticked by.

'Have you forgotten something, sergeant, or do you wish to be paid for the delivery?' Again, the brigadier didn't raise his head.

'I was under the impression I was here for a monthly check up, sir, and a medical maybe, that's why I was requested to attend, and by your own order.' It was a strange situation he was in as no enlightenment came back from the brigadier.

'See you next month, sergeant. Close the door on your way out, there's a good chap.' Still the brigadier didn't look up.

Sean wanted to call him a pompous prick, but he couldn't, as there was something about this officer, something he couldn't quite figure out. 'Who has the bigger dick?' Doyle muttered, smiling to himself.

'Everything okay, sergeant? Do you have another question?' smoothly enquired the officer.

'No, sir, everything's good, on my way.'

Charles gave a grin and wrote a number on a sheet of paper with a time and a strange location. In walked a second female. She said nothing just relieved the brigadier of the envelope, which now contained the bit of paper, and she left. Walking at speed as she passed Doyle, her shoe heel gave away. 'How clumsy of me.' She leaned on him whilst she adjusted her shoe.

Outside the office he started putting two and two together as he walked over to Miss Crown: "feedback sheets and his mate Carl".

'The delivery address is on this card, sergeant, and here are the two envelopes we require you to deliver.' She passed over the deliveries. Before proceeding to escort him to the main door, she asked for his visitor's ID card back, and she left. Out in the fresh air he looked at the card.

'Here, mate, do you know where this place is?' he asked a suited passer-by.

The wide lapelled jacket wearer took one look at the address then at Sean. Puzzled, he spoke and pointed. 'There, the third building along.' His arm pointed to a building not more than 60ft away from where they stood. Doyle gave a semi-embarrassed smile. 'Thanks, mate, not from around here.'

The suit left after giving him another strange look.

Miss Crown could have popped next door on her lunch break, he thought, but he was more aware than most that procedures and orders are to be followed, no matter how ridiculous they may appear at the time of following. The temptation was there for him to take a quick look at the feedback sheets then get in touch with his mate, plus, his own curiosity could be satisfied. Sean had known Carl a few years and he never failed anything. But he knew he wasn't going to look because although he was intrigued, being a professional and carrying out an order was ingrained within him like Blackpool rock.

He entered the posh building and asked the receptionist to sign for the documents. This was over in less than half a minute. 'Thank you,' said the receptionist.

Job done, Doyle left and set about returning to the parlour.

'Sorry, mate, really sorry,' was the man's words as he bumped into Doyle.

'No harm done, don't sweat it,' replied Doyle and walked off hoping to sight a taxi. He received a text, just as the man who knocked into him called a number. The text read, "Our Bev is having a bit of a party tonight. You're invited". He called the text-sender's number. 'Can you sort me a taxi back to the parlour?' Straight to the point.

'Why, where are you?'

'Whitehall.' He turned to see names or numbers.

'I've left work, Sean, but I'm not far from there. Wait, I'll come for you.' She pressed the end call button on the screen of the Mercedes.

The Whitehall secretary returned into the brigadier's office but couldn't talk as he was on a call. "You placed the note in his pocket, you are certain of this?" she heard him say.

'Good work.' The mobile back on his desk he looked up, removing his glasses.

'Papers, sir.' Miss Crown handed back the feedback sheets to the brigadier and continued, 'Loretta has called. Sergeant Doyle handed over the envelopes very quickly, and there were no interference marks found on the envelope, even under the ultra-violet light, sir.'

'Thank you, that will be all, Miss Crown. No, actually, I have a favour to ask, but it is to remain between us.'

'Not a problem, sir,' she replied, knowing full well the level of secrecy, but to her it was an everyday occurrence.

'Could you ensure this person is invited to a meeting with myself, at the time and location written on here.' He passed over half a sheet of paper. 'Oh, and use a cold phone please, Alison.' Her first name was used to say thank you for the discretion afforded.

'Of course, sir. And the outcome will be confirmed with your afternoon tea.' She left the room.

The brigadier pressed three digits on the phone.

'Have you a moment?'

'Yes, of course, sir,' replied Tanya.

9

BROWN EYES BLUE

'Feck me, you look proper,' a cheerful Sonya shouted through the window, leaning over to the passenger side. She hadn't really had to try too hard to find Sean, even with the drastic ten years change. Six-foot-four and broader than Arnold Schwarzenegger, at first Sean hadn't a clue who had pulled over as she sounded half - London, half -Aussie, her telephonist tone left back in the office. You getting in then? You're holding up the traffic.' And at this Sean noticed all the car drivers looking at him, driving by slowly.

'You've blossomed,' complemented Sean as he pulled over the seat belt.

'Yeah, I know, they cost me five grand,' she replied with her head out the window edging the Mercedes Sprinter forward and further into the reluctant traffic.

'And you ... yah prick. Get a life.' She responded to the butcher's van's horn being used continually, then what followed was a quartet of similar sounds, but she still edged in. Twenty-five minutes later, Sonya pulled over behind some buildings on a wasteland and looked at a surprised Doyle. 'Come on then, give me a bit of body heat.' Not waiting she moved in to hug him.

Trapped by the door, he had no escape route, and hugged him she did; he would have to have his shirt pressed again. Five minutes saw the pair of them in the back of the van which had been converted into a camper.

'This is professionally done,' commented Sean as the surprise hit him. He was up for what she wanted but, 'Sto...'

'I'll give ... yah the tour after,' replied Sonya, her rapid fingers twisting his shirt buttons open.

Her hands came away from him but only for a couple of seconds, to pull off her top; the same hands flew around her back to release the catch. Coming back round, her shoulders came forward, and the red bra fell. Sean now saw the family resemblance. With his height, he was forced over in the van. She pulled the curtain across; his hands slid down and took hold of her ample cheeks. Sonya was off the floor. He walked four steps and she was on the bed, lying on her back, her skirt up, his finger slipped in, the white pants pulled aside...

'Cup of tea?' she asked, wearing only his shirt.

Sean had wedged himself into the small seat. He pulled down the leaf tabletop on her instructions; it rested on his thighs. His eyes were fixed on the gorgeous Sonya.

'What's with the van? You, living in here?' His words were backed perfectly with the frying of the bacon.

'I've only been back home a month or so, I dropped out of college at seventeen ....' She stopped, both talking and turning over the rashers; the buttered bread would have to wait.

'Sean gave it as long as he could but was forced to flip the table up and grab the pan as the smoke detector sounded. He slid the van's side door open and fed the birds. Back in, he opened the roof vent and windows. His finger pressed on the red button, the noise stopped.

Sonya still hadn't moved or said a word. He turned her and sat her down on the tiny chair. He placed the tabletop down; it didn't sit on her thighs. The tin kettle had started to whistle, he finished the teas by putting two sugars in Sonya's cup. Both cups in one hand, he lifted the table, sat, and rested the top back on his legs. 'Drink this, but I'll warn you I'm not the best at making tea.' He slid the cup toward her.

'Sorry, Sean, sorry, sorry it's just sometimes, well, it still overwhelms me. And more since I've returned home and thank you.' She placed her fingers through the handle her second hand wrapped the cup. She tried to look at him and smile but didn't pull it off. She wanted to tell him everything, but she had already spoken with ten therapists, and nothing came out.

'I'm not very good at this,' offered Doyle, 'Just remember Mary giving people tea when they were upset.' He posed his face, and a quarter courteous smile was held.

'It's not your problem, I'll be fine in a few moments, it always passes. I have to think positive thoughts.' She drank some of the tea.

'You never said why you were living in a van.' He attempted to switch the conversation.

Then it all came forth, unlike talking to the counsellors and doctors, with Sean she felt safe and protected. 'I left here five and a half years ago. I'd not quite turned eighteen. We have relatives in Sydney, Australia. I flew out there a week after the event. I stayed with my mam's brother and his family up until about six months ago, then I came back for a couple of weeks but still couldn't settle, so I purchased this.' Sonya pointed to the van's interior with a wave.

She reached up to a shelf and pulled off an album and opened it to page three then twisted it around. Doyle looked at the page then pulled the book over, closer up he recognised the setting. He was staring at eight young kids all wearing some form of swimming attire. They posed in front of an old oak tree, himself with his arm around Beverley, to the left was Specks, close, even touching John Ash, and Kev was behind the pair, one hand on each of their shoulders, then to Sean's right was Sonya. He looked harder at the picture, then up towards her and her short real blonde hair, then back down to the photo.

'I know, not much of a resemblance is there? Well not no more!' She said. She undid the shirt and lifted up her ample breasts. Shattering Sean's family resemblance theory, and then it registered with him what had cost her five grand.

'Twelve months ago, I had these done,' she explained as Sean looked at the neat fading scars under the breasts. In the picture her hair was long with Shirley Temple curls and as black as Whitby Jet, as was her sister's, Beverley. Doyle continued to look between Sonya and the photo. He sipped at his tea while she re-fastened the buttons.

'I'm known now as Tamara, now a cousin from Australia to Beverley and Sonya, and it seems to be working.' Her hands went to her eyes. He watched as she popped out contacts: her brown eyes became blue. All Doyle asked was, 'Why go to all this trouble? What ar... or who are you hiding from?'

'I wasn't like our Bev; she had got more than her fair share of the femininity and outward personality. I was the geek of the family, skinny, flat chested and a full-blown introvert. I dressed more like a boy, but I was happy, my party time was spent in the library and there I was content with my head in the books. Career choices came and I decided that I wanted to be a reporter, more on the research side than in the field.'

She sipped more tea. 'Our Bev asked Alex Warren if I could tag along with him. He was a freelance journo by then and had left the cops. I figured that the experience would help me with getting into a good university, plus he had a cool office with some great computers. And Alex was good at what he did and worked hard. I went everywhere with him for a few months, but he was working on one case that I was not to become involved with.

Two days after he told me to stay away from this particular case, he was shot, killed I believe, and I was kidnapped on my way home from college. I spent the following three days in some dark, wet stinking room. I saw no one, had nothing to drink or eat. I laid on the floor – I was naked – my skin crawling with insects and cut from being dragged about like a doll. Still to this day I don't know how I got out of the place, but the police told me I was found naked and wandering near the old Victorian warehouse down by the dock with half my mind missing. I was in hospital, they had a cannula fitted in me and nearly all my blood was missing, While there, in a dream, all I remember was a woman came into the dirty room. I was strung up from a rafter, she cut something, I fell on the floor, and she placed a knife to my throat. I don't know what she was saying. I was too tired to listen, or it didn't register but it was definitely a well-spoken female voice. I remember being so thirsty – my insides felt dry. I opened my eyes, I think, but no ... it was a dream, I'm sure of it. It was a dream.' She sipped more tea, her head moving a touch. She gave a quick glance to Sean, making sure he was still there.

'I was kept in hospital for another two days after being found by the police, I'd only been back home for a few hours when my phone rang. A posh female voice told me, *"The next time you will not escape. I will slice you from your left ear to your right ear! And you will join your mentor, Alex."*

I instinctively knew it was the "Bitch" I just did. Alex was investigating a local gangster, name of Ahmid, yes the same one from school, and he had also made some headway towards discovering Ahmid's links to the Bitch and her identity, he was certain it was a female, a lot had the thought it was a male using the name bitch to help with securing his identity.

Sean, by his own statement, admitted he was no counsellor, but he could listen, but now was the time to say something.

'I don't think it was a dream. Was it?' Sean placed his finger on her throat, touching softly the small well-faded scar.

'No. It wasn't, Sean, but I have to believe it was!'

10

DEATH WARRANT

Shoebridge dialled another mobile number immediately after the Texan had contacted him all the way from his homeland. Half a million dollars was on the way to his offshore account and that was only the beginning. The Waterfront was going to be the UK's version of the American Bones and hopefully as profitable, a cleverly designed charlatan charity with profits an oil company couldn't dream of. The phone was answered, but no words were spoken by the receiver.

'Uguba, there will be no more deliveries to you from me.' The minister spoke into the mobile with his ingrained arrogance.

'As you wish, sir, it is your prerogative. However, you still are outstanding on the last one, are you not? The meat you brought over was contaminated, rendering its value worthless to my people, remember?'

'Well, my good man, Dr Uguba you win some – you lose some. Chalk it up to experience and move on.' Shoebridge laughed.

Now the Americans were on board he didn't give a shit

for Africa, the direction of his life was all one way and that was inwards.

'I don't think you want to do that. It wouldn't be in your best interests, sir,' warned Uguba.

'I think I do, and I am very good at looking after my own interests.' He laughed again, increasing his condescension for Dr Uguba.

'My people will not be happy with you, and rest assured you don't want to be upsetting the likes of them.

I see it as my duty to warn you of the danger you could find yourself in by not fulfilling the order.' The African Witch doctor and British GP told him the truth.

'Why? What are they going to do, dance, cut a goat's throat and put a curse on me? Magic isn't real you stupid baboon.'

'Have it your way, sir. I will see you before you see me. I may appear, I may not, yet my soul will be known to you as you die, you will slowly lose life, as you will suffer greater than any other. You will not be dead – but they will believe you are.' Uguba finished the call.

Shoebridge didn't give the threat a second thought. Dismissing it as more superstitious nonsense.

Glasgow hospital.

A 46-year-old, overweight woman hobbled slowly down the hygienic corridor. Slightly out of breath her hands came from the pockets as she stopped and knocked on the door. Not needing to display her warrant card to the two-armed officers, from her station, they parted after the shiny clinical door opened. A voice of calm authority was heard.

'Helen, thanks for attending, please come in. Lady De Pen Court has only just awoken, but she is willing to talk to us.' He spoke warmly with a posh Scottish accent. His uniform was immaculate with one pip and a crown displayed on the lapels. His full attire was the polar opposite to Helen's with her 20-year-old tatty trench coat, under which she wore a trailing dress, shredded at the bottom and severely worn walking boots.

The inspector stared at Helen, trying with his eyes to point out the dried dinner stuck to her top. She knew his intention but didn't respond. She just didn't care for his or anyone's opinion. She got results and good ones, which brought in the trash and in numbers that no one else came close to matching.

'Helen is that you?' croaked Lady De Pen Court, turning from the left onto her back.

'Do you know Lady De ...' The inspector tried to ask.

'Emma, please, let's drop the formalities for the moment shall we, inspector? And yes, Helen and I go a long way back, don't we, Helly?' She smiled at the detective inspector. Her next words were in the form of a question. 'How is Alaskin? I don't remember what happened to us, is he here with me, in the hospital? ... Did we have a collision...?' Her voice was tired and still croaky.

At first the room remained silent. 'Let me adjust your pillow, Lady De Pen Court,' sheepishly said the nurse, really not wanting to be in the room.

'Helly, do tell me the truth, please. What has happened, please?' Emma stared at the detective and former friend; confident she would answer her.

'I'm afraid he didn't pull through, Emma,' interrupted the inspector, sensing some delay from his inspector.

Emma looked at him then sharply turned away,

keeping her stare on the wall. A tear formed and was noticed by Helen. 'Maybe we should give Lady De Pen Court some time to wake up properly, sir, she has been through quite an ordeal, after all.'

'Yes ... y ... of course, a good suggestion, inspector. We will return when you have rested a while La... ma'am. I will inform the officers outside that no one is to enter, other than hospital staff, of course,' he added after the nurse looked puzzled.

'Thank you, that is very thoughtful. Helen, will you stay for a moment, please?' softly asked Emma.

The rest of the room was cleared. Helen hadn't moved at all. It was true that Emma did know her and had done so for a lot of years. From nursery school, in fact. However, what neither of them disclosed to the chief was that their friendship had been dissolved twelve years previously, after Helen had discovered Emma's involvement in a local kidnapping of a child and murder of a bank manager.

She overlooked the facts and never mentioned it officially, because Emma had chartered a plane and paid for Helen's mum to have medical treatment in the USA. Unfortunately, she died only days after returning home to her beloved Highlands. This was the only time Helen had overlooked anything criminal in her long police career, and it never sat well with her. A lump in her throat she would never get rid of. She had never spoken to Emma again until today.

'Do you still blame me for your mum dying, Helen?'

'Is that what you think this is all about? You believe I never contacted you for all these years ... because of my mum? You are unbelievable.'

'Yes, I do actually, as the NHS consultant said Megan would have lived for maybe three months longer if she hadn't made the journey to the States. I'm so sorry if I robbed you of that precious time with your mother, really, I am. I know how close you were and how big a part of your life Megan was, Helen. But you must know how much I liked, loved, and respected Megan. I would never have done anything to hurt her, or you.' Her voice had lowered but was clear.

'My mother wanted to take the risk, and I was really appreciative of your generosity, there was no way we could have afforded the £30,000 but no, that was not the reason. You're not to blame for my mother, or her demise.' Helen's voice had raised. She had unwittingly joined the conversation.

'I don't understand then, but thank you for explaining about Megan, that is a relief. So, what did I do for you to forsake me? In such a way.' responded Emma.

'You're a real bitch, a real piece of work! You really are. I have no words. Yo... ...' Helen stopped talking and shook her head in disbelief.

'I'm sorry, I really am, Helly, for whatever you believe I did. Let me make it right between us, please, I miss our friendship, it has never been replaced... it couldn't be replaced?' reflected Emma still unaware of what had caused this rift between them, but very sad it did.

The door opened and the nurse's head appeared. 'Not now! Get out!' shouted Emma. The two armed guards looked at the nurse then at each other. The door was closed.

'Tell me Helen, what did I ever do that caused you so much pain? I need to know.' Emma tried pushing again for an answer. She watched as Helen paced, her anxiety growing.

'The Richardson kidnapping! There, you happy now!'

'What are you talking about? What has that got to do with our friendship?'

'The Glaswegian bank manager who was kidnapped, and well, well … killed? Mutilated!' stated Helen.

'I am aware of the case. It was all over the news. What has it to do with us? Me?' An answer didn't come straight back. Emma had pushed herself up the bed. 'Speak to me, you owe me an explanation at the very least. Or is it a lot of piffle you have blown out of proportion. We had been inseparable since, well, I can't remember when weren't together.' Emma's face showed discomfort.

'How dare you come across, whole innocent. You know damn well what I'm going on about. We arrested one of your thugs, come-would-be minders. I always knew you dabbled in things that weren't always clean, but the kidnap and murder of a respected member of the community,' Helen had stepped closer to the bed, 'That I never imagined, never in my wildest dreams, could I believe you were capable of such violence.' Helen had walked away from the end of the bed; she couldn't get any further away without leaving the room.

Gloves off.

'You say a respected member of the community, are you joking?' Emma laughed and took a painful breath and started again. 'If your lot had done their jobs in the first place when the two young girls went missing and were discovered mutilated and dead, it wouldn't have happened. And what about their kidnapping, their torture, or didn't it matter! Because they were from a "site"? Did you read the autopsy report on those sweet young girls? Did you, did you, Helen?' Emma meant what she said and no longer was she going to stay quiet. Never mind gloves off, the cat was well and truly out the bag.

'He tore out the girls' genitals – and while they were still alive. Burnt them with cigarettes at least a hundred times each. Not satisfied with that he used a blow torch on them; can you imagine what they felt? One had to watch this happen to her friend knowing it would be her turn next!! The coroner wrote one died at this point, Jessica, but Sunshine lived another hour, after he started on her, she must have been terrified, as the autopsy report stated the wounds were inflicted 30 minutes before and after life had ceased.'

'There wasn't enough evidence, we tried, no one would talk to us, a wall of silence was their reply. And what has that to do with the bank manager? And how did you see the autopsy report?' defended Helen, but the memory sickened her as it had done years ago.

Emma wanted to shout and tell her former friend the full account, but she couldn't. All her life this lady's dad had, had to make so many sacrifices, as had her ancestors for hundreds of years. But the friendship of a real, genuine person may be a step too far for her.

'Helen, please, can I ask one last favour of you?'

The female detective with her back to Emma stopped from leaving. Her thoughts had spun back to been a child when both her and Emma were waiting for Helen's Mum Megan, the pair of them knew they would be told off for using all Megan's make-up. The two little girls stood there with their heads down, Emma spoke first and said it was her who had used the make-up and not Helen. Megan made them tidy up, but followed this with a make-up lesson, then her famous hot chocolate before bed. And today Emma still applied her facial dressing the same way, Helen didn't wear any.

'What's the favour? And then don't ever speak to me again, Emma.'

'Visit the estate. Caroline will have something for you to read. All I ask is that no matter what you believe, or imagine right now, you go to my home with an open mind, then you promise me, ... that you will destroy the files afterwards. I will honour your request if that's what you wish. But your law cannot always be the answer.' Emma was taking a huge chance with what she was about to do.

The conversation had become less heated as it drew to an end. The nurse knocked on the door once more, only to be ignored. Another knock came, a louder one that was repeated and re-repeated.

Helen asked through open the door. 'Who are you?' she demanded to know, then mouthed off to the armed guards, 'Do your job, get rid of him.'

The police officers closed the gap. 'Please leave, sir,' said the older of the two.

'I'm here to see Lady De Pen Court, it's important.' Sean's voice was loud and masculine and easily recognised by Emma. 'Let him through, please. I know him, I've asked him here.'

'I will send someone back later to take your statement, ma'am,' said Helen, and she vacated the room, forcing past Doyle.

'I see you get on well with the local plod, Emma.' Sean laughed.

'She's not just local plod! We are friends all the way from school. Just having a little tiff as us ladies do. Now explain what brings you north, Mr Doyle. Not that I'm not pleased to see you.'

'I contacted your estate last night trying to get hold of

you, and they informed me you were still in here. I've discovered a connection to both your attempted assassination, and I believe the murder of your son.'

'What about my Henry? Are you telling me you have discovered who killed him and why they would commit such an act?'

'Yes and no, well yes, and how he was killed and this whole situation has expanded and is still expanding. And unfortunately for you, Emma, someone is trying to clean up the mess that has been created here, and to them you are just a loose end to be tied up. The one thing I can assure you of, is the person behind this has a lot of clout.'

'Explain yourself, Mr Doyle. I am still a little dazed, and your investigation seems to have escalated substantially since our last chat. Do you have any names? And / or places for me? And how certain are we of the guilt of these names?'

'At the moment I'd say 85 percent. I know he is the one giving the orders for your assassination attempt and more than likely the money behind it. I'm still finishing the canvas, and for that I'll need a couple more days.'

'You have done very well, Mr Doyle, very well. How about I give you a very large bonus, ... shall we say £50,000, and in return, you leave me the name of this money man? I'm sure that will make us both happy.' She didn't smile but there was definitely a different expression on her face, even after he told her that he hadn't located the child.

'I would sooner complete my work, Emma, then pass it all over to the police, let them deal with it.'

'If that's the way you wish to play, Mr Doyle, so be it, but you still deserve a nice bonus. Before you leave and return to London, I would like you to visit my estate. I do appreciate that it's somewhat out of the way, but I'm sure it will be worth the journey. I will call in advance to let them know you are to arrive. A folder full of information about your family will be waiting, just as I promised. You may as well take it away with you.' She sounded tired and had naturally slumped in the bed, the day's events finally taking their toll.

'Much appreciated. I'll leave now if that's okay, let you get some rest, and I need to be heading back to the city tonight.'

Emma held out her hand. Pointing to the door, her eyes had begun to close, but she resisted. Sean exited the room. It would take him 90 minutes to reach the big house.

'The De Pen Court estate.' Is how the phone was answered.

'Caroline.'

'Lady De Pen Court, ma'am, how are you feeling?' enquired the housekeeper.

'I'm feeling fine. Two instructions for you. My friend Helen is coming over. Have ready a copy of the bank manager's execution file for her to take away and the consultation papers for the two gypsy girls, and I want their pictures in the front of the folders! Ensure the papers inside have no trace to us. She will arrive at any time, please make it so.

'Secondly, there is a Mr Doyle on the way to the house as we speak. He doesn't leave the place, but I want him alive, not harmed, do I make myself clear, Caroline?'

'Yes of course ma'am, he is not to leave ca....' She shushed quickly as Emma began to speak again.

'Who is on duty tonight at the estate?'

'Lance and that new guy, oh, and my Harold is coming over soon to pick me up.'

'Not good, that may present a slight issue. Lance has become friends with Chalky, and he's Sean's good friend. Tell Harold to call me the moment he arrives I need to make sure those two are out of the way – and for the full night.' Emma had begun to sound more tired.

'What shall I tell them, ma'am?'

'Think of something, Caroline, think woman!'

Emma ended the call. She wanted the name of this money man, as Doyle had put it.

And she would get it at any cost.

And if he believed the police were going to be involved with this whole mess, then sadly he was very much mistaken. Hopefully, she wouldn't have to neutralise him, but when dealing with men like Doyle, being lenient could be the equivalent of signing your own death warrant. However, she had done intensive research for a long time on him, much more than any other, and she believed she could ensure, without the use of violence, that he saw things her way. It just may take some more time.

And if this wasn't the outcome, she would have misread a lifetime.

Doyle had been travelling for well over an hour, or longer, forced to slow as the roads became tracks and not flat ones.

'Fucking hell, where's this house?' Sean pulled over to use *Google Maps*, but there was no signal. His arm went out the window, but the page still buffered.

'Are you lost, son?' was shouted from the heights of a tractor window.

'Looking for the big house, mate. Lady De Pen Court's place,' shouted Sean, ensuring he was heard over the decibels of the large engine.

'You've taken the wrong turn back there at the ford, lad. Go back down to the water, through the ford, then it's a sharp left. Looks like you are coming back on yourself, but the road turns slowly. You'll see an old grain store on your right. After about a mile keep straight from there and you be fine.' Sean could see his eyes moving, recalling the details, and good details they were but he hadn't finished.

'Stay on that road for ten miles. It narrows a lot, but you'll see the estate, and you cany not miss the house, nothing else out there.'

'Cheers mate,' shouted Sean and backed it up with a hand gesture.

'Wait a moment, lad.' The tractor door was pushed open. Doyle could see the 12-gauge fixed to the inside of it. The farmer was coming down the steps on the vehicle. 'Just a second,' he said again as he disappeared around the back, reappearing holding two pheasants. 'Give this brace with my compliments to Caroline and tell her thanks for the pies, her best ever.' Doyle's arm was still out the window holding his new passengers. He watched as the old farmer somewhat awkwardly pulled himself back up the heights of the vehicle then gave a wave and went on his way.

Sean looked at the two dead birds now on the passenger seat. He gave a small shrug then completed an about-turn. As he turned left at the ford, he was practically forced off the track by an old Land Rover. He looked twice semi recognising the detective from the hospital. Within 40 minutes he pulled up outside the estate. The door opened, exiting was his mate and Lance.

'Sean, what you up here for?' Chalky was pleased to see him. Five minutes of chat followed before Lance prompted Chalky. 'We have to go. We'll miss the ferry sailing. Nice to meet you again, Sean, Chalky has told me a lot about you,' added Lance.

'And you.' Sean shook hands with Lance.

Chalky slapped his mate on the arm. 'Thanks again.' And the pair were gone.

Caroline was waiting at the main door. She had deliberately allowed time, seeing them talking, her arms crossed for warmth not attitude. She began to speak as she watched him walk around the car. 'Lady De Pen Court has informed me of your arrival, sir. I have a parcel waiting for you to collect. I believe that is your purpose for visiting us, Mr Doyle.' Caroline was clearly on edge. Surprised, she spoke again. 'How very thoughtful of you, Mr Doyle.' Her arms came loose.

'Sean, call me Sean, and I'd love to take the credit, but these are off an old farmer. He gave me directions then said I was to give these to Caroline and thank her for the pies. "Best ever" he added?' Sean slammed the passenger door, holding up the brace.

'Mr Doyle, please, please, will you come in, and can I get any refreshments for you?' Caroline was too ingrained and had been a housekeeper for too many years to call any guest by their Christian name, even if prompted.

She led the way, going back inside the mansion after relieving Sean of the birds. He followed the plump welcoming party whilst looking around the place. He was impressed with the exterior of the building, yet he'd seen it before somewhere, but couldn't recall from where and this was his first time in this part of Scotland. He patted the head of one of the large lions positioned on each side of the door. The pair stood at four feet and had been carved from local stone which was a smooth granite. The poly creatures had heads that were ugly being some type of bird of prey, and their feet were weird too, they were hoofs instead of paws. Then human arms held out a shield in front of their chests.

Each shield had a coat of arms depicting an axe severing a chain. Above this sat an old helmet followed by a dagger which crossed the axe's handles. Below the weapons and expertly chiselled into the stone were some words these seemed to grow around the shield, a strange language that was clearly very old. Where had he seen these before? he questioned, again a feeling of deja vu.

He followed Caroline in through the large door, automatically wiping his boots on the bristle mat cut into a steel grate.

'I have your parcel behind the desk, Mr Doyle.' Caroline made the journey to the other side of the counter that filled the far wall. The counter was erected in the late '80s when the castle first opened its doors to the paying public. A necessary sacrifice to bring in funds, as these buildings were over 600 years old with maintenance issues.

'Beautiful place this,' said Sean, walking across the stone floor.

Hanging on the wall above the reception desk was a collection of framed photographs. 'That's where I've seen it before,' said Sean out loud. The photo he was looking at was of all the cast members who starred in the *Highlander* movie.

'Most of our guests have the same reaction, Mr Doyle.

The house has been a star in over fifty movies to date and several series.' She produced a box file from behind the desk, it was closed and sealed with tape. She hesitated, keeping the box close before passing it over.

'I hope I am not speaking out of tern, but Lady De Pen Court mentioned you were intending to drive all the way back to London tonight, Mr Doyle. Surely, sir, a good night's rest and an early start would be a much more sensible solution, would it not? It's a long way,' said Caroline on the move.

She looked at him and spoke again. 'We have three rooms made ready, with beds turned down, and plenty of hot water, Mr Doyle, and if you have an appetite, I could rustle you up a supper. Maybe one of the pies the farmer mentioned?' Her professional smile was waiting.

Sean didn't need much persuading. It had taken him a lot longer to reach this place than he thought. 'If it's no trouble, I'll take you up on the room offer. I wouldn't mind stopping here tonight, loved that *Highlander* film. One for the bucket list, this is.'

He knew it was a full day's drive from Glasgow to London alone, without his little excursion added on.

'Let me show you to your room, Mr Doyle, and once you have settled in, I will send up your supper, ham carved off the bone with lashings of garnish all tucked into freshly made pastry,' said Caroline who was short, stumpy with wide feet, dressed in attire that would match the counter in its heyday. Sean was forced to follow at her pace, meaning he had a brief wait on each step.

'Here we are, sir.' She stopped and unlocked the room door, turned, and gave him the file. 'Twenty minutes and your food will be with you, Mr Doyle. Hot cocoa?' she tempted.

'Thanks, and yes,' said Sean, who couldn't remember the last time he had cocoa. He closed the door and walked to the bathroom.

Caroline had reached the end of the long corridor and began the descent of the steep staircase. A large figure waited at the bottom of the stairs holding a gun.

'Harold, put the gun away. He's stopping the night and having a bite to eat, then leaving at six in the morning,' she sniggered, 'Or so he believes.' Her face changed. 'I'll spike his hot chocolate; he will be sleeping at least 'til lunch. He looks like he could do with a good rest, I'll be doing him a favour,' Caroline said from relief rather than success.

'Whatever you say, love. Can I get some supper, hungry.' replied Harold, breaking the barrel of the 12-bore and popping out the shot.

'I'm making a pie for our guest, so I will do the same for you, but after you have called Lady De Pen Court,' answered Caroline. She collected the brace off the counter and set off for the kitchen. Harold followed weapon across his arm he began the questions.

'So, what's this Mr Doyle like? I've heard that much about him from Chalky, you'd think we had Jack Reacher upstairs.'

'Who?' asked a semi-interested Caroline, pulling ingredients from the cupboard.

'Jack Reacher, you know, ... from that great author I like, Lee Child. I have all his books and Reacher is his main character.'

'Oh, yes, that's right, I remember, I bought you a book for your birthday,' she replied, slicing through the homecooked ham, she hadn't a clue who this Jack Reacher was. But she stopped, 'Wait a minute, Jack

Reacher, how could he be like him, I saw the film, Tom Cruise isn't that big?'

'Don't go there!!!!!' Harold placed the shotgun on the counter then got his hand slapped attempting to pinch a piece of meat.

Two days previous

'You've become very attached to Tony's old Mac I see.'

'It's warm, loose fitting, and comfortable. What's not to like?' Sean nodded with his answer, slipping his arms through the sleeves, catching his fingers again on the torn liner in the left arm. 'Was it his then? I don't remember him wearing it.'

'Tony's Christmas present to himself a year or so before he met Mary. It was his rain Mac for the funerals. He didn't wear it that much, because he thought it made him look larger than he was.'

'But it's well worn.' Sean emphasised this. His left-hand finger wriggling in the torn lining.

'You know how careful Tony was with his pennies, Sean, he brought a whole new meaning to being frugal didn't he? He purchased it from the Oxfam shop on the High Street. He would often say he paid two pounds for it and found a fiver in the lining, had to cut it to get it out.' She took the sleeve and wriggled her fingers through the same hole, then smiled at Sean.

'I'll sew this up for you later it won't take me a minute.'

'No, thanks but I'll leave it as it is, and frugal isn't a bad trait, people get it mixed up with greed,' defended Sean.

'Oh..., no dear, I wasn't saying that he wasn't greedy, not at all, he believed in choosing where his money went that's all. I didn't mean to imply ...' She felt bad.

'I know, I apologise, it's me, Ann. I feel like I didn't have enough time with him, I always have felt like that. He was a good man, in fact a great man. If I had one wish it would be to have him back, even if it was just for one day.'

'I agree wi...'

'Sorry, Ann, gotta take this call.' Sean turned his head; phone went to his ear. 'Chalky, how's the job going?'

'Great thanks, just thought you'd wanna know her ladyship was shot a couple of days ago. She's in hospital now, her butler was killed outright at the car, three shots in him, but one went through and hit the boss. She's been wounded but it looks like a full recovery will be made. At least that's the brief we've received from Caroline. There'll be two of us stationed at the house round the clock in shifts from now on, ensuring this place is safe for when she's discharged. There 're armed cops at the hospital. I'm guessing it was a professional hit, a sniper. We'll carry the shifts on when she's back home, at least until further intel changes the game.'

Chalky sounded happy, he was doing what he was born to do and more so now the heat had been turned up. This made Sean smile. His mate had found a life again and Emma had a good man on her team that was for sure.

'Text me the details of what you know, and I'll come back up there. Pair of fresh eyes on the situation may help.'

'Back up a minute, Doyle, what? You've been up here already?'

'Yeah, but it was a little tricky, and I was informed she was on the mend. With everyone fussing, I came away, back to London, you know I'm not one for crowds,' informed Doyle.

'Fair enough. Do you have an email address? Text it me.' Chalky touched his phone.

'Send it to the parlour in a secure attachment. Text me the password.'

Sean quickly fished through the paperwork on Ann's desk, searching for an email address. 'Here, you ready; info-at-Barchardsward.co.uk, cheers.' Sean placed the phone back in his pocket.

Chalky switched off from the call straightaway and set to typing on the laptop. The "send" key was pressed as his orders came in. 'You're on midnight 'til six with me. You okay with that?' asked Lance.

'No worries. You heard how the boss is doing?' he replied verbally whilst sending a text to Sean's phone. "22Reg!" was received on Doyle's phone.

'Ann, I may be away for a few days. Anything you need from me before I leave?'

'A holiday? And, no, no. Yes, sorry it nearly slipped my mind. The salary cheques will need doing, it's the bonus month, so not just a bank transfer,' explained Ann.

'They're done, all signed and waiting on the new desk. I also left an envelope for you as you hadn't given yourself a bonus.' Sean gave her a look.

'I won't take it. I'm telling you now, LAD, we need to sort the bank out first. That was the plan ... remember and ... I, ... I, I have the new flat, that's bonus enough. I love being in there. It keeps Mary closer to me and it as central heating!'

'And you remember, I'm dealing with the big picture. Enjoy it, treat you and hubby to a good night out, it's not that much. Spend it, Ann, or I'll double it next month and again the month after.' Sean watched Ann screw her face up, and it was obvious she appreciated his thought.

Sean was off, the green holdall in hand. Ann went to the window and pulled back the clean net curtain; she watched him walk around the corner. She slightly smiled to herself before dropping the net, just for a moment her world was regaining some normality, - is it what she wanted. The just past middle-aged female closed her eyes tight, took in a deep breath, a wish was made.

Reluctantly she made her way to the office still thinking about Sean and Mary. Sitting behind the old desk, her breathing accelerated, and her fingers tapped at speed, in rhythm at first, then they became erratic as her concentration focused on what she would say.

She told herself to calm down. The soft spoken newly appointed and trusted manager rummaged through the second draw, a sense of relief displayed on her face as she took hold of the phone, she quickly called a number on Mary's old mobile, a phone that Sean wasn't even aware existed. The number she dialled was listed under "Emergency funds". This phone number had called Mary's mobile 197 times over the last two weeks, leaving messages on each attempt. Ann pressed to call, then pressed once more on the speaker icon then placed it on the desk and listened.

'The Waterfront. Lexi speaking, how can I help you today?' is what Ann heard.

'Could I speak to Doctor Moe, please,' quietly asked Ann, keeping herself calm as best she could. Her fingers still tapping but on the ink pad, not the wood. She knew what was happening but had never done this before; she knew the process but had never carried it out before, she had been Mary's wing man and saw it from the sidelines.

'One moment, please, I will try and connect you,' eloquently answered the receptionist.

'Dr Moe speaking.'

'Do ... doc ... doctor, it's Ann. Can you stop contacting this phone, please? You are aware Mary has gone. And I cannot facilitate your needs like she ... '

'Now, now, little Ann, play nicely unless of course you want to join your dear Mary.'

Moe came across as creepy as a person could. Ann didn't know what to say in response. She had only called the number because the last time she checked the phone the 197th message read, "If you have not made contact within the following 24 hours, we will contact you in a different way"!

She didn't think too much of it but a couple of days later and Ann's husband had been knocked clean off his bike. The police later filed it as a hit and run, but no witnesses came forward, so no one was caught or convicted. The car was later found up on the heath completely burnt out. The Ford Fiesta had been reported stolen off the estate the previous night. Soon after, Ann received a bunch of flowers and a card sending her condolences for the loss of her husband, with his name, place of work and his local pub written on the card. Petrified that what the note said would come true, she quickly texted the number, explaining she would be back in touch when they had capacity, and with Sean now gone, she made the call as promised.

'I can't continue with this, doctor. Mary wanted to stop all of this business. You know that ... she... she ... told you ... it was to end.' Ann was shaking, fingers frantic and back tapping on the wood.

'She did, you're right, and look how she ended up! Now tell me what I want to hear, little Ann. How is your husband doing after his accident?'

'We have two days whilst he is away, and four services booked in. Have you a need?' asked Ann mimicking Mary's words. The confirmation of the services spun her back years to that day Mary first asked for her help with all this – "cloak and dagger business", as the pair would refer to it, later it was given a code name – one which they could use without people becoming suspicious; "heavy coffin".

'I have two in need of disposal. I will arrange to send them both over immediately,' replied Moe, enjoying her surrender.

'Th ... the ... there's a ... matter we need to d d d... discuss first.' Ann went silent: being brave for her wasn't easy, her fingers took hold of the pen, it scribbled down numbers.

'And what would that be?'

'The price, ... doctor.' A large gulp of air was taken in, arms out, her hands open she slowed her breath, recalling what her friend had told her about dealing with these types. "Never show your fear to the monster" Mary would say.

'The cost of each disposal will have to double.' She waited for the eruption, and it came.

'Double! Twice as much! Three thousand pounds each! You need to rethink your calculations,' angrily replied the doctor.

'The risks are much greater now. With what happened to Mary, the police may still be sniffing around. And then there's Sean, if he finds out I'm involved in all this, and that I knew about Mary's death, I'm dead. Especially since I had to remove the object from her cold hands.' Ann shivered at the memory of that one event.

'That's not my concern, is it? You took the money from

Shoebridge not me. I don't know why he wanted her dead. But just remember that the greedy bird will be pecked by the others as they arrive. I'll pay you an extra £500 for each recycle, and that's the last I'll hear of it. Be satisfied with that or I will tell your Doyle chap myself.'

Phones down. Ann left the office fuming that she had been told off, but still an increase in the price she had gained, and that was the same amount what Mary had asked for from Shoebridge. So, in her own way she had done it for Mary.

She threw her hand on her chest, sat at the desk for a good ten minutes, contemplating what she had just done. Only a few days ago the world was rosy, what with Sean being back and her new manager role, there was hope back in the air. Doyle, like the first time he arrived, had brought again a fresh energy into the parlour. She made herself go out into the yard for some fresh air.

'You startled me, sir, we're not open at the moment,' she said, craftily wiping away a tear.

'I am hoping to speak with a Mr Doyle. I believe that he is the proprietor of this establishment. Am I correct with this assumption?'

'He is, sir; however, if it is a bereavement you wish to discuss then that would fall under my remit, as I am the manager.' Ann had knocked up her articulation a notch. This was a daily occurrence for her as at the parlour someone from every walk of life could wander in at any time, it was in no way patronising it was the personal touch.

'No, it's a different matter I wish to discuss, and it is Mr Doyle I need to speak with,' came back, polite yet blunt, but not offensive.

Tongue   twisted   by   the   gentleman's   lack   of communication, Ann informed him that Sean had left and wouldn't be back at the parlour for a couple of days. Maybe longer as he had some business to attend to out of town.

'Thank you, good lady. I shall return if I still require his presence at a later date.'

'Can I say who has called, sir?'

The immaculately turned-out gentleman didn't reply. Instead, he chose to turn and leave the yard.

Perplexed for a moment Ann remained in the arch adjacent the parlour. She watched from the cover of the bricks as the gentleman broke cover from the far end of the long Victorian archway.

The gentleman was soon back on the public highway, the umbrella flicked up whilst walking to a waiting limousine, then down it came again on arrival. The driver watched the gent closely as he approached. Two metres away from the car and he was out to take charge of the wet umbrella. 'Thank you,' was said. The vehicle's rear door was opened.

'Mind your jacket, sir.' The material was pulled in, the door firm in place and the umbrella was shaken several times then placed into the boot.

'Any luck, sir, finding him?' asked the driver on re-entry.

'No, well yes, this is the correct place, but I seem to have missed this Doyle character. Get someone on it. I want him located asap. A stupid private investigator messing up things is the last course we need to take right now. Do I make myself clear?' His tone had changed rapidly.

'Yes, sir, and I'll sort i...' Andrews didn't get a chance to finish his reply as the glass divide closed between them.

The gent switched on the TV, the driver called a mobile number; the phone rang in another car.

Across London.

The passenger smiled as he read the window stickers on the vehicle in front. "Baby on board", "Future princess", "Precious cargo".

'Put yah foot down, Sligh,' demanded the passenger.

'The lights are changing,' replied the driver.

'And? Just fucking do it,' ordered the passenger.

The Range Rover's speed increased; the lights did change to red. The Rover's bumper pushed the Micra's rear end right in. The female driver was out of the car, straight at the rear door, frantically checking on her child. The relief was plain to see on her face that the kid was uninjured and smiled back. She stared at the driver of the Range Rover, who looked at the passenger.

The female was at the window. 'What were you thinking? The light's red, innit,' she demanded and started to shout again.

The first reply came from the driver. 'Is the child, okay?'

'Yes, but no thanks to you,' stated the irate female then heard the second reply, this time from the passenger.

'Shame, it won't be next time. Tell your idiot boyfriend to stop selling shit on my turf unless it's bought off me? Now move that piece of shit out da way before we have a second go.'

The female stared at him, she saw darkness in his eyes, the chavy girl dressed in a shell suit silenced herself – her head stopped pecking at him, her skinny arms fell to the sides, she returned to her car.

The Range Rover's driver was gobsmacked, about to say something when a mobile sang. 'Ahmid, I've got a job for you,' said Andrews.

'How much and when? I'm busy right now,' were the first words out of the mouth of this six-foot-six, skinny, Asian, with eyes the colour of coal.

'A grand, but I want you on it now, today, none of your usual bullshit, you listening – I need this person found, so, stop with the "I'm busy" crap, I've had my fill of wankers today.' Andrews hated dealing with these cardboard gangsters, but needs must, and they would do anything for the right price.

This honour among thieves was the biggest load of shite going. Ahmid had already given over four of his so-called close friends.

'What is it? Someone upset your governor again and they're in need of a slap?' replied Ahmid, watching the female drive away. He waved.

'No, well not right now. We just need someone in your neck of the woods locating. We don't want them spooked, only located then call me. I believe he may be a private eye, name of Doyle, Sean, lives at the f...'

'I know where he lives, but I thought he was in the army,'

'You know him?'

'Yeah, I went to school with him. He left the area at the first chance he had, scuttled away like a wounded dog, tail between his legs. He joined the army. And like I said, I wasn't aware he had returned home.' Ahmid was now very interested in this job and not just for the money; that had become secondary.

'Will this friendship present a problem to you?'

'No, there won't be a problem. Never liked him as a

kid, can't see him growing on me now. I'll find the cunt for yah, it'll be my pleasure. Have the cash ready.' End of the call.

The passenger remained quiet, the driver wanted to ask again what was happening but still daren't, his hands twisting the leather on the wheel. Ahmid leaned over and started pressing the horn and flashing the lights at the Micra, the young mum panicking turned off and drove to her gang. Ahmid laughed dropped the glove compartment pulled out a small plastic bag, he flicked it ensuring the white powder fell to the bottom.

11

WORRYING

Specks had returned to Sean's tin-can with Kev later that afternoon, unaware Doyle had left town for a couple of days.

'Do you think he's different now?' She was dressed in baggy sportswear, but still immaculately turned out.

'Who? What? Different?' Kevin was counting out the welding rods into lots of five, their conversation echoing in the partially empty container.

'Sean, of course. Who else would I be asking about? Are you even listening to me?' Her head shook.

'He's filled out a lot that's for sure, bit of a hunk now and doesn't talk as much. At school he wouldn't be quiet. Remember?' Kev started changing into his overalls, dropping his clothes next to the paint cans.

'Well, to me he seems somewhat at a distance and when he does talk his emotions are restrained, like he's always holding things in. I knew he always could be the deep one at times, especially after Tony passed, but this is different somehow. I can't put my finger on it?' She looked at Kev. 'How is your bottom?'

'Just pass us that box, will yah, Soph, I don't wanna talk about that.' He was holding a handful of rods, deliberately not going there. Sean was back and that made Kev happy. 'Thanks, and yes you're right, he did seem a bit distant to me the other day. Outwards he's happy until anything from the past emerges, then he clams up.' Kev placed the rods in the box. 'I'll need more of these,' he mumbled, picking up his order book.

'It can't be good him looking into Mary's murder, and I'm convinced that's half the problem, did you know he had a copy of the police report on her. Has he discovered anything? I know he has. Kevin.' Specks may as well have been talking to herself as Kev was distracted with the build.

Kev started to chalk lines, making up squares on the container wall, a long yellow spirit level in hand to aid his accuracy, but a secondary check with the tape measure, from top to bottom; measure twice, cut once.

He put down the tape. 'You're over analysing things, Soph, you always do, stop it. I'm just glad he's back, really glad. Plus, we don't know what shit he did in the army, do we? And naturally he's going to want to find Mary's killer.' Kev scribbled numbers on the wall, calculations of some type. To Specks it resembled theoretical physics.

'And why does he want to live in this container? It will be freezing, dismal and dark. It's not healthy for his mind, it can't be? Do you think he's depressed?' She was still talking to herself as much as to Kev. 'I'm worried about him, I really am... I have a spare room. He could stop with me, until he gets sorted. I do understand he may not want to stay in Mary's flat, memories an all that comes with familiar surroundings.'

'Hey, less of the dark and cold. When I've finished

here this'll be fantastic, especially if he gets the money from them rifles and what about them suits of armour and the shields? Did you see them shields? Like brand new!' Kev started to draw the shape of a shield on the wall. His head turned, 'Hey! The spare room at yours is where I stop.'

'So, you are listening? But you're moving in that new flat with your mum at the end of the month. Sean needs support now because I know he's not himself, I just do.' Specks slowed her words, but she still spoke out loud yet didn't care if Kev was listening anymore.

But he was. 'Now who's getting depressed, snap out of it, he's not himself you say but you don't know him now and we're not kids anymore – he's an adult. Like I say I'm thankful he's back and reached out to me, we just have to be here if he wants us. Now tell me about these rifles and the other gear we've discovered?'

'You're right, I'm worrying for the sake of worrying. We will know how much they're worth by the end of play Wednesday at the latest, and I believe we'll all be pleasantly surprised. The auction room will be full to capacity. The Internet has been going mad with enquiries, especially regarding the two duelling sets as they're made by one of the best gunsmiths of that era. And most likely the best examples out there today.'

'Is that yours or mine?'

'What?' Sophie frowned, staring at him.

'A phone's ringing, you deaf?'

'Oh, it is mine? Sorry, I was miles away and it's a new ringtone but I don't recognise the number though. Work's phone.' She turned as she pressed the answer button.

Kev watched when she answered, sounding so upper

class, so professional he didn't recognise the voice she used at all.

'Louise King speaking, representative of Christies auction house. How can I help?'

'You can help by telling me is your little boyfriend Doyle back home?'

'How did you get hold of this number, Ahmid?' demanded Sophie. At the same time, Kev froze on the stepladder, his gloved fingers gripped tight to the rails upon hearing the name Ahmid mentioned in the conversation. The lightness of the day being washed away by that NAME.

'I know your number and everything about you, my sweet love. Did you think changing your name would hide you from me? You can take the girl from the gutter but she still smells.' He laughed, playing the game she started.

'What does that even mean? Don't ever call this phone again! Do you hear me?'

Ahmid continued laughing even though Sophie had sharply ended the call. She remained silent looking at the phone's screen. *Not a bad bone in her body*, Kev thought but Ahmid was the exception. She hated him.

'W...hat, w...hat, did he want?' Kev was petrified and he had every right to be, he had seen what Ahmid could do and had been a victim himself on more than one occasion, he even had the scars to prove it. Ahmid, a few years ago found out Kev was gay. He and two of his crew ambushed him tossing him against a wall. Taking a Stanley knife, they "striped" him, two big cuts sliced into both his buttocks, each was an inch deep. Gangsters liked this act as if you did get caught you couldn't go down for attempted murder. Eleven weeks Kev was off work, and he still had some complications today. Ahmid also outed Kev with the offshore lads and some of them made his life hell on the rigs, which he why he wanted off.

'He was asking me if I knew that Sean was back home. It's freaked me out. I don't know how he got a hold of my number. I've changed my name to lose my past and not still be branded with my family name. The number, it's my works number, it's not available to the public. How did he find – MY NUMBER?' Then she remembered it was now on the Christies website. But still he must have gone searching for it, for her, and found out that she worked there.

'What do you think he wants Sean for?' Kev quivered.

The room inside the steel container was cold and quiet and the joyous reunion that was blossoming between these three old school pals, had somehow been tainted with the name "Ahmid". The darkness that November brought around so quickly was upon them. Specks stared out the hole cut in the side of the container; the canal water glistened from the moonlight.

'Do you think Ahmid is looking for Sean to hurt him, or see if he wants some work?' A few seconds had passed, and she hadn't received a reply from Kev. Posing the question again, 'Kevin, are you listening to me? Why do you think he wants to get hold of our Sean?' Still no answer, she turned. 'Kevin, what's up?' she found herself watching as her friend of many years sat silently whilst tears rolled down his cheeks. 'Kevin, come on, I'm here, it will be alright. Sean can look after himself, ... more now than before. He's been in the army, remember – he's our warrior now. You'll see.' She smothered Kev, holding him tight, rocking slightly, warming and supporting him like a big sister.

'No, no he can't, not against Ahmid and your fucking

brother. They'll kill him, you know it! He's not nasty like they are, look what they did to Alex when he tried to stop them.' Kev was genuinely upset and frightened.

The last couple of weeks he'd been so happy. His old friend was back and a new purpose had materialised in his life with the container build. He loved Doyle and not like that, yes he was gay, but these three were more like family.

'I'll kill him, I will, I'll kill Ahmid if he hurts Sean. I'll get a gun and I'll kill him, even if I go to prison for it.' Although his words were only heard by Specks, he wanted Ahmid to know as well, he was still crying but he meant what he said. Well, the intent was there and even if he stood a chance one to one with Ahmid, how would he get him alone? Ahmid had a crew of over twenty and never went anywhere without, at the least two or three of his cronies and his paranoia grew as his empire extended.

'Shush, shush,' said Specks still cradling him. She knew that Kevin was no killer he wouldn't hurt a fly and Ahmid already had two tears tattooed just below his left eye as did Specks' brother, Gary. The only tears Kevin displayed were real ones.

12

TATTOOED TEARS

T wo years earlier

'Ham aapako tab le gae jab aapake paas kuchh bhee nahin tha, aur aap hamaaree dukaan se drags bechane ke lie hamaare lie sharm kee baat hai.' shouted Ahmid's uncle as he approached him outside the fish shop.

Ahmid walked over to his mum's brother, watched by ten of his gang and a dozen under 12s, all holding a small see-through plastic wrap.

'Davaon ke saath band aur naukaree pao,' said his uncle.

'Speak fucking English, you've been here 25 years,' demanded Ahmid.

'How dare you disrespect me like this? I am your elder, you bring shame on our family. What will my sister say?' His uncle was aware the group of thugs had cut him off. People in the street had started to disperse. The blows came fast and hard; the under 12s ran to complete the deliveries.

'Enough, get him in the car,' ordered Ahmid and his unrecognisable uncle was thrown into the boot of the Range Rover. Two miles the journey took, and the last hundred meters Rajas was awake but struggled to breathe or see out of his beaten face.

The white Range Rover pulled up outside the mosque. Rajas was dragged out of the vehicle and into the place of worship. A young man on the door tried to intervene but Ahmid head-butted him then pushed him away. No shoes were removed by any of the thugs. The mosque was half full; they all got up off their knees, flabbergasted at the scene unfolding in front of them.

Women and children at the edge of the hall began to scream. Rajas was held up by three of the gang. People felt sick at the sight of his face and head. Two of Ahmid's group walked over and locked the room's doors.

'What are you doing, Ahmid? Who has done this to your uncle?' spoke the imam.

'Shut up and watch because this is what will happen to anyone who disrespects me.' He pulled out a blade. 'Hold his head!' Two hands grabbed Raja's head and a second pair ripped open his mouth. In front of the full room Ahmid cut out his uncle's tongue. The coughing and spluttering started – blood running down his throat – out his mouth – down his chest where it soaked into the ripped shirt.

'Anyone else want to say ought?' Ahmid held up the tongue.

No one uttered a word; the mothers held tight their crying children.

'Have you anything to say?' Ahmid looked at the

imam, who didn't reply; instead, he turned his head not from fear but from disgust. Rajas was set free of the hands. He flopped to the floor and the thugs followed Ahmid leaving the holy place. Inside the mosque the good people ran to assist the uncle. One of them was on the phone calling 999.

'HELP, HELP?'

'Please calm down, sir, I need to take down some details,' said the calm voice.

'I think he's dead … his face is smashed in … they cut his tongue out l, l, l, lots of blood everywhere, we're in a mosque, how c…' he began to cry.

'Sir, the police are on the way along with the ambulance. Can you tell me if the patient is breathing?'

'Yes, but he's coughing up blood, WE DON'T KNOW WHAT TO DO?'

'How is the patient positioned?' asked the emergency call taker.

'We have him propped up against a wall.'

'Could you lay him down, turn him onto his front and lift his leg up towards his chest and pull out his arm on the same side of the raised leg? Place the other arm down by his side. Turn his head and ensure his airways are clear, his tongue may have folded backwards,' he calmly continued to instruct.

The mobile phone had been switched to loudspeaker and the instructions carried out as they were repeated. But not regards the tongue, as the operator had remembered what had been said.

Outside the mosque the two white Ranger Rovers and silver Passat drove off, back to the fish shop. On entering the place Ahmid dropped the tongue in the batter and from there into the fryer. 'Get the van and empty this place now,' ordered Ahmid. Five of the crew left to follow the orders. 'Plant, take over, we'll all have chips,' said Ahmid.

The dumb looking, big eared, skinhead tipped in the chips. He was forced to rub his forearms as the hot oil landed all-over his skin.

'We're not open officers,' said Ahmid sarcastically; the crew backed him up with laughter.

'Ahmid Rajas Basheeme, you are under arrest for the attempted murder of Rajas Dinesh Basheeme. You do not have to say anything, but what you do say will be taken down and may be used against you in a court of law. Do you understand?'

Four of the crew stood in front of Ahmid. He walked back behind the counter. He heard a whistle.

'That's alright, lads, the officers are just doing their work. 'I'm happy to come but first have some food.' Plant opened the box with a cartoon fish on the front. Ahmid took the scoop and first in the box was the battered tongue.

Ahmid came back around, and the armed officers moved into the shop, pushing back the thugs. Ahmid held out his wrists he was cuffed then was led out of the fish shop and into the awaiting van. The whole street was out to watch the spectacle. He was still smiling as the female officer closed the mini cell door and then the van door.

A shot was fired inside the fish shop, and four more armed police cocked and lifted their weapons. Plant was bleeding from the chest, just lying on the floor. One of the officers had fancied a snack and bit into what appeared to be a fish fritter in the box. He spat it out and then removed the rest of the batter, looking at the cooked tongue. His weapon fired the round entering the laughing Plant.

'GET DOWN ON THE FLOOR! HANDS ON THE HEAD!' shouted the officers all together, as the cardboard gangsters were dragged out one by one and forced down onto the concrete pavement, hands tie-wrapped.

An ambulance arrived on scene; the medics rushed straight into the shop. Plant didn't make it.

A police officer squeezed past the rescue team. 'I'll just remove this.' And he picked up a small pistol next to Plant's arm. The medics looked at each other. 'You saw me collect this, didn't you?' said the officer. The medics looked at each other again and remained silent but still didn't reply to the officer. Plant, or Liam Maffat was taken into the ambulance and pronounced dead on arrival at the hospital. The fish shop was transformed with tape and notices into a CSI scene.

'I'm entitled to a phone call, I believe?' mocked Ahmid.

'You're a sick fuck who shouldn't be entitled to oxygen,' bit the cop.

'I'll make sure to let my solicitor know your concerns, officer.' Ahmid still held the sick expression on his face. Another officer rushed across the room to stop the cop from killing Ahmid. 'Get off him, Barry, he's not worth it. He's doing it to make you lose your job.' Alan had got in front of Barry. Ahmid was still talking and baiting Barry, his neck outstretched as his arms were cuffed behind his back.

'Come on, Barry, take a shot, I'll let you. Come on, you want to, I can see it in your eyes you hate me. Oh, wait a minute, you wanna be me, you're jealous of all the pussy I get, including your Jackie. She's a good fuck for a fat bitch but very grateful and sucks forever.' Ahmid laughed.

Alan had to wrestle Barry out of the room. 'Enjoy it while you can, Ahmid, you will be going away for a long time. Why take the evidence back to the fish shop? I really thought you had brains.' Barry was locked out. The sergeant sat on the chair opposite Ahmid and went silent.

'So, do I get a phone call, Stewart?' Ahmid waited for an answer.

'Why have you got to be such a prick all the time? How can I protect you when you behave like this?'

'Who's paying for that house, in the Caribbean and wouldn't your bosses like to see the photos of you there and how old was that girl? That reminds me I must compliment my photographer. He got some lovely shots of you with her.'

'You really are a prick Ahmid. I hope you do go down for this and don't worry about me I'll just disappear. It'll be worth the hassle to know your rotting away.'

The sergeant vacated the interview room. 'Allow him his phone call,' he told the uniformed officer waiting outside.

'I want to be out now, so get a move on,' Ahmid said into the phone.

'Don't bark at me you low life. I take my instruction from elsewhere,' answered the smart voice. Ahmid laughed in response. 'Today,' he said.

'I will be in touch if I receive instruction to do so.'

Four days later at 1520 hours outside the fish shop

.   .   .

A crowd had gathered which included Ahmid's uncle, Rajas, aunt and two cousins although Rajas was in a wheelchair. The police had finished with the premises and the family were to take it back. The crowd consisted of friends and members from the mosque, all there to help and reassure the family. Sixteen-forty hours and the fryers were hot enough to cook chips, this was a thank you to the many hands that helped, and not only today. They and others who knew the family had given the place a full makeover in an effort to lessen the bad thoughts on returning.

The street party was over, all was well. The family believed they were home and safe.

2320 hours that same night

The first person in the street was out and they witnessed the flames bellowing out of the top floor windows of the fish shop. Within minutes several more of the neighbours had joined him. They were out to see the large shop front window explode. All of them ducked and their hands flew over their heads as the fire engines pulled into the street followed by the police and ambulance.

Impressively under a minute and the hoses released water into the shop. The full street was witnessing the courageous acts of the firefighters entering the burning building: they looked like astronauts wearing the air tanks as they entered the inferno fuelled by the oil in the friers. On their return they handed over the lifeless bodies of the family to the medics waiting in the garden – the police were preventing the friends of the family getting too close, people were crying and wailing at the loss.

'He's alive, he's alive!' shouted one of the medics. Another came over to assist. A young boy of teenage years had survived. The firefighters and police joined by the crowd, cheered. The rejoice was short-lived as the three other bodies were brought out into the open transported to the ambulance, two adults and one small girl were zipped up in black shiny body-bags.

The police had begun taking statements from the neighbours and friends, but no one had seen anything. Ahmid had been released that night on bail at 2220 hours. Three weeks later he walked free from court on a technicality; his £2000 an hour barrister had ripped apart the Crown Prosecution's services team.

The case they had put forward was built on two witnesses – but neither of them made an appearance. They never showed because one was now driving a BMW and the other had gone on a two-month vacation. So, the CPS had no option but to divert all their efforts onto the evidence brought back to the fish shop, allegedly by Ahmid.

But because the police officer had bit into the tongue then spat it out and add to this that it had been deep fried, and after that he removed the remaining batter from it, the defence had two expert witnesses to prove that under no circumstances could the meat give up any DNA, so it could have been anyone's tongue. It was said to be contaminated. Wilson and Wolf put forward the argument that the cutting out of the tongue act was all down to Liam Maffat (Plant), as was the beating of Rajas Bashmeere earlier that same day, and it was his idea to go to the mosque where the horrific act took place. Ahmid and the others only followed him as they feared for their own lives. Liam Maffat was the leader of the gang which is why he carried the pistol and aimed at the copper, which ended with him being fatally shot. The defence lawyer made a point of thanking the officer for entering the pistol into evidence.

Mr Wilson rested their case and sat back down next to Ahmid who wore a tailor-made suit and make up that hid the two tattooed tears under his eye. His earing had been removed and his coarse black hair professionally greased back. During the trial he'd been portrayed as a selfless individual who placed others before himself, constantly giving back to the community.

At least ten character witnesses backed up each other with nothing but praise and examples of the charity work undertaken by Ahmid. Even coming from a local priest and imam. Ahmid should have been up for an award instead of being on trial for the murder of his uncle and his family.

The jury retired and returned with their verdict in less than four hours. 'Not guilty on all three accounts, your honour,' spoke the forewoman.

Sitting in the public gallery taking notes throughout the proceedings was Alex Warren. Two minutes after this Ahmid walked free from court two hours later.

An hour later he walked into the fish shop with eight others.

Twenty minutes after entering the fish shop, the grease was out of his hair, his suit removed, face wiped, his tattooed tears re-appeared under his left eye.

13

ENCRYPTED

S ean had been given a small tatty notepad and over thirty sheets of folded paper from the eccentric poet who he had met at the pumping station the night of the explosion. He had been knocked unconscious jumping into the cellar. The young girl must have slipped the book and notes into his Mac pocket before she covered him up with it. The only problem was his little swim across the canal had resulted in the pages merging and it was two days later when he'd discovered these. Looked like she wasn't as messed up as he had first thought or somehow, she had only a partial grip on reality, in and out of the "normal" world. Doyle had seen this before many times, and lots of people talked about reality when they had never had to face it?

To him this made things much more sinister. In his mind it was clear reality was created by men, but not all were able to sustain the images and gave in to others. But the poor girl was petrified and that wasn't faked, so he had to discover whose reality she had been living in for the last months of her life, and when he found the devil he would alter it at any cost.

What the fuck is unfolding here? he asked himself, slicing the edges of the pages with a razor blade. Each of them had been filled with multiple pieces of paper and each containing dozens of letters, numbers, and strange symbols. All of them as random as her altered rhymes and again this was a clever play on her part.

Each strange song that she sang was recognisable in tune and pitch perfect in a cappella. Yet the words had been doctored by a true wordsmith. Each altered song Sean was trying to recall at this moment in time, but he couldn't, even with the old tunes running through his head.

Refraining from the lyrics he allowed only the notes to be heard. Still the old tunes played, yet none of her new words came forth, radio on and turned up loud.

Then the pages became a diary of events. *This girl had without a doubt missed her true vocation* imagined Sean, as he read her words with ease and pleasure. Also feeling some sadness and anger for people of her age having to live on the streets in derelicts, gathering in clandestine groups for safety then being treated like scum by people who believed they were better because they paid rent.

But the words in fact, were only part of the puzzle – all over the tatty pages wherever there was a blank space and no matter how tiny, she, like many of the great poets, authors, and songwriters, had drawn a doodle. A sign or a number. There were parts in the book in which the writing was so small Sean couldn't make out the letters.

'There's something here, there has to be, it's too random to be random, I just can't see it. What is the fucking link? Why did she pass it on to me? Come on think, think, is this a code or is it

simply the ramblings of a deranged young woman leaving her mind?' He was getting frustrated.

Taking each page and the images they contained, he stuck them with Blu Tack onto the makeshift board. It was no good he was too tired for all this. He also couldn't stop thinking about the image of Mary holding something clasped tight in her hand. The base of it was shiny and the top pointed or maybe squeezed. He needed the image enhanced on the picture, and to be able to read the tiny writing – but how? It was an illegal crime scene photo. And a bog-standard magnifying glass wouldn't do. The image wouldn't leave his mind. He didn't want it to vanish permanently, but a rest from it for even a few hours would have been nice, allowing him some shut eye.

It wasn't going to happen.

'Run, go for a run. Clear me head,' he said, just as his mobile rang. 'Kev, what's up, it's late?'

'Burnt my hand and it's bad I think.' Kev sounded quiet.

'Location?' asked Doyle.

'What?'

'Where are yah?'

'Oh, yeah, the yard, Sean. I'm in the top container.'

'I'm coming, two minutes.' His planned run became a sprint.

'What the fuck, Kev. What you still doing here? Let's have a look, your head is cut as well.' Sean was mad but happy to see Kev not seriously hurt.

'My head.' His hand flew up. 'Shit, it's blood. I think I must have passed out then. Oh, yeah, I was on the stepladder.' Kev turned pale seeing the blood on his hand and the side of the step ladder.

'Sit down, before you fucking fall again and hold this

against the cut, press it hard.' Sean gave him a towel. 'Harder.' he was up and called Specks.

'Sean, have you seen what time it is, I was asleep, … is everything okay?' she asked while yawning.

'Kev's injured, could you come over? I'll go for some first aid stuff, but I can't leave him on his own.'

'Ahmid, what has he done to him now?'

'Ahmid? What made you say his name? He's fell at the yard, off a ladder. Not sure if he was concussed.' Sean turned to Kev.

'I'm on my way, I have bandages and stuff here. Twenty minutes. Keep him safe,' she told him, then cut the phone off.

'Why did she think Ahmid had hurt you?' asked Sean, looking out the window then turning back to his mate.

The blood was still trickling slowly down his face. 'Err, err, not sure why,' he replied, his finger stopping the blood before it dripped off his nose. 'Hold the towel tighter,' demanded Doyle.

'Okay, okay, but don't tell her I told you, promise me,' asked Kev like a ten year-old making a pinkie swear with his best mate.

Sean nodded to him. 'Well?'

'Ahmid rang her on the mobile the other day when you had left for a few days. He wanted to know if it was true that you were back home from the army, and did she know where you were.' His finger wiped again.

'He has her phone number. Do they socialise?'

'No, God no. She hates him and was fuming when he called, asking where he had got her number from. Like I said, she despises him especially after …' His bleeding had stopped and so had the conversation. It was too painful, too personal.

'After what?' Sean pressed another cloth on top of the towel.

'I can't say, it's in the past anyway...' Kev's stare altered. 'Sophie, you didn't have to come. I'll be fine it's just a scratch.' Kev couldn't look back at Sean. Sophie entering then, was perfect timing.

'There's a lot of blood for a scratch and why were you here alone at this time? You will have to go to hospital – I think that will need a few stitches,' suggested Sophie, kneeling down and lifting the towel. 'Here, drink this.' She passed a bottle of sports water to him as she opened a bag of bandages and other dressings.

'I'm not going to the Royal, no way, not at this time. I'll be okay. Stop fussing over me, I've had worse.'

'Yes, and at the hands of our old friend Ahmid it appears. Is someone gonna explain?' Sean was tall and with both of them at sitting level they didn't have a lot of options but to talk. Sophie gave Kev a look. 'I couldn't help it, and you mentioned Ahmid's name on the phone to him,' explained Kev.

'I didn't want to scare you off we had just become friends again, sorry. And it really is hard for me to talk about,' muttered Kev.

'Scare me off, from what?' Sean laughed.

'It's not a laughing matter, Sean Doyle. Ahmid is in charge around here everyone knows it. He's untouchable, and if he is looking for you then I'm afraid for you, truly I am.' Sophie sounded scared, but she continued. 'It may be better if you left here again and for good this time, don't come back. Just leave Sean. You can't help us.' she added, as she placed a clean dressing on Kev's head.

'This still doesn't tell me what happened to you.' His

stare was straight at Kev who simultaneously looked for support from his surrogate sister.

Her arms and shoulders raised. 'Maybe we should tell him, you're not working offshore anymore. He can't keep blackmailing you. It will be alright. I won't let him hurt you again, I'll speak to him.'

Kev's head dropped to his chest, deflated listening to Sophie.

She tied off the bandage and placed her hands on him, kissing him. She spoke softly. 'We will get through this, you and me like we always do.' She kissed the top of his head again.

'You're forgetting me,' said Sean. 'Let's get one thing very clear. I'm going nowhere and as for being scared of fucking Ahmid, that's farcical.' Sean pulled over the chair, spun it round sat and rested his arms on the back rest.

'Now, shall we start from the beginning? Tell me everything that's happened in the last ten years, then we'll take it from there.' He looked at the pair and waited.

The three of them talked for a couple of hours at least. Kevin and Specks left Sean around three am in a taxi. At least the evening's events had cleared his mind of Mary's image. Sean managed to grab a couple of hours' kip.

He was up again at six. His run today would take him back to the door of the old pawnbroker. Six miles later and he heard the familiar sound of the Victorian bell. 'Hello again, Mr Doyle, always a pleasure. Can I tempt you?'

'You remember all your customers and offer them coffee?' asked Sean, slightly surprised at his name being passed over so fluently.

'No, I don't, Mr Doyle, but not everyone brings me a ring with such intrigue as you did, and being a

Sphragistiphist your band was like the holy grail to me?' replied the Fagan lookalike, showing Doyle the coffee pot again, although he was much more well fed than the Dickens character. Sean smiled as the man's fingers rubbed together subconsciously.

'I'm here on a different matter today, but I've also come into some cash, so I'll take you up on the offer to have the words on the ring translated, whatever it costs.' Sean was as intrigued as the pawnbroker.

'And the second matter you seek advice with, Mr Doyle?'

'Have you a strong magnifying glass, a really long one?' asked Sean, as the man walked away. He fished for the ring in the small zipped pocket in his wallet. His brain's memory lit up. The face of the ring had the same crest on it that had been chiselled on to the shields held by the lions standing on guard at the De Pen Court estate.

'I have this one and it has a light-built in.' Fagan flicked the switch on and the 12 by 12 sheet of glass illuminated.

'How much?' asked Doyle with a small nod.

'Let's call it a thank you for easing my curiosity, sir. When one has all, he wants, curiosity is a rare and sought for commodity.' The strange man wrapped the lens.

Sean looked down at the ring it and passed it over to the strange man, relieving him of the magnifier. 'How long will it take before I have it back?'

'We should allow four weeks, sir,' replied Fagan.

Sean nodded in acceptance of the timescale.

'Would you like a receipt, sir?'

'I don't think you're going to cheat me, are you?' Sean left the shop, the chime of the old bell bringing him back once more into the 21st century. Doyle tucked the magnifying glass in his trousers, and he hit the tarmac, gaining speed.

Inside the shop a moment after Doyle had left

'You were correct my old friend, the ex-soldier returned just as you said he would, and he indeed wants to know what the words scribed inside of the ring mean,' advised Fagan, while pouring coffee.

On the other end of the connection the recipient smiled and said, 'You know what to do.'

He replaced the receiver.

A week later, somewhere on the campus Oxford University

'The ring is most definitely authentic, sir, and after removing the incremental band, it showed the number **thirteen.**'

'Are you sure about this? We thought that one was missing, at least that's what our files say, and if I recall correctly the last person's signature against it was...' Several pages were flicked over in the long book.

'Here we are, the finger went down the page, it was in 1785 and the name attached to it is ... well, well, I didn't see that coming!'

'Who was it then, sir?' asked the quiet voice.

'You know better than to ask? And the band you have there is without doubt in your expert opinion, ... the number thirteen? I will have to go to the table with this information, so I have to be one hundred percent.' informed the confident voice.

'I'll email you the blown-up photos and a transcript of the words discovered under the band.'

'Thank you, but I still find it difficult to digest, as up until a few months ago we only knew twelve rings had been smithed.'

'As did I, sir, but recently further research disclosed that in the year 1598 a further eight bands had been commissioned, and by her majesty Elizabeth herself. They also contained her signature as did the original dozen, plus one significant detail that is different on the eight extras which is not present on the original twelve.'

'And?'

'Cum sicario disputabo. Meaning "Assassin", sir.' The quiet voice rose.

'Interesting and signed by Her Majesty herself, you say. But wasn't the Queen dead by that year?'

'No, she lived another five years, sir, until a good age of sixty nine.'

'Send me what you have so far and a copy of the documentation that goes with the discovery of these new bands. I wasn't and I don't believe that any of the table are aware of the extra ones. Whilst I think on, don't email any information regarding the new finds, not for now, we wouldn't want it falling into the wrong hands, not with those words engraved into the gold. And we know "others" seek the bands.'

'I will set up a dry file presently and have it with you by the morning. Good night to you, sir.'

The room from where the quiet voice had called was twenty feet deep by same width and not quite seven feet high. Yet the only space available was less than five feet and no walls could be seen due to the crazy number of boxes stacked so high. It appeared like they held up the ceiling.

This remaining small space is where Jonathon's desk sat. The onyx green light only illuminated downwards. Piles of papers in an organised mess spread everywhere. A handful taken and the forty something man stood and did the sideward shuffle to the door.

In contrast the photocopying room he entered was akin to a clinical theatre.

'Hello, sir, would you like me to do those for you?' a young woman asked whilst nudging her glasses back up to the bridge of her nose.

His head shook awkwardly; and he began to sweat, this was Johnathon's reply as it was all the other times. His stare remaining at the floor where he spotted a paperclip next to the machine, he fixated.

'Paper jam,' she read aloud off the digital screen then started to press a couple of buttons on the touch screen. "Drawer three" were her next words read.

Jonathon's stare no longer took in the small bit of shaped wire lying next to the photocopy machine. He began to overheat as his eyes saw the back of her legs; he even dared to look as high as her thighs.

'Got it.' The crinkled piece of paper came away in her hand. Still bending over her tight skirt rose above her knees. Upright once more she looked at the nearly middle-aged academic. 'Are you feeling alright, you appear flushed? Professor.'

No answer.

She continued to speak, 'I'm free most nights if you would like an assistant. I have all my qualifications and it would help with my university course. I am reading advanced librarianship and Latin. So, I wouldn't need any payment, as we would be helping each other, wouldn't that be nice?' She lightly kissed his cheek; the colour transformation was spectacular. She vacated the room her arms crossed securing the mass of papers to her chest.

He placed a piece of paper over his mouth and tried to slow down his erratic breaths. Nearly every day and some nights for at least a year he bumped into Stacy, yet not one word had come from his lips, well not in her company.

Back at the desk the dry file had been completed and closed, his index finger and thumb pulled the tiny chain. The green light was out; he finished the contents of the glass, and again the piles of papers were fashioned into a pillow.

The following morning

'Wakey, wakey.' Her hand moved some of the papers allowing her to place down the hot Costa. 'Wakey, wakey.' Her sweet voice repeated.

'Wakey, wakey.'

This time he came around slowly. His eyes picked up an image of Stacy, but he often saw her in his dreams when he was sleeping.

'What? What are you doing down here? No one is allowed down here. Leave, leave now, now.' Jonathon's face showed the despair that consumed him. He was shocked.

'Did you fall asleep here last night? It's seven thirty in the morning. I heard an alarm going off and came to investigate. Why are you sleeping down here?'

Stacy, a geek in her head maybe – but she was pretty, next door pretty and able to give Holly Willoughby a run.

This was underneath the woollen fashion of her choice, which was finished off with the hand knitted yellow and white Balmoral she wore on her head. Her eyes would seduce most men, not just Jonathon.

'I meant what I said yesterday, professor. I really would like to help you around here and it looks like you could do with a hand.'

She began to tidy the desk.

'Stop, please, stop it, you don't understand. I have my own system.'

'Really?' She continued to shuffle the papers into neat piles. He was of course lying. It had been a year at least since he had looked at any research for the university. The dean had tried on several occasions to help Jonathon, but each attempt fell by the wayside.

Forty-two years of age and he had never known any world outside of a university. His father had been a resident professor and then moved to the role of dean at Durham. Jonathon had been tipped early on in his life to be a scholar, and he would be up there amongst the highest in the world. The only obstacle holding him back was his debilitating phobia of people – especially females.

'Drink this while it's still hot. It cost me £2.40, and I don't have money to waste, professor.' Stacy picked up the cup and pushed it towards him. 'Drink!' she insisted.

'Wh ... st ... get o ... out, OUT NOW!'

Realising she wasn't going to leave he grabbed hold of the folder and tried to squeeze by Stacy. He accidently touched her soft bottom and began to hyperventilate, causing him to drop the folder. Both bent to retrieve it, clashing heads.

'Ouch, that hurt. You have a hard head, professor.' She

rubbed hers better then kissed Jonathon on the forehead. He started to cry and break down.

At the door appeared the dean. Stacy saw him, but said nothing, she concentrated on the papers and the dean left after putting his thumb up.

Most educational establishments would have dispatched with this man's services by now, but Jonathon was a real genuine genius, well liked, and also to his benefit he had a long running contract with a government department that paid his board and lodgings, as well as part of his salary.

Stacy held him tight. He felt secure but not enough to prevent more tears.

Twelve minutes past nine and Stacy was summoned third hand to the dean's office. Jonathon with the geek's aid had calmed somewhat and left the building to deliver the folder.

'Stacy, thank you for coming, could you enlighten me on this morning's events. I've been concerned for a while now regarding Professor Smith.'

'Am I in trouble, SIR.'

'Not at all, Miss Bella, please take a seat.' The dean was half out his chair and pointed to the chair in front of his desk.

'I found him fast asleep on his desk, sir. I heard an alarm sounding so I went down to the cellar to investigate. He tried to get rid of me, but I couldn't leave him, not after seeing all the mess. He started crying like a small child. I was trying to console him, and that's when you arrived at the door, sir. I spent another hour consoling him after that. Are you aware he has been sleeping at his desk?'

'I am and it concerns me? How many hours currently

are you with us a week?' asked the dean, opening a file on his desktop.

'Twelve hours over three days, sir, as the assistant librarian,' answered Stacy. A strange feeling of fright entered her head: why was he asking?

'Would you be interested in an increase in your hours?'

'Yes, yes sir, I would,' she instantly replied.

'Oh, right, that's a relief then.' A small chuckle, 'I was actually worried that you wouldn't want to.' He laughed more chuckles.

'I love the library, sir, it's my life.' She also needed the extra money but didn't say that.

'Well, that is just it, Miss Bella, I would like to offer you an increase which would triple your current allocation, but not in the library, I would like you to assist Professor Smith with his, ... whatever he does down there, it's beyond me. You may also have to go for an interview elsewhere, for some clearance?' The dean's eyebrows moved around. He scratched his face dry skin fell.

'Yes, that would be acceptable, sir.' Delight showed clear on her face.

Stacy had her eye on this department for a long time. Professor Smith had completed some outstanding work on historical points of interest which had been published in a lot of papers. Some even shattering pre-formed ideas from some worshipped academics.

'When would you like me to start, sir?' was her next question.

'As from now, and feel free to book some overtime, at least for the first few weeks then we will have a review of the situation. First off, I would like to see the cellar in some reasonable state, it's a bloody fire hazard, then secondly the professor no longer living down there. I am convinced it will help Jonathon – and thank you for taking this on, but I warn you now, he does have some strange ways to him. Yet I am convinced we haven't seen an end to his genius.' The dean felt it was his duty to tell her the truth, or at least part of.

'I will be fine, sir, and we all have some oddities, don't you agree?' Stacy pushed back her chair and left the room dialling on her old mobile.

'I've got into the department.' The joy was growing in her voice.

'Well done, my love, I knew you would, it was always just a matter of time.'

'It all starts here.' Stacy ended the call.

London bus stop

'Thank you, could I give you a tip?' said Professor Smith quietly, as he exited the bus. The driver didn't reply, he wore a blank expression and just looked at the tweed wearing man holding an old attaché case.

Jonathon held on to the steel support tube at the front of the bus. Ready to brave the step, he turned.

'Don't go so fast around the corners, try and make haste on the straights. The scheduled time for this journey is 75 minutes. You have managed to reduce this by nine full minutes, but this was at the cost of both the comfort and the pleasure of your passengers. And if you studied the numbers, I would wager that at least two people would have missed this bus today causing them problems which would in turn cause others some issues, and so on.' Johnathon smiled at the driver and continued exiting.

Anyone listening to his last words would have him down as sarcastic or arrogant, but none of these descriptions were correct. His words had all been said with genuine intent and he was of the belief he really was helping by informing people of their misdoings.

Off the bus and walking, he kept his attention just six feet in front of him and a tight grip was on the case, as around him were way too way many people creating anxiety enough to freeze him to the spot. His destination being on the other side of the road this meant he would have to cross the busy road and then there would be no more than twenty metres. This was the third time Jonathon had made this harrowing journey. He was going through purgatory to get here as far as he was concerned, but what drove Jonathon was the research he carried out, Hell could have been the destination, and he would go there, if it was needed for his precious research.

'Are you lost, mister?' asked the young lad.

Jonathon looked at the boy. He was wearing imitation Nike trainers, jogging pants and a sweatshirt with the same name printed on that was on the front of his trainers. Jonathon gripped the handle harder then pointed to the other side of the road.

'Come on then,' said the young lad, who looked at two of his associates standing afar. The lad took hold of Jonathon's arm and started to cross the road.

'Thank you.' managed Jonathon as they reached the safety of the opposite curb. The lad's associates had crossed too. Jonathon pulled forty pounds out of his pocket, and he was about to give the lad a twenty.

'Thanks, mister, that'll do.' He grabbed both the notes and ran, thinking he'd outsmarted the tweed jacket, but Jonathon knew that twenty alone wouldn't have saved the case, the decoy had worked – and he was now only feet away from the building.

14

FROZEN CHILD

The Waterfront Hostel, London

'Minister, sorry I wasn't aware you were here. Did we have a meeting arranged for today?' asked the doctor.

'No, Moe, there is no meeting scheduled – just visiting. I am the patron of this place, remember.'

'Yes, yes, of c ... c course, sir, just never seen you here before,' nervously replied Doctor Moe.

'You're too paranoid, Moe, relax a little. Chill I think the yobs say.' the minister was pushing down the air softly with his hand.

Shoebridge was well aware that he made most people feel nervous, or at the very least put them on edge. But Dr Moe was his best toy.

'There is one situation I have been meaning to talk to you about... ...' he deliberately slowed the words down. 'But quite frankly ... ... I never found the time. Today I was passing so I popped in to see how things were doing.' Shoebridge looked around the room, again deliberately allowing several seconds to tick-by before resuming his words. 'Now is as good a time as any I thought.'

His walking was slow around the lab, touching things at his pleasure, knowing the suspense weakened Moe's resolve and his pacing carolled the doctor into the middle of the room.

Shoebridge stopped and walked towards the exit to the relief of Moe, but he stopped again at the door, and locked it, pushing down the handle not to test the lock but to ensure that Moe knew there was no way out.

'And what's that, sir, how can I help you? You know I will if I can,' replied the doctor, with no eye contact.

'Remember a couple of years ago when I set you up, employed you, put some money in your account – even though the GMC had struck you off the register, and making sure those sleezy charges went away.' Shoebridge began his pacing again; Moe only nodded.

'We had a conversation, at that time did we not? ... About you only working for me, yes me, with regard to DNA experiments. Do you recall this conversation? Doctor?'

'I do, d ... sir, and you are the only person I do w..w..work for in that field. What's brought this on, sir?'

'You wouldn't lie to me now.' He paced more. 'Would you Moe? I cannot abide lying!' enquired Shoebridge, moving closer to the doctor.

About to reply, Moe was shushed as Shoebridge continued. 'Do you know a Lady De Pen Court?'

'I, yes, I, ... I do, but le...let me I, I can I explain, sir, ... please ... please allow me to tell you what happened. It's not what you are thinking, I I I can promise...' Moe's begging rambled on, it turned into fear; he was dreading the consequence to come.

Shoebridge left the room for a moment, but not long enough to give respite to the doctor's growing fear.

Re-entering the clinic room for the second time closing the door behind himself, once more the key was turned, and the door shown to be locked.

He leaned over the desk with his arm stretched out. Doctor Moe cringed, shrinking in size.

Shoebridge picked up the receiver and dialled a number; a phone rang downstairs in his limousine.

It was picked up on the seventh ring, the whole thing orchestrated earlier by Shoebridge himself. The effect was clear on the doctor: the waiting game is not good for someone in fear of his life, and Shoebridge was one of the best players.

'Andrews.' is how the phone was answered, clear and confident.

'Bring up the container, please, there's a good chap.'

'Yes, sir, I'm coming right away.'

Andrews was out of the car. He popped the boot and took hold of a square blue and white plastic box; this was slipped into a hazardous waste bag. The boot closed itself as he walked away.

Ten minutes is all it took. The minister opened the door. 'Thank you, Andrews, come in and then please remain outside and guard the door – no one in … or out.' Andrews placed the cooler box on the doctor's desk, never said a single word, but the face expression he wore was enough. He left the room, remaining outside as instructed.

'I want the child that you Frankensteined in that box … and before the end of play today. Will that be a problem for you?' Shoebridge tapped on the container. 'Moe.'

'Yes, yes, I mean no, I'll, l, l, l … can, of course minister.

I'm sorry, but sh...' He shushed himself realising his other benefactor was a real bitch and was as bad as the one who was in front of him at this very moment, if not worse.

'As long as we are all on the same page. A small bit of advice for you, doctor. If you wish to dance with more than one devil at the same time, ensure to pick the tune you like most and be loyal to it!'

Shoebridge had his hand firmly on the door handle and was about to press down. 'Oh, ... silly me I almost forgot, there is a present for you in the box, just to show you there is no hard feelings between us.

No need to thank me. It's just a small reminder that I don't like being taken for a fool. Now you have yourself a good day, doctor, and don't be worrying about how to return the container to me. A courier will be here to collect the box at 4 o'clock – sharp, and if it doesn't contain a frozen child, he will f..., well let's just imagine what he will do, shall we.' Shoebridge was outside the room. He deliberately remained stationary for a few moments.

'ARRRRR!' screamed the doctor. The lid clattered on the floor as he was violently sick, after the third time vomiting his eyes closed tight, as he curled up in a ball praying, he was in a nightmare and would awake soon. The minister remained outside the door as two of the nurses ran to the room to see why the doctor was screaming.

'It's okay, ladies, nothing to be concerned about. I have just had to inform the good doctor of the death of...'

Inside the room Moe had stared into the box at the floating head of Nurse Fuller.

'It may be best to leave him alone for a while, let him come to terms with the bereavement of his close friend.'

The minister walked off, guarded by Andrews as the nurses returned to their station.

Back in the car he asked if there was any news on the whereabouts of this Doyle chap, the private investigator.

'No nothing as yet, sir, but the man I have on it knows him. He was at the same school with him, I believe. He did confirm Doyle was in the army. Have we any background on him, sir?' Andrews glanced in the rear-view mirror.

His boss didn't answer as he was too busy looking through the contacts on his phone. The mobile dial tone was audible through the rear speakers. Andrews heard the start of the conversation but not the middle or the end.

'I would like to speak with Charles Howlett.'

'I will see if he is taking calls, sir, one mo...'

'Just put me through – he'll take my call.'

'Brigadier, really sorry to interrupt, I have minister Shoebridge on the phone and h...'

'I know what he's like put him through and don't concern yourself over it.' Charles was annoyed but not at her, he gave a small smile.

'Putting you through now, sir.'

'Allister, how can I help?'

'I am after some information on a chap, name of Doyle, Sean. Ex-military, so of course my first point of call was yourself, Charles.'

'As I have said before, I am not military personal. And what is the reason you seek information on this Boyle character, are you looking to recruit?'

'No, not at all, he happens to be meddling in matters of which he has no understanding – issues above his comprehension. And I don't appreciate insubordinates interfering in my business affairs.'

'Tanya,' whisper-shouted Alison, pointing to the brigadier's office.

She turned in time to catch Charles beckoning her to join him.

'Allister, leave it with me for a day or two, I'll make a couple of calls, see if I can find out any information on this chap and get back to you. Simon Boyle, was it?' he stalled.

'Doyle, are you losing your memory Charles? Sean Doyle, and I would appreciate some urgency on the matter. I don't have a couple of days.'

Shoebridge hung up.

'Close the door, take a seat. That was Allister Shoebridge on the phone. He was asking questions about your "lost soul".' Charles spun in the chair and grabbed a black folder from the shelf then faced front.

'Doyle, sir?'

'Yes, apparently he's "meddling" in his business or Allister's pseudo government business more like. This all happened whilst he was playing at being Magnum, apparently.'

'An ice-cream lolly? ...' replied Tanya, not up to speed.

'I forget your age, girl. A private investigator.' He had the cup in his hand and a pill jar in the other. There was a knock at his door.

'Come in!' shouted Charles, throwing the words over Tanya's shoulder, then swallowed three of the pills, all washed away by the thick black coffee.

The office door opened slowly. 'Sorry to interrupt, sir. I thought you would like to know that David Sissons has arrived for your meeting, he does appreciate that he is a good bit early.' Alison said, smiling at Tanya.

'Thank you, Miss Worthing. I'll be five minutes. Let him know will you.'

She closed the door and made the short walk to the old-fashioned foyer.

'The brigadier will be five minutes Mr Sissons. Would you like a coffee or tea while you are waiting?' So polite was her question.

'Dave, please, Alison, none of this "Mr" shit, and a strong black coffee would be great. I'll be over near the lift.' he turned and walked off.

Back in the brigadier's office

'We will need Doyle to come back in, and sharpish to find out what he has done that's ruffled Allister's feathers, and ruffled enough for him to want to track Doyle down.' Coffee to lips, and back to the desk. 'Because I can assure you that's what will be happening right now. We have already had several personnel disappear. Can you make some clerical error up? I don't want him being spooked.

'There is one more thing regarding Doyle that I may have neglected to say ... and the direction things are going you will need to know,' He paused, holding his tongue. He looked at his wrist. Realising Dave had come early because there was a lot to get through. 'I will have to fill you in later regarding that issue. We must prepare for tonight's operation and I know David has a lot to do, so I mustn't keep him waiting.'

It wasn't only the time that stopped Charles saying anything more, he remembered that only three people were in on this. But Tanya was aware of everything as a rule, so even for Charles it was awkward.

'I'll get straight on to it, sir. I'll have him back in today, it's been a week nearly. Shall I ask Dave to come in …?'

'Yes, … No, I need to stretch the old leg, the walk will do it good. In fact, we'll use the war room as we're prepping for tonight's operation. To be careless is to be sorry, and to be unprepared means the funeral suit out. And that's been out twice this year.'

He raised himself: his collection of war wounds and injuries from all over the globe were making themselves known.

'Give him my regards, sir.' Tanya turned to leave the office.

'Before you go, lass, how are you feeling since the operation? I thought I'd lost you. Are you positive that you're well enough to be back at work?' questioned Charles, but this was as a father asking.

'You forced two weeks leave on me; that was enough. You heard what the doctor said at my last check-up. I am on the mend, and he is pleased with the results, he couldn't see any reason why I should not return to work.' She gave him the facts, but he wanted truth and real confirmation. 'But yes, I'm fine, still very weak but that was all the blood transfusions and the last one of them was on Tuesday last. Their team told me it could take up to a year for normality to return.' She came around to give Charles a hug and a peck on the cheek, something that you would have never seen previously between these two at work.

'If you need anything, Tanya, talk to me. Promise.' Charles insisted.

'Of course.' She returned to her office to discover a courier-delivered envelope waiting on her desk. Still standing, she opened the brown delivery. After reading it she rushed off to the war room which was located in the basement of the building.

Charles hadn't been in the room long himself; he had stopped to make a call on his way down.

'Hi, Tan, you joining us?' asked Dave, as she burst through the door.

They hadn't been surprised as the only way into the secure part of the war room was by index finger and thumb identification. And the individual was identified inside the room by an audible computerised voice statement.

'Dave.' She acknowledged him instantly, before switching to Charles.

'This has just arrived; it is regarding this evening's operation.' She began to read.

"Miss Howlett, Tanya, forgive the last-minute warning. I have decided to send you this information regarding your team's work this evening. I – the author of this letter must remain anonymous, as I am sure you would expect in our line of work.

However, recently you showed great kindness to a fallen comrade's family, when you did not have any duty to do so; this is the sole reason I pass on this detail. Be it a small amount of information, I feel to you, it will be received as monumental".

She paused for breath. 'It changes here into Russian, sir, and fluent, not a Google version. Translated it reads that the submarine you are greeting tonight is a ploy, designed to lure you in. Your team will be annihilated.' She looked silently at both Dave and her boss, but her eyes registered a long-time friend and her father.

'It's an attempt to scare us away, that's all, don't worry about it. We've had challenges before, par for the course, and it keeps us on our toes.' acknowledged the brigadier. Dave agreed but remained silent his head nodding.

'But it mentions the submarine, how would just anyone be privy to that fact?' Tanya tried again to convince the pair of the danger.

Dave broke his silence. 'Charles is right, Tan, they're aware we have some intel. They aren't sure exactly how much or what, so they're fishing, nothing to worry about, we'll be fine.' Dave was marking points on the plans.

'I don't like it, sir. The letter was written personally to me, and at the last hour.'

Dave stood and placed the drawings into his case, the lid closed.

'I'll see you tonight at the pickup, Charles, and Tan, don't be worrying, we can look after ourselves. You know that?' Dave squeezed her on the shoulder and left the building.

'He's right, girl, don't give this note a second thought, we'll be fine, I promise.' Charles followed Dave out of the war room and walked with him to the underground car park.

Back in her office she tried to focus on contacting Doyle to get him to come in for further talks, but the courier letter would not vacate her mind.

Who sent it? Who would be capable of receiving the sub information? She questioned and began to write down all the people she had helped over the last couple of months. *But how long should I go back?* And she had aided so many – over hundred in the last year.

She gave up and dialled Sean's number.

'Sean Doyle.' she heard, and the reply came quickly.

'Sean – Tanya, I need you to come into the office today, now - please?'

'Can I as...' but she had gone. 'Guess not, then.' Sean pocketed the mobile and turned. 'I'm off, Kev. Got to get to an appointment. Will you be okay on your own here?'

'Yeah, yeah, go, leave me, I'll call Shorty to bring some food and drink, and he can fire watch. I'll be here still when you get back. I need to get the windows cut out.' Kev was only interested in the building of his designs. Gas turned back up; a nod brought the mask back down. The blue flame was back and cutting through the steel where it had left off.

Sean made his way to the front of the funeral parlour. He'd only been there a few minutes when the overhead doorbell charmed away.

'Can I help you, sir?' asked Louise from behind the ancient reception desk.

'Is Mr Doyle here and is he available, please, and if so, could you inform him his car is waiting,' said the man with an adjustable walking stick.

'Sean, there's a man and car here looking for you apparently,' called out Louise, as she gave another glance to the man's leg.

'Thanks, I'm expecting a lift,' replied Sean. He chuckled, just about how efficient Tanya was. Coming through the door into the parlour's reception, it was as if he was staring into a mirror. In front of him was an ex-squaddie – it takes one to know one. Who in his head was still serving, a part of something much bigger than he was or ever would be, and with that thought came a form of solitude.

'Sean, Ann asked if you could pop up and have a word before the accountant arrives,' passed on Louise.

'When I get back, I shouldn't be long.' He looked at the young receptionist who sent back a nervous smile, which she used in an attempt to cloak her crush on the boss.

Outside, Sean was impressed with the waiting black Mercedes. The driver proceeded to open the door for him, even though he needed the stick for support whilst doing so. 'Thanks, mate.' The car journey wasn't long in distance, yet the sheer volume of London traffic made it last twenty minutes.

'Who did you serve with?' enquired Sean, out of interest.

'Queens for eight years.' He tapped the leg. 'Got shot by a sniper.'

'What happened?'

'It was halfway through selection we realised something was wrong.'

'Wasn't that when that nutter was sniping at th...'

'The lads! Yes, I caught a 7.62 in the lower back, it ricocheted and came out me leg. Never walked properly since.' interrupted the driver.

'I was brought in on that selection to hunt the fucker down. Wait a minute, was it you who dragged an injured soldier to the farmhouse while we caught the twat?' realised Doyle.

'Yes, took me nearly a day to do a lousy mile.' laughed the chauffeur.

'Your mate survived though, didn't he?'

'Alan, he sure did, and made a full recovery. Went on and passed selection the following year.' The chauffeur glanced in the rear-view mirror.

'Hang on, that wouldn't be Alan Bench?'

'Yeah, it is or as we called him the clock,' answered the driver, enjoying the chat.

'He was in my squad, yeh, a good lad, he ripped his knee a couple of months ago and from what I heard he's just gone with a private outfit in Dubai, security at the airport. So, you're Scotty then, and I never figured out why Alan's nickname was the clock?'

'I am Scotty, how did you know? And didn't yah notice his hands?'

'His hands?'

'Yeh, one hand bigger than the other,' replied the driver.

It took a second but then the penny dropped with Sean, he started laughing, 'Clock, one big hand, one small hand.'

'Fuck, you may have not passed selection but every time we had a difficult operation, Alan would say he's taking you on it.' Sean noticed the smirk on the face of the driver, he continued. 'So, tell me, what's this mob like? They've summoned me here for the second time this week.' Sean fished away.

'Tanya, the pretty one, she visited me in hospital two days after my regiment had been in and told me my army career was over. I was in bits. No thanks – or kiss my ass, nothing – just a lousy three months' pay and then sort yourself out.

Tanya was brill and the brigadier, seriously, a real stand-up guy. Don't take no shit though, and one of the best your regiment has had serve. He didn't get his beret back door like a lot of the officers. He earned it.

Within a week of me being discharged from the army I was on their payroll. Even though I couldn't walk properly for another two months, they kept their word and got my physio sorted. They also helped the wife with some counselling, then sent all of us, me the missus and all three kids on a two-week holiday to Greece, just before I started with them. Like I said she is brill, I do a lot of the driving about, on call 24/7 and deliveries for them, but the brigadier also allows me in on a few operations and if I'm honest they keep me sane.' He indicated for the turn.

Sean began to rethink the earlier deception. He wasn't a daft lad; he had figured the letter drop was a test, but that fact alone made him more pissed.

'We're here, mate. Good luck and nice to have met you, Sean,' said the driver.

'Likewise mate, not every day you get the chance to meet a real hero, and that's what you are Scotty a real hero,' replied Sean, offering his hand over the seat. After slamming the door he banged on top of the car; the window came down.

'Here, I have something for you.' Sean pulled out his wallet and removed a cap badge with two wings and a dagger. 'It's yours, you passed, it's your reg as well. Anyone asks where this came from – tell them to call me, Sean Doyle.' He gave another tap on the car roof.

Sean looked up at the old Whitehall building. It was still as daunting, more so even on the second visit. Working for this lot was one thing, coming here "to the office" was another.

Staring at the massive building Doyle felt the same emotions as he did when he walked through the gates of IJLB, at 16, all of them years ago in Folkstone.

He didn't show nerves then, and he wasn't going to start today. Still thinking, his arms and legs began to move.

Behind him in the car Scotty hadn't moved yet. He was

wiping his eyes after the tears had stopped. What Doyle had said and gave to him meant a lot, especially coming from the David Beckham of the special force's world, everyone knew Doyle. He felt a prat when the traffic warden tapped on the driver's window, then pointed to the sign. He nodded and moved off. Nothing could spoil his day.

'I've been asked to come in and report to Tan...'

'Yes, Miss Howlett is expecting you, and thank you for your promptness, Sergeant Doyle.' She shuffled some papers on her desk. 'One moment and I will page her for you, sergeant. Please take a seat. – Miss Howlett, could you come to reception, please.' The perfectly groomed female was pretty, sexy, confident and yet still very professional in her manner. Sean replied with his eyebrows and again made his way to the outdated sofas.

Waiting wasn't his strong suit, not unless there was a point to it. And he couldn't see one. He was also aware that being here was not part of the brigadier's brief. So he decided that he was neutral.

There were three sofas positioned in a horseshoe formation and all of them facing a walled end.

Fixed to the wall was a 60-inch TV with no make or model displayed. No one had ever watched the screen, the only pictures and audible the blank screen had ever produced were reversed, as it captured images from the seating area then relayed them to a couple of monitors. One in the brigadier's office and the other in the war room.

A few moments had passed. He'd done the normal shit of checking the place out, after wondering if anyone else had worked out the TV's true calling. He leaned forward to pick up this month's copy of – *Soldier of Fortune*.

'Sergeant Doyle?' asked the female.

Placing back down the glossy mag. He rose to greet her. 'That's me.'

'Would you please follow me sir. I have been asked to escort you to Miss Howlett, she is expecting you.'

It took a full ten minutes to arrive at the door; no conversation had taken place. Sean read the plaques on the walls as the receptionist knocked on the door.

In an emergency call 999 and vacate the building

Follow the green running man

Maintenance should always be carried out under the codes on the agreed work permit, followed by. *All maintenance must be cleared at the correct stat...* The door opened.

'I have Sergeant Doyle for you, Miss Howlett.'

'Thank you, Victoria. I'll take responsibility for him from here.' The secretary turned to her right and set off back to the elevator. Sean's eyes followed her all the way.

'Enjoying the view are you, sergeant?'

He smiled bringing his head around to her, the grin remained as he spoke.

'Unusual venue for a meeting.'

'Please enter, sergeant.'

Standing aside, she allowed him in. He saw a tall very well-built uniformed man standing in the far corner. He was holding a foot-long baton-shaped object.

'Please stand on that circle, sir, spread your legs to the width of your shoulders and raise your arms, if you will.' He pointed to the centre of the room with the baton.

Sean obeyed without a flinch, relaxed, as he had already figured out that the baton was a metal detector, he'd used enough of them himself. He was about to be swiped for weapons. A *Beep* was heard.

'Lift up your right trouser leg please, sir … slowly if you will?' asked the officer, pistol drawn and held with two hands and without any doubt it was aimed at Doyle's chest.

The denim was raised six-inch from his boot.

'Freeze!'

Tanya moved away several feet.

'Hands on the back of your head, fingers locked tight, do not move!' ordered the well-built man, who knew how to handle a weapon. Doyle obeyed him without question; his grin still held.

'It's a gift from an old Scottish friend, a skean dhu.' He broke his fingers and went to retrieve the blade.

'Freeze, do not reach any further, remain like a statue, I will shoot. Place your hands back on your head and lock your fingers,' ordered the man with no emotions attached to the words. His index finger clearly visible on the trigger of a Browning.

'Why do you have the knife on you, Sergeant Doyle?' Tanya asked.

'I live in a rough neighbourhood, why else?' The grin never faded.

She moved forward and bent over in front of him. 'May I?' She looked up.

'Help yourself, darling, but I must warn yah, it's bigger out of the sheaf. It must be eight inches.' His grin grew.

She mirrored the smile but hers said something different to his. The knife in her hand, she then placed it on the table. 'I suggest you get yourself a new tape measure.'

Her body turned. 'Thank you, Paul, I'll carry on from here.' She nodded to the guard.

'Are you sure, ma'am?' he asked still looking at Sean the Browning in the process of being re-holstered.

'I'm sure. Paul: the sergeant here means me no harm.' She gave a glance towards Sean.

'Ma'am.' And the officer left the boiler room, acknowledging Doyle as he passed him.

Tanya reached across the table for the skean dhu and turned towards Sean. 'Here, next time let us know in advance, please.'

'Thanks, and you know men see things bigger, and I apologise for the surprise it gave, but it was a good test. And yah man there, ... was impressive I do believe he would have shot me!' His grin still there.

'Enough, I really don't have the luxury of time. Can I trust you?' She went straight in for the jugular.

Sean gave her a funny look but said nothing.

'Like I said, sergeant, I am running out of time. I need to protect some people close to me. I know this isn't the correct protocol, but remember I've read your file and obeying rules isn't your strong point, is it Sergeant Doyle?' She was just about to talk again, well aware for the first time in her career she was jumping in feet first. And that wasn't her, she was more the cool-headed analyst, every stone unturned and every piece of data read and re-read, turned upside down and looked at again before a move was made.

'Are you in trouble?'

'At the point of preventing trouble.'

'What is it you need or want me to do?' asked Sean.

15

AUCTION DAY

Present day
    The room was at the maximum capacity, yet still he wasn't here.

People that had pre-booked seats had started to sit down. Around the perimeter the standing became still. Two rows from the front Kev had yet to sit, obviously on edge as he was imitating a meerkat looking for his friend.

'Hurry, it's about to start. I thought you weren't coming. Come on hurry.' Kev remained standing in the aisle just his forearm waving until Sean was up to him.

They both sat down together.

'I was waiting outside for Specks. Not seen her yet, have you?'

Kev pointed to the front of the room. Standing behind the polished wooden lectern was their Specks.

'Bloody hell, she does scrub up well. Is that really our little geek who wore boys' clothes every day for school?' Sean was impressed.

'It is, I'm really proud of her she's not only become successful, she's saved me.' Kev said, feeling emotional.

'Me too,' agreed Sean, followed by, 'What do you mean saved you, from what?'

His questions were drowned out by the room applauding.

The clapping of hands slowed, and Specks began to talk; the hands stopped.

Sean stared at the name plate on the front of the lectern. "Louise King", in a posh 3 - D font, cut out of stainless steel. Believing the wrong name was there, he whispered to Kev.

'It's her work name,' Kev replied, but didn't hear the come-back as the applause started again.

Specks leaned in slightly and spoke with her mouth close to the microphone.

'Ladies and gentlemen, thank you all for attending today and joining us for this special auction that Christies have the pleasure of hosting. We are set to deliver one of the best presentations of antique weaponry that we have ever had the pleasure of bringing to you.'

Now standing upright her words flowed perfectly,

'This is truly an outstanding collection. So, allow me to start by informing you all, that an American anonymous buyer has offered to purchase the full itinerary, and he would pay the full expert's valuation. However, he went on to disclose that all the items would be shipped back to his home in the States to become part of a private collection. The owner of the weapons refused that very generous offer.' she looked in the direction of Sean, 'Stating he would like them to remain in the UK. Also, the owner has currently sold two of the flintlocks at a very reasonable price to local museums.' Specks turned her head to check the pictures had begun appearing on all four eight-foot screens surrounding her at the rear of the platform.

'As you can see from the photos, these flintlock rifles are in immaculate condition. And you would be forgiven for thinking "forgeries", but we truly have a wealth of documented evidence and a well-formed backstory that could be made into a film ... Ladies and gentlemen...' She smiled, stopping for a moment as the audience laughed a touch as well as becoming excited. '...These papers will prove to you all that without a shadow of doubt, and with no room for error, all the items in today's sale are authenticated.' Another breath was taken and a sip of water.

'A copy of all the relevant paperwork will be provided with each purchase made, as well as our usual Christies guarantee certificates, giving you, the buyer complete peace of mind and a purchase of a lifetime.

I feel on this occasion I must ad...' The audience interrupted and burst into applause once more; she again allowed some time.

The hands slowed once more, 'For your interest none of the weapons have been fired; however, for those of you who wish to have the barrels tested, of course this can be arranged, but after you have purchased the item. I am sure you will all understand.' As Sophie, or Louise, said the word "fired", a single picture appeared on all the screens. A close up of the hammer and cup on the flintlock.

The pictures changed again from the current single one to some showing large antique books and all of them were hand bound ledgers from the maker of the weapons. These stated names and addresses – plus the sums of money originally paid for these rifles in the year 1838. Just before the pictures changed once more, Sean moved forward – closer. In the sales ledger he could see the address for the delivery of the rifles, and it was the De Pen Court estate. The screen flashed and the pictures changed. The whole room were shocked because on the screens in front of them now, were several photos of a full complete suit of armour, immaculate in its appearance.

'As you can see, ladies and gentlemen and I can definitely see from all your reactions, this is, if I say so myself, most likely one of the best and complete examples of a 13th century suit of armour…'She played to the crowd perfectly. 'That anyone today will come across in the world.'

As she explained, several smaller pictures of armour in museums around the world appeared, 'And yes, we do have a wealth of providence for this item also. We believe that the suit was commissioned by and belonged originally to the De Court family from North Darlington.' The photos remained the same but were magnified to highlight individual segments of the suit itself.

'We will start the auction with this magnificent suit. Shall we?' Her voice became full of excitement. It increased in volume but remained perfect. The images had become 3 - D and were rotating on the screen.

'Will someone start me off at… £35,000? … … Thank you, madam.' Specks pointed over Sean's head, then he heard, forty – fifty – fifty five – sixty – seventy – eighty – eighty five. Kev kept on tapping Sean.

Her arms were pointing everywhere, and a small breath was drawn in as she glanced around the room. Specks was off again, arms moving at speed.

'Ninety thousand from the tall gentleman standing at the back of the room. Hold up your paddle please, sir.

Ninety thousand in the room and now we have...' she touched her ear, 'On the Internet, ninety five thousand. I will take increments in ones, if that makes it easier for some. Thank you, ninety six thousand again, sir. I can see you want this beautiful specimen. Come on! Think this through people, when will you ever see another example as good as this one? Don't lose it for a mere thousand pounds.' A few more words came through her tiny, shiny earpiece. Specks threw these out to fuel the room even further.

'Just to remind all present – there is no VAT on this lot, only on the house's sales commission, AND we have just waived that!' The speech worked as planned.

'Thank you, madam, Ninety seven – ninety eight – ninety nine thousand.' Her arms once more flying around the room as the numbers rose rapidly, as did the tension in the audience.

'Wow! I would never have guessed, it's gonna reach a hundred grand, and you have another one of these suits.' Kev was excited, much more than Sean himself, it appeared.

'I do but I intend to display that one in the container and you can give your notice in on the rigs if you still wanna. We start on the container tomorrow,' announced Sean.

Specks showed her skill and played the room perfectly yet again.

'Is that the last bid I have? One hundred thousand pounds! Ladies and gentlemen.' She went quiet for a moment as her eyes checked the room for late bidders. Nothing 'Going ONCE, GOING TWICE. GOING...' She counted to five in her head. 'SOLD!' Her gavel went down, the crack amplified by the mic.

The crowd began the applause.

Kev kept nudging Doyle, before he spoke. 'Yes, of course I'm in. I can't wait to start properly instead of a bit here and there, really up for it.'

Over in the far left corner an eloquent lady turned and walked out. She headed straight to the sales office. 'Invoice the De Pen Court estate. I have arranged for two of my staff to remove the item later today.' She waited.

'I'm sorry, ma'am, we have to have cash or a bankers draft before the release of any of the items,' said the young girl.

'That's fine, Alicia, I'll sign the release form,' the manager said, approaching the desk.

'You have purchased a grand suit there, Lady De Pen Court, and of course we will invoice your estate. Can I ask though...'

'Yes, the De Courts are the same family line, the Pen was added through marriage ... I believe in ... 1610, but don't quote me.' She indulged his history interest.

'Well, I'm happy it's going back home ma'am and I'll have the item crated for travel. If you would like to leave us a contact number for your men, I will personally call them in a couple of hours when it is ready.'

'Thank you, Sebastian, it is always a pleasure. How long have I been doing business with you now?'

'It must be over twenty five years, ma'am. Yes, yes it's my silver anniversary next month. I started here a week after I married. You were my first client and I will never forget I broke that small statue which you had only just purchased, and you were so kind telling me not to worry, you would claim it on your insurance.'

You could see the memory in her eyes 'I too remember I still have the item, never claimed, I spent an afternoon with my Henry, and we fixed it with glue, now its priceless. You are still married then, Sebastian? Have you purchased a present?'

'Meaning to, ma'am.' he chuckled.

'Suggestion?'

'Please, ma'am.'

'Have you a piece of paper?' Emma started writing, "Four nights residency in the Willow Suite, the De Pen Court estate inclusive of full board and amenities". She signed the note.

'Thank you, ma'am, but that may be a little pri...'

'That's what my signature is for, Sebastian, it's nothing for the service I have received from you all these years. A week's notice we will appreciate, and when you're with us please ask Caroline to inform me. I would love to meet with your dear wife. And I must add we have an extensive old library; I believe you will find it fascinating.'

'I ... d ... d ... don't know what to say, ma'am, I re...'

'Say nothing, words are not always required. See you soon. My men will be here in a couple of hours, they will wait, no need to call them.' And she was gone.

Back in the auction room

'After that excitement. ... We will take a short interval of thirty minutes or so. If there are any persons who have not viewed the flintlocks or the duelling set, and of course the bayonets, please approach me or a member of the team during the next ten minutes and we will escort you through to the viewing area – where you can take a look at these delightful weapons. The same goes for the paperwork we have available for your inspection.' Specks left the stage walking down the seven steps like a film star at the Golden Globe awards.

She began mingling with the people. Sean watched. She was a true professional working the crowd at ease, yet she was so shy at school, a wallflower he remembered. He couldn't have been prouder. He knew what she had been through with her family and yet here she was a real winner an inspirational person.

Waiters and waitresses were all over the room passing out sparkling wine and water accompanied by food that Sean hadn't a clue of the name. He spotted Specks talking to an older man. The pair walked off down the corridor, clearly well acquainted with each other. He knew the man from somewhere, just couldn't put his finger on it. Then remembered.

'Over there, that's the dog walker who rescued me from the cellar,' semi-shouted Sean as the crowd was loud.

'Can't be, mate, sorry, that's Sir Shoebridge. He's some sort of government minister. He's here tonight on behalf of the museums, some culture thing he does. He represents the couple of museums that you sold those rifles to. He does some fundraising for them.' Kev had a drink, 'I often see him leaving Sophie's place when I visit.'

'I guess that makes him her boss at the museums then, my mistake but coulda sworn it was him.'

'Yeah, her boss,' semi answered Kev, busy watching the room.

'I don't usually forget a face but given the night and the circumstances you may be right.' Sean swigged back the champagne not giving him another thought.

'How are you finding it? Enjoying yourselves I hope?' Specks asked, approaching the two of them.

'Yeah, and the free booze, good gig,' replied Sean, lifting the glass up towards her.

'We did very well with that suit of armour of yours. You should receive ninety two thousand, give or take the coppers.' Specks was impeccably turned out; you couldn't fault her dress, make up or hair.

'You really know what you're doing with this buying and selling stuff,' said Sean, smiling genuinely, looking into her sky-blue eyes. He never saw her beauty in this way before.

'Guess what, g... g... go on – guess, guess.' Kev didn't give a second for her reply. 'I'm off the rigs, we're starting full-time on the container house tomorrow.' interrupted Kev in a childlike manner, due to being so excited, plus he was at least a couple of times over the legal limit, and not a big drinker.

'Really happy for you, Kevin, come here.' Her arms opened and they hugged.

Kev wasn't selfishly taking Speck's limelight he just couldn't help feeling the relief and passing it on. These two were so close and leaving the rigs for him was the climax of a few years of pain and suffering.

'Where's the gents, Sophie?' asked Kev, as the tears formed. The drink had become an emotional trigger. Daft as it may seem but to him all that was happening was too much, life for him had become good at last. And all of a sudden aided by too much complimentary champagne he found it overwhelming.

'Go back out into the hall... and, here take this with you show it to the assistant at the entrance. The staff toilets will be empty at this time they're all backstage getting ready.' she gave him her swipe card.

When Kev was out of earshot she turned. 'Thanks, Sean, and I really mean it.'

'I should be thanking, you, I think...?' A slight frown.

'You don't know what you have done for him, do you? Kev's wanted to stop working offshore for such a long time, ever since ...' She stopped herself, realising it may not be her place to inform Sean of the reason.

'Hey, let's not forget he's building my house, it's not charity and since what? I get the feeling I'm being mushroomed.'

'No, it's not charity! You have enough of them! You're turning out to be a bit of a nice guy.' She smiled, determined to deflect him away from the "reason".

'What time is the next auction starting?' he asked. Stopping the waitress as she passed, he removed two long and very thin glasses and offered Sophie one.

'On duty, sorry.'

'Good dodge.'

'It should start in around ten minutes or so but on this occasion may be closer to twenty as quite a few people have gone behind to take a look at the flintlocks. And my boss says the Internet enquiries have nearly collapsed our lines. The interest regarding the duelling set has been phenomenal. I don't believe Christies have ever had such a response to any item, ever. You're going to have a very nice tin box coming today.' She left just as Kev returned.

'Sophie,' Sean spoke, semi-loud.

She didn't hear him.

A relief really as his emotions had taken over his voice box, aided by the champagne. He was relieved as he may have said words he would have regretted later. He proudly watched as she took her position back on the stage, professionally placing her hands on the sides of the lectern.

She waited a few minutes, allowing the audience time to settle. The music that had been playing during the break slowly faded out and the wall behind her filled once more with images of the items up for sale.

'Allow me to welcome you all back for this second, and very exciting, half of today's special auction.' Her professional persona cloaking her once more, there was a bit of small talk and some questions whilst the remainder returned from the viewing.

Specks placed her index finger to her ear. 'Well, that's a surprise and even to me. We have just received a buy it now, offer for the duelling set of £100,000, ladies and gentlemen. A round of applause, please, come on, join me.' Her hands were together.

'This is like that *Only Fools and Horses,* episode,' said Sean.

'The watch episode, I know,' added Kev, clapping like a seal.

'Yeah, and I'll be the one passing out. Can't believe it, a couple of days ago we were broke. At this rate we can square the bank up and have some left over. And all thanks to you, mate.'

'To me?'

'You were the one who went looking around the sheds, putting me on to this lot. I'd have got someone in and skipped it all, making space for the workshops. And don't forget we have that £84,000 from the timber. I gave your old man five grand as commission, he sold it all and sorted it to be picked up this morning.

The sheds are virtually empty; we have a lot of space. He asked me how you were doing? I didn't tell him anything, but he sounded pretty concerned.' Sean had the glass back to his mouth.

'It's too little – too late, the fences have been burnt and the bridges have collapsed where he's concerned. ... I can't go back there again, it hurts, he only wants other people to think he cares. He's broken me and more than once. He left me feeling like a freak, a pervert, a piece of shit on the bottom of his shoe. Please, Sean, let's not spoil today by bringing him into it. It's your day, mate, enjoy it, but I'm looking forward to seeing the space at the yard. Will get all my stuff over. I have most of it in storage down on Walker Street. Been buying stuff for years, got about £60,000 worth for £15,000 bankrupt buys and auctions.' Kev returned to applauding the sale of the duelling set.

'Twenty thousand pounds!'

'What? It's just gone for a hundred grand,' replied Kev.

'Twenty thousand for the machines, and all the other stuff you have,' replied Sean.

'I'm not following yah?'

'I'll buy the stuff of you, for twenty grand!'

'No, there's no need. But I see where you're coming from, and thanks, but gimme ten thousand and we are partners in the shop?' Kev's hand lifted.

'Deal?' added Sean. 'Another word and the build's off.' glass back to his lips.

Kev was going to cry again, he wasn't going to call the build off, but too nice to take all the money of Sean.

Both the day and the auction ended on a high, with total sales accumulated from the shed finds coming to £678,000. Sean received £630,000 after Sophie worked her magic on the commission. All the funds would remain in Sophie's private account, because, like she explained to Sean it would be better for tax and VAT if he divided it independently between the charities in the form of investment grants, and the businesses, it was safe with her for a couple of weeks.

The three of them spent the rest of the night together, celebrating the day's success. A few drinks followed by a meal at the Golden Ruby if they could get in.

'Kumar, it's Kev. Sean Doyle's home from the army. I know it's a bit late, but could we come over for a meal at the restaurant?' Mobile remained close to his ear, as Kev waited.

'Come yes, we have some curry left, can you come now I'll set a table.'

'We're on our way – thanks.' The mobile off Kev listened to Sean.

'Thanks all hard work and all that went, was in. You're good. I, I, I, have I told yah, you're good. You selling that stuff, Soph, you're really good at it. I so impressed. You're good. I want to give you ten grand from me to my geeky friend,' slurred Sean.

'You're not making sense. Are you drunk, Sean Doyle? I get paid for selling antiques, remember. It's my job. I don't need ten thousand,' she replied in amusement, and surprised at the very generous offer.

'A liiittlle ma'be.' And he stared at her, his eyes full of respect and genuine admiration, but also love but he didn't know that.

Kevin watched the pair. It made him happy. Thinking he'd give them a little space, so he left the table and spoke to the owner and friend, Kumar.

'Can I have a bag of chips to take away, and will you wrap them in newspaper please?'

'Newspaper?' Kumar queried.

'Yes, *The Sun*, *Daily Mirror* or local rag, don't matter which as long as it's got print all over it.'

'It's great to see Sean back. Did you tell him the meals are on the house?'

'I did, but he said no, and to send the bill to Barchards and he'd sort it later, he doesn't want freebies. But he appreciates the offer,' replied Kev.

Kumar looked at the old Asian man stood a couple of feet behind the bar. Kumar raised his shoulders in answer to a question posed in a foreign language (Mandarin). Thanks to the food and Kev saying hello to the big white telephone, he wasn't so drunk now.

'Is there another problem, Kumar?' he asked as the old man kept on at him, chirping away in the same language but the speed of the strange words had increased.

'No, it doesn't matter, I can handle it,' answered Kumar.

The old man began shouting at Kumar and his hands started flying everywhere. Then he looked up at the big clock above the bar.

Kumar retaliated verbally and started shouting back at the bold, old man. He won; the old guy left.

'Sorry for you having to see my grandfather like this, he is worried. He's not usually like that. Kumar looked up at the same clock. Gold around the outside, a strange cat in the middle, its front paws telling you the time.

'You will have to leave, Kev. I need to close up the place.'

'Come on you two, we've kept, Ma, up too long already,' he beckoned, and all three of them left.

Twenty minutes later the trio were sat on the old railway bridge sharing the chips. Kev produced a cold can of Coke out of his pocket, finger in, he pulled the ring, took a swig and passed it on.

'Thanks, Kev,' they both said together. As the warm scent of salt and vinegar hit them, the years melted away, and for a couple of minutes they were all twelve once more. Sophie took a drink and then passed it to Sean.

Kev smiled. 'Right, I'm ringing for a cab. You sharing, Soph? I could stop at yours.' He dialled on the mobile.

'Yeah, will do, and anytime, you know that.' she replied.

Sean took hold of her arm.

'Tell you what, Kev, you get a cab. I'm going to go back to the office, get the paperwork signed off. I don't want any hiccups with this sale. It's a lot of money!' She looked back at Sean; her eyes twinkled.

'As long as you two remember you're not married.' He laughed telling them "Night" as he received the text from 45 – 45 – 45. 'Your car is waiting. A silver Ford Focus, SL15YR.'

'Are we going back to your container? Is that your plan?'

'We are.' His voice changed, no longer as merry. 'And you're gonna tell me what the fuck is going on with Kev and that shit Ahmid, and most likely your brother will be involved.' He may have felt strongly for her, but what drove Sean was protection of those who could not protect themselves, especially a close friend who wouldn't hurt a fly, and who'd give someone his last penny.

'Romance isn't dead then?' said Sophie, standing and backing away from the bridge.

'What?' asked Sean.

'Come on, you're right I'll tell you all I know about it. But you must promise me.' She wiped bits of chips from his top, 'You won't say anything to Kevin, and you will not challenge Ahmid. I don't want you getting hurt. Sean.' Her fingers still touching his shirt, even though all the bits had gone.

'What is it with you two and me getting hurt? Do you have a clue what I've been doing for the last thirteen years?' Sean put his arm around an old friend, a close friend, now a real woman, but he wasn't sure which he wanted tonight.

It took the pair nearly an hour to get back to the container; it was a 30 minute walk sober and in daylight.

'Who's that over there with Mr Doyle, Danny?' asked Lisa, as she pulled the door closed, giving it a little shake for peace of mind. The pair were outside the community café.

Danny had returned from a run, panting hard as he replied. 'Not sure but she's a stunner though. You're working late.' he noted, somehow feeling less agitated around her.

'Yes, late.' clearly sidetracked she focused, 'I'm applying for a National Lottery grant. The application forms are something else. I agree she is pretty. Goodnight then, Danny.' Lisa walked slowly not wanting to bump into the pair.

Inside the container

'Coffee?'

'Haven't you any bottles of beer left?' replied Sophie, taking her coat off.

'You like your drink?'

'We're not all fitness freaks are we, and treating our bodies like temples?' She opened the fridge herself and removed a bottle of Becks for her and grabbed the carton of milk for Sean.

'That's worse than the beer. It's produced by an 800 pound mammal to fatten up her calf and the chemicals the food industry puts int...'

Specks shook her head as she re-opened the fridge. The milk was returned, and a second bottle Becks was taken out and passed over.

'Just drink – and shut up about the milk.' Her lips landed on his without an invite; without a doubt a connection occurred. And Doyle wasn't bothered about these chemicals entering his body.

'Sean,' she moaned out loud.

16

SEAN'S DREAM

Earlyish the following morning Sean was woken by the loud sharp sounds of metal banging against metal, thick steel ensuring the sounds echoed.

'What the fuck?' He was up and looking at the old clock on the upside down crate, with seventy percent of his eyesight he saw: 0640. He looked over to the other side of the mattress.

'What time is it? ... Oh, my head.' Her arm was covering her eyes, her long previously perfect hair was now in disarray, yet she was still appealing, if not more so.

'Time for you to do a Paul Daniels,' answered Sean, pulling his trousers on.

'What, ... what do you mean?' she twisted her palms over; the sheet falling away – her breasts bare.

Sean enjoyed the view as he pulled on the T-shirt, 'Disappear!' his voice kept low.

'Oh, you're one of them happy morning people.' Her arm was back over her beautiful eyes, deflecting the new sunlight 'Don't I even get a coffee?'

'No ... Unless you feel the need to explain to Kev what you're doing here.'

He heard someone shouting from outside.

'It's too long we'll have to set it up out here or remove that stone gate post. Your choice Kevin my dear and you only have me here 'til one o'clock today, remember. I'm booked in at the docks after that, right 'til next Tuesday, on a big job, I am.' Kev heard the bragging in Derrick's tone.

'Okay, Derrick, okay you don't have to be such a drama queen all the time. Just give me a minute to decide.'

He heard the steel door clatter up above.

'Morning, Sean,' shouted Kev as the steel door was closed. The sunlight was bright, but November ensured there was a nip in the air.

Sean didn't reply, instead he pointed to his watch, a stalling tactic while Sophie dressed.

'Is there a back way out of here?' He heard from behind him and also then from in front... 'Sorry, I got the crane cheap, and we need to position the four containers putting them in place ASAP. It's the priority, then we can get started on the welding,' briefed a new Kev, wearing all his offshore safety gear. 'You go get yourself a coffee and get out of my hair 'til dinner, but I'll need you back for just after one.'

Kev was clearly in charge.

Sean saluted. 'Yes sir.' And returned into the container.

Derrick had climbed out of the crane. 'I see why you like him, you and him... he's a real man, a young bear, I wouldn't m...'

'Just set your legs up and get the machine operational. I want this done before you leave. And make sure you put plenty of wood underneath the hydraulic feet. This yard is hundreds of years old, plus it's part of my planned design, so I want as little damage as possible to the sets, they're original,' ordered Kev.

'Get you and your new job.' Derrick's head wobbled side to side while the mocking took place, he ended with - 'And don't forget Kevin... you promised to pay me in cash no receipt.'

'How much did he say he'd pay?' asked Sean as he pulled up the collar on the Mac.

'A, a ... a oner, sir, yeah, a, ... a hundred pound and in cash,' spoke a surprised Derrick, having not noticed Doyle approaching.

'Here, and Kev'll give you an extra fifty if it's all completed to his satisfaction.' Sean passed him a hundred notes then turned. 'Can I fetch anything back with me boss? In fact, Kev can you walk with me, I have that information in the front office?' shouted Sean, needing to be heard over the old crane's engine, he coughed once then dodged the thick black smoke.

'What information?' thought and spoke Kev.

'It won't take two minutes, the gym's room idea,' reiterated Sean.

The pair set off.

Her hand slid down the wet handrail, a quick wipe on her dress as it came free, she seemed to shuffle at the bottom of the stairs, as if to ensure her shoes were on properly. Sophie smiled at Derrick as she rushed by. Her hair had been put up in a bun.

'The walk of shame, you're a lucky girl,' said Derrick.

Sophie smiled half in agreement and half out of embarrassment; so, did Derrick.

'Has that fax arrived, Ann?'

'No, ... what fax?' she replied, as she turned towards the machine.

Kev looked at Sean. 'I have to get back. Derrick won't do anything without me. He's a great operator, but a lazy one.' He frowned. Sean tried not to laugh.

'I'll walk with you,' offered Sean then he stopped. 'Can we empty the pot, Ann?' he asked pointing to the glass round jug. 'Yes, go on. I'll do a fresh one in a minute.' She looked at the clock, 'The staff will be in shortly.'

'Is everything okay? Are you alright, Sean? I've started too early. Sorry.' asked Kev, realising he had been keen. Ann looked over, also puzzled.

'I'm good, nothing wrong. Just spending time with a friend. Anything wrong with that? Here get this down yah.' Sean passed him the white mug.

Kev looked at Ann; her eyebrows raised. 'Guess not,' he replied and relieved him of the mug also grabbing a couple of biscuits from the tin.

'There will be something wrong...' loudly said Ann. Sean gave his grin Ann looked out the window and sharply back to Sean then spoke. Both the lads stopped and turned to look at her. '...If them mugs don't return here! I have just bought them.'

Back outside in the yard, Sean asked Derrick along with a pointed stare, 'Nothing happened has it, mate?

'No, no, nothing just me waiting here, for his nibs there.' Derrick winked at Sean.

'Make that an extra fifty if this man gets everything done for yah, Kev, even if it takes longer than one o'clock.' He looked at Derrick who nodded his head.

'And are you sure I can't get you anything when I'm out Kev?'

'No, I'm fine, just yourself and don't be late back or it

will hold me up.' Kev started rolling out slings and chains with gigantic hooks and carabiners attached.

Sean walked off quietly laughing he had got her out without Kev knowing. And talking about Kev he was fired up about this build, Bob the fecking Builder on speed but it was good to see a friend happy.

Nine o'clock that the same night and the four containers had been finally welded in a hundred and eighteen carefully chosen spots. Each weld designated for the stabilising of the now very large steel box.

'Pub, come on we've earned a drink,' suggested Kev.

'Agreed, you call Soph. I owe her one for the auction.'

'You call her,' came back from Kev.

'Busy – I've to go sort something out.'

'I'll do it but it's like dealing with a couple of loved up teenagers. Her trying to second guess your thoughts and emotions, always asking me what you were up to and what you were in the army. And now there's you not talking to her apart from business. If you fancy her just ask her out? I'll tell her to meet us in the new wine bar, she likes that place, its posh. I'll bring along the designs for the lounge and office. We could get her feminine thoughts on a few things. Her apartment is really well designed. Between the two of us we did a great job. Well, I sort of live with my mother now as she left dad couple of weeks back.' Kev dialled Sophie's phone as he continued the waffle.

Sean was virtually out the door.

'Meet you around the front. I need to have a quick word with Danny. He's been asking me for some more gym equipment, for when the extensions finished. We can afford it now, thanks to you two.' And Doyle was off realising Kev had just told him he sort of lived with Sophie.

Kev had cut and fabricated a gate into the steel fence separating the yard from the undertaker's side, so the journey wasn't as long, if you chose to use it.

It took Doyle less than five minutes to be in front of the old stables. Only one light on at the back gym, his eye caught some movement in the far corner, so he slowly pushed open the door.

'You're looking in good shape, and still got that right hand I see!' shouted Sean, as he watched his old trainer and mentor working out on the heavy bag. The fifteen stone dead weight was swinging slightly as Danny stood away, panting, his gloved hands dropped to his knees. No one else was about as the 48-year-old ex-cop, ex-trainer - was regaining his youth.

He straightened up and started to do twists. 'Yeah, I'm getting there I think and it's all thanks to you. Anyway, what you doing here at this time? Don't tell me it's to complement me on my fitness, or is it?' Danny laughed then looked up at the massive clock. He tried to free the gloves from his hands. Doyle pulled them off.

'Thanks,' said Danny putting the gloves away.

'Don't mention it. How many times you pulled mine off?'

'You were a good fighter, in fact, a great one, easily professional material and a chance at the world titles, you rea...' Danny spoke whilst walking to the office, a small walled-off square at the front of the building, concrete blocks painted white at the bottom, with glass and wood in the middle, finished with a plywood sheet as a lid.

'It just wasn't for me, Danny. I needed a different fight,'

said Sean, sitting in what they all called the "pep" talk chair.

'I know that Sean, just as a trainer, someone like you only comes along once, maybe twice and you want to take them all the way.' Dan sat behind the cheap desk.

'What about Spider, that Mexican lad? He was coming up behind me and he had talent.'

'Yeah, yeah, he was good, bloody powerful right for a middle weight, and you couldn't knock him out, so he had a bloody good chin.'

'So, what happened what was he called?' Sean now needed to know.

'Ahmid, that's what happened, that fucking Ahmid. And his name - Juan Junior and he was from a nice family as well.'

It was rare that Danny swore.

'That was it, Juan. Well?' Doyle waited.

'He got into taking a bit of the nose candy, and to pay for it he was doing a bit of running for the Black Devil, then he went down the road – juvey; got six months. I feel shit about that and it's never really left me.'

'How's it your fault he got sent down?'

'I was asked to give him a character reference and they wanted to know if I'd take him back at the gym as the court had been told he had real potential and may be a future champ. That's if he was bound over instead of getting a custodial.'

'And did you?' asked Doyle following the saga.

'No, I wanted to, really did, but ... I was on my own then, remember when Joe buggered off to New Zealand for six months to see his daughter. Plus, fifty odd kids were coming to the gym then. What sort of message would it have sent to them, especially as there was you, Laker and Jesus, as they called him?'

'Jesus? He wasn't that good.' Doyle's grin appeared.

'It was his middle name, you ape.' Laughed Danny, a real laugh as well.

'You had no choice. Shame though, I liked him. I remember he would always watch me and Laker sparring then beg us to let him have a couple of rounds.

Darren used to get him in and tease him but tell yah what, he had some grit. So, what's he up to today, you heard?'

'Not recently, but I know when he got out of juvey he started working for Ahmid, bullying, collecting and shit like that. Anyway, enough... enough of the past what did you want to see me about?' Danny twisted off the lid of the Lucozade bottle.

'Remember that gym stuff at the bankruptcy auction you told me about. What was the buy it now price?' Sean had his notebook out. Danny had a drink of the Lucozade.

'Two and half grand, but if we turn up with cash in hand... I knew the old trainer years ago, you know, before... so I reckon we'd score it at two-two, or somewhere near that. Retail price, we'd be paying over seven big ones and that's a lot of dosh.' More Lucozade. 'But don't sweat it. If we can't afford it, we'll pick bits up here and there. Someone has already donated a rowing machine.' Danny rubbed his face and head with the towel before sipping more of the fluid sugar.

'Is it all good stuff?'

'Yeah, some of it's like new, the old gym went bankrupt. The building's been taken over by one of the chains and it's been totally refurbed, just for the image really.'

'Organise to go tomorrow afternoon. Have you got any wheels?'

'No, unless you count my old trolley.' Danny laughed again.

'Hire a van in the morning. I'll sort the cash and leave it with Ann. If the gear is as good as you say, just buy it, Dan, don't lose it for a couple of hundred. But for the pull-down machines, I'm gonna get Kev to make some, so grab as many free weights as you come across.'

Danny smiled.

Sean was at the door.

'Sean!' Doyle turned, catching the glass door before it came to a close.

'Yeah?'

'While I have you here, we received an invitation from the Albert Hall. The free style fight night is back on. Do we want to book a table? All the proceeds go to a local charity, minimum though is a ... monkey and that's for the table of four.'

'Not sure, leave it with me for a day or two. I'll let you know before the weekend.'

'Course, and don't lose any sleep over it. It's one of the events that shit Ahmid puts on, trying to be a modern-day Robin Hood. Somehow, he believes doing this charity stuff makes people forget he's an anti-social psychopath.' Danny pulled off his T-shirt.

'Ahmid!' Sean stopped himself, turned and re-entered the gym. 'Explain.'

'He's got his fingers in a lot of pies. He puts on this tournament every year. Any style of fighter can enter, well, providing they come up with the £500 entrance charge. Winner receives a purse of £10,000.00 but Ahmid wins every year. Well, no, two years ago your old buddy Darren

Laker beat him, but he was hospitalised two days later after being mugged on the way home from the gym.'

'Yeah, Darren was good. He should have achieved something.'

'He boxed with you for a while, but then took up karate just after you took the Kings Shilling. He did really well, scrapped for England in the Olympics twice then became a stuntman in Hollywood. He had come back because his mother was ill.'

'Book the table and enter me for the fight night.' Sean turned to leave again.

'What! ... To fight? You?'

'Do you have a problem with that?' Doyle's tone was different, his eyes not so kind.

'No, not a problem, but Ahmid is a real nasty shit, and I mean, really nasty and to be fair to him he can handle himself as well in the ring as he can on the street. Last year, he thumb-screwed his opponent's eye till he was wrestled off by the ref and security. When was the last time you had a one to one fight?'

'What the fuck is it with everyone and Ahmid being this monster? I knew him at school. He's just a fucking bully. I sorted him once, twice ain't gonna be an issue. Book the fucking fight, will yah!'

'Sean, I've seen him scrap. He takes pleasure from the torture. It's not just the win he's after.

Sean didn't say a word.

'Listen to me. You really don't want to get in his sights. Please listen, people are just looking out for you, that's what it's all about.

'To beat the likes of him you have to be like him! But you're the boss, and if, ... you're sure.' Danny began wiping the whiteboard where the ring was booked for sparring time, another source of revenue for the community fitness club.

'When is this "terrifying" night to happen?'

'Twentieth of December, three weeks away. It's on a Friday night. Starts at three in the afternoon for the fighters on a knockout get through basis. Then the doors are open to the public at seven. There's an hours break for the fighters whilst people take their seats, get drinks. And off the record this is when all the betting is finalised, and the devil runs the books; that's the true reason for the contest. Several hundred thousand will change hands; you'll see the corner that's full of Chinese. The contest itself starts for real at eight and goes on 'til around 12 to 12:30. Any fighters who have a qualifying record can get a pass 'til the quarters, if the organisers see them as a worthy opponent and they pay a £750 entry, not the £500.'

'Book me in, straight in for the quarters. I'm not pissing about with the dancing in the afternoon,' demanded Sean.

'What's your record and style you'll be fighting in? We have to show something?'

'Just state the truth. I've already had a couple of fights with Ahmid and won one.'

'That was at school though and many years ago.'

'When he sees my name, he'll accept me in, ...' a nod and the grin full on, 'Don't worry about that. What styles are listed?' Sean walked towards Danny.

'Boxing, karate, Judo, Brazilian, freestyle, cage, mixed and a few others, including street. And the only rules are, you can't bite, and you have to accept a submission from your opponent. That's it.' Danny read from the brochure at arm's length, giving away his age.

'Put me down as freestyle, "in five" if you wanna be

accurate.' Sean took the whiteboard marker from Danny's hand and wrote his name on the sparring board, an hour a day for two weeks. He opened his wallet and passed Danny one and a half. Danny didn't want to take it.

'I'm paying, this club has to make some money, or it won't be around in a year.' He put the money in the top drawer and walked out of the office, followed by Danny.

'Let's see what this "in five" is all about and what sort of name is that?' Danny threw some gloves at Sean, hard enough to state game on.

'You sure about this ... old man and its correct name is, well I still can't pronounce it?' Doyle laughed, pulled off his top and performed a few twists and stretches then secured the Velcro on the sparing gloves.

A few minutes later.

'You okay? Breathe, Danny, come on breathe.'

'Bloody hell, where did you learn that?' squeaked Danny, arms on his knees, short breaths taken.

'We picked it up from a couple of Shaolin monks, a good few years back now - pretty effective.'

Doyle left the gym. Danny had changed his mind, no longer was he worried about him in the coming fight. He went to the board started ringing round for sparing partners for Sean, the amateurs wouldn't do, Doyle would kill 'em. His last phone call wasn't to a paid fighter – It was to a small shop.

'Mr Wang, have you started taking notes for the city hall bouts?'

'PC Rhodes! Now there's a voice I've missed. Last, I heard you was down on your luck?'

'No longer a copper, and well ... let's say I've finished

punishing myself, Mr Wang, so I'm just a punter now, yah gonna take my money?'

'Of course, yours is as good as the next. Who are you staking?' Mr Wang twirled his finger whilst on the phone.

'Sean Doyle, two K, to win.' Danny had to sit down.

'That's a lot of money, Mr Rhodes, Are you sure?' Mr Wang's fingers twirled again. 'I'll bring it over tomorrow, you still at the laundrette?'

'What odds are you looking for on this fighter of yours? I've never heard of him.'

'Ten to one. He's an ex squaddie, just returned to the area, he was at my club as a lad.'

'Has he any professional record?'

'No.'

'Done, but 6 – 1 and I look forward to your visit.'

The phone call ceased. His finger stopped twirling, in front of him the muscle-bound Chinese man stopped spinning the chair. Mr Wang's head gave the slightest nod. The chair spinner pulled out a small Colt fixed with a silencer. Mr Wang gave a second nod, the trigger was pulled, the debtor sat in the chair was dead.

The following morning soon came around Danny was up with the Larks, still not accustomed to being back under a roof. A cuppa in his hand, he watched a cat stalk a pigeon from the window of the medium sized flat above the workshop.

Ten minutes later and he pushed open the parlour's front door.

Some chit – chat took place he declined a coffee then

he was ready to leave. 'Thanks, Ann,' said Danny, relieving her of the envelope she was holding.

'Good luck with the auction, and there's an extra twenty in there for expenses. And don't forget, we'll need a receipt. And what have you bumped into? That looks nasty,' asked Ann noticing the black eye.

'Sean. I bumped into Doyle in the ring last night.' Danny smiled.

'Does it hurt?' she asked, leaning over the counter for a closer look.

'Yeah, like hell. Me, own fault tho' I was goading him a bit about Ahmid.'

'What has Sean got to do with him? I know at school they were always fighting, but Ahmid is a gangster now, with real guns and that.' Ann was scared.

'Don't be worrying yourself, Ann. It's to do with the charity fight night, nothing personal,' lied Danny, he knew anything between them two was going to be personal, after watching Sean's reaction, and that... was just to Ahmid's name. Then, feeling the wrath he dished out in the ring, Ahmid should watch out.

Danny had trained Doyle a lot of years ago and he always knew he had real potential, but this new thing he had going on... whatever these Shaolin monks had given him, was for real the next level, and with his time in the Special Air Service he was ready to sort out a gangster.

17

THE DOLL

Houses of Parliament, London – 1400 hours
'Well, Allister, how did you find your first
payment, satisfactory I do hope?' asked the
Texan, his accent jovial in tone.

'Very satisfactory, very. I take it that the goods were
acceptable?'

'They were and I am looking for six more for our
Arizona plantation, we will require four females and two
males. They must all be healthy, and of a breeding age
fifteen to nineteen ideally for the egg layers, and eighteen
to twenty-five maximum for the swimmers. It will be a
live-in position. Both sexes will be required to help with
the animals that we husband for pharmaceutical
intervention. The females have to be tested for
childbearing at your end, and for the males a sperm count
is required. We will pay $40,000 for each female and
$30,000 for each of the males. And of course, we shall
take care of all the shipping. We want assets with no
family or ties, and of low spirit as I am sure you will
understand.'

'Of course, that makes perfect sense, no visitors, as they would be a nuisance. I will set to on recruitment today. Could I ask what their duties will consist of, apart from the animals that is?'

'Let's just say that after the animals have given us some data, we use humans on the next stage. This way we are guaranteed no lawsuits when we go into the trials, as we know they don't affect people. Also, long term we will aim to breed the females with the two males.

These should produce a harvest of twenty two offspring over a decade. After two litters we will have the adults removed and the offspring will never know of the outside world – we will literally have human lab rats.'

'That is forward planning.'

'Oil is running out of popularity and to be frank it's becoming expensive to rear beef, and the green world is causing a stink with all the trees being felled.' The cowboy laughed then spoke more. 'It's easy to keep people fat and sick, we don't want them dead, just convinced they need treatment, and the ironic thing is, the medication they take causes complications.' He laughed more. 'So, the bloody fools need to buy more medication from us, again causing more complications.'

'You are a visionary my friend,' commended Shoebridge.

'Oh, and while you are recruiting keep an eye out for golden bloods. I pay $22,000 for each of the rare ones.'

'Golden bloods?' Shoebridge's ears rose on hearing the G word.

'Yes, the rare blood groups such as all the negatives and of course Rhnull blood and for that one I'll open the cheque book as I have a couple of clients in Saudi with medical issues.'

'Intriguing, I will have to visit this new Utopia in Arizona.'

'We will arrange it.'

The international phone call was over.

'Coffee, sir?' asked Askins, approaching the minister with the silver tray in hand.

'Yes, place it on the desk. I have some mail it appears,' he replied, walking from the window to rendezvous with the tray.

'You do, sir. It was delivered a few moments ago by courier. Security have checked it out and nothing flashed up.' Askins poured the coffee.

The hot liquid released an aroma that turned the minister's head. 'Is that a different blend, Askins?'

'It is, sir, sent over by your American friend.'

'Very considerate of him. I can definitely see a special relationship developing between us.'

Shoebridge sat down and tasted the gifted coffee as he proceeded to open the small very neatly wrapped package. Askins stood near the door semi on guard. As the final piece of paper was pulled away from the parcel it revealed a smooth white box, another sip of coffee and he removed the lid – time stood still for him; his brain froze.

'What the! Aaarr!' His fingers quickly released the box as he screamed. Tossing it back onto the desk his eyes digested the thing some more before frantically pushing back his chair and escaping. His back clattered against the bookcase knocking over the dozens of first editions he cherished.

'What's wrong, sir?' asked Askins rushing to his aid. He'd not ever witnessed his boss scared or flapping like this before or anyone for that matter.

'That? Look ... a ... at that, lo...'

Shoebridge was forced to stop talking as his own hands shot up and grabbed around his neck. His two thumbs squeezed into his throat, and he began to choke himself.

Askins ran to his assistance but even with his powerful biceps he couldn't pull Shoebridge's hands off from around his own neck.

It was hopeless.

He was left to watch the minister turn a shade of blue in front of his eyes, then the image of the minister's fingernails drawing blood. He couldn't comprehend the visualisation of this strange event.

Shoebridge literally was standing in front of him strangling the life out of his own lungs. Askins, after trying again to release Shoebridge's hands, decided to pull away his arms and give up. He rang for help. Two security officers arrived quickly but by this time the minister was unconscious and had collapsed to the floor. Yet somehow his own fingers continued to carve into the bloody mess that was once his throat.

The two guards looked at Askins. He shrugged his big shoulders, half miming, half talking; they were frightened all three of them. No rational explanation was available for the scene occurring in front of their very eyes.

The ambulance team ran through several sets of double doors and along the joining corridors, finally coming into the minister's office.

Moments later they were followed by two armed police officers. Askins was taken aside to be questioned. He began to tell the police officers what had happened. Not that he really knew anything and what he did know he couldn't explain in words. And if he tried. Would he be believed? The minister was still lying there with his hands around his neck his body stretched out fully on the floor, his left leg started to twitch then convulse like roadkill. The whole room had an appearance of a Quentin Tarantino movie set.

One of the policemen had moved towards the desk, carefully he side stepping on his toes around the medics and blood. The other remained next to their main suspect and Askins was well aware of how this must have looked.

'Take a look at this,' said the police officer shocked by the unusual, strange object, gazing at the thing that only moments earlier the minister had thrown back on to the desk.

Measuring a mere six inches in length the thing had fallen back and out of the box – It was leaning against the still steaming cup of Texan coffee, but it didn't quite hide the printed red letters: "Best dad in the world".

The strange man-made object was stitched together from what appeared to be human skin and with real hair on the tiny head, the teeth and nails fixed in expertly. The Voodoo doll uncannily, DID resemble the minister, Shoebridge.

The mimicking doll's hands were tied around the thing's neck. The police officer picked up the packaging that the doll had arrived in.

'There's a note in here.' The paper was flattened and then he read it out loud.

'*We warned you and you took no heed. You will now bleed and bleed. Breathing shall slow but you will not die, no, you will not die – only appear to do so in front of other eyes. You should have never messed with our creed! You were warned and warned again. Three opportunities were given, and you declined each and all. Now bleed and bleed until I squash you and you once more become seed!*'

The officer looked at the others before speaking again. 'Call the boss, Steve, seal off the room. This is some weird shit right here. Fucking weird!' The officer dropped the note as he himself had become frightened that the same thing might happen to him as he watched the fingers on the minister's neck. They continued to cut deeper into his own throat, even the medics couldn't release the clam like grip as the long skinny fingers just about touched each other.

The paramedic injected the magnesium. She looked into Shoebridge's eyes with the intention of working out if the muscle relaxant had worked; instead, what she saw was the unbelievable reaction that told her he was still very much awake and crying out for help from behind his pupils. Her thought was to get some tube into the lungs and stop the bleeding, but first she had to stop the grip. 'Pass me the tongs.' she cut each of his fingers off just below the first knuckle.

Shoebridge's office was battened down, no one in – no one out while awaiting the arrival of the forensics team.

A few hundred metres away Uguba watched the ambulances and police arriving. His reflection showed a smile in the rear-view mirror. His lips parted just like a talking horse his teeth oversized for his mouth and whiter than white, the only imperfection was the large gap in the centre, his recorded age was 55, yet you would believe he was no more than 30. He pressed in the ignition key quickly, checked the mirrors and pulled out. To many of the onlookers he was just another black cab joining the mad traffic on the chaotic London roads.

The window came down. He tossed the second identical "doll" out and into the rush-hour traffic. Back in Shoebridge's office the female paramedic was forced to snatch away the oxygen mask from the minister's face. The blood coming out of Shoebridge's mouth was like nothing she had ever seen. The volume alone didn't feel correct, and the pressure was that of a full-on tap. Uguba drove faster his smile growing wider after seeing the second doll being crushed by the wheel of the red double decker bus.

The female paramedic leaned forward to place her fingers on what was the minister's neck. She announced, 'Life ended 1545 hours.' She went quiet as the blood reached her knees and began to soak into her green trousers.

'He's been murdered. Inform the security teams,' shouted Askins, unaware of the big picture already beginning to unfold.

Eight uniformed police officers had attended the parliament building. One stood back and spoke clearly into his radio using a low tone, out of respect, I guess.

'HE 16, speaking, can you patch me through to the boss, in fact, ask him to call me back on my mobile and inform him it's a matter of urgency.' He stared at the minister from the back of the office next to Askins and another officer who threw up.

The blood was still oozing from Shoebridge's mouth – his chest had sunk – flattened literally to a thickness not much more than his spine.

It was drastically concave. The officer or anyone else present could not give a rational explanation for what they all had just witnessed. The room was discombobulated into silence.

The theatrics of the minister's demise appeared to be at an end when there was a second powerful eruption of blood from his mouth. Followed by his upper torso deflating even further in front of their eyes. In a few seconds it was as if his chest had been vacuum packed.

'Sir, thanks for calling back. I'm in Minister Shoebridge's office, he's dead... sir.' The officer who by now was physically shaking from the horrors he witnessed, walked to the door and out into the corridor, a breath taken as he listened.

'Are you sure, and how...? Never mind set too, secure the area. I'm coming over.' The chief inspector immediately called the press liaison officer. 'Meet me in the car park. Now!'

'I'm halfway through a...' She tried to get out of the request.

'Now, Sandra, and I mean, NOW. I'll brief you on the way. This is a matter of national security.'

She followed his orders and ended the meeting with several east-end community leaders. Ten minutes later she was sitting next to the inspector in the back of a black Lexus as it pulled out of the underground car park. The driver nearly deafened the couple as he switched the sirens on a moment too soon. The solid concrete walls sent back a bellowing echo.

'A senior cabinet minister has been murdered in his own office in the parliamentary building.

We're on the way there as we speak, and you'll need to be prepared for when we arrive as the gates will be swarming with press. The incident has been leaked already; don't ask me how.' He was angry. The inspector switched on the small TV monitor which was fixed to the back of the vehicle's chair. The screen instructed him to answer the incoming call.

'Thank you for being prompt with your reply, sir,' answered the chief inspector.

'What is the emergency, Clarence?'

'Allister Shoebridge has been killed, sir.'

'What? How? Was it foul play?' questioned the Prime Minister.

'Yes, sir, it most definitely does appear that way, however, I will be more accurate shortly. I am en route to parliament as we speak and for the moment all I have to go on is a report from one of my officers and he categorically states foul play and some "weird shit" his words, sir. I have ordered the inside of the parliament building and Shoebridge's own office to be shut down.' Clarence spoke well but panicked a tad when speaking to the PM.

'Are we thinking terrorist involvement? One moment, Clarence.' The Prime Minister turned his head. On the monitor in view for Clarence to see was Brigadier Howlett. A brief exchange of words took place between the high ranking officer and the PM. 'Apologies for that interruption, Clarence, I have cha...'

'I can see him, sir. Will you be sending him over to Parliament?'

'If you have no objections, Clarence. I would like him on the ground, so to speak, just in case it is political, and we need to instigate, Fallen Bird. But I don't want to be heavy footed at the moment, it's still your circus, Clarence. However, if there is clear motive or a sniff of terrorism, I will not hesitate to hand it over instantly, I am sure you understand?'

'I have no problem with him attending, sir, but could we give forensics an hour? I will willingly hand the case over to Charles myself after that if we have nothing to go on, of course,' returned Clarence.

'That is acceptable and thank you, inspector, for both

your time and understanding and your request will be adhered to. I will ask that he keeps you abreast of all that's happening if he does become involved.' The Prime Minister waved for Charles to come over and sit down.

'I look forward to receiving it, sir.'

The monitor was switched off from the Downing Street end halfway through the inspector's goodbye.

Clarence sat back in the soft leather of the Lexus. Sandra placed her hand on his thigh. 'Are you okay, sir? You seem a little agitated.' Sandra's Polish accent barely came to the surface. Her pale grey and blue eyes stared at Clarence as her hand wandered.

'Fucking Howlett, the PM's puppet. He's always interfering in my affairs; I despise the man.'

Sandra's fingers pulled at the inspector's zip. 'Shush, relax, sir, please, relax, remember what your doctor told you about your blood pressure.' Her Polish accent had returned intentionally; the sexy accent fed him the words then stopped and her tongue caressed his ear.

'We're at the gates in two minutes, sir,' announced the driver who was aware of the back-seat massage taking place. The car had stopped the door was only open ten inches, but the noise was loud and becoming louder.

'Can you tell us if it was a terrorist attack, sir? Can this be confirmed.' shouted one of the press pack. Another wanted the chief inspector to confirm that a minister was, actually dead, and which minister was it? Could he name him?

'So, they don't know everything then, that's a plus,' said Sandra to Clarence.

'You stop at the gates and keep them at bay but don't give anything away.'

'I can't, I don't know anything, sir, remember,' replied Sandra, back to no sign of the Polish accent.

'It won't be hard to follow my request then, will it!' He glared at her behind the guise of a professional stare as he forced her out of the car.

The gates were closed by four officers quickly behind the inspector's vehicle. Sandra smiled to herself aware he hadn't zipped up his fly.

At least two dozen press from all the TV stations and papers were present and they were all surrounding her. Four extra police officers had been drafted to the gate; protocol was well in place.

Not that this would mean much to see. If a terrorist attack or a suspected terrorist attack happened, Parliament would be totally sealed off. Partly visible with uniforms these were more for reassurance, but mostly with the use of clandestine officers which is where Charles Howlett's department came in to play.

Thirty-eight feet above Parliament – one mile away

The helicopter was airborne and travelling at fifty miles per hour as it began circling before it descended.

'Sir, all external exits are sealed off and are now monitored. We're starting at the west side and clearing our way to the centre, over,' informed the confident voice.

'Roger that, number six. Is number nine with you, over?'

'No, sir, number nine has been setting up a secure comms in the designated safe area waiting for your arrival, over,' replied Kelly.

'Roger that, two minutes, out.'

A very similar message came next from number seven,

but the main difference was seven was clearing from the east to the centre.

'Roger that, number seven, out.' The brigadier made a quick call on his phone while he looked at the scaled plans of Parliament.

He felt the thud whilst removing the headphones as the Lynx helicopter landed with a bounce on the top of the parliament building.

The brigadier leant through to the front. 'Good flight, thanks, lieutenant.'

'Anytime, sir. Do you wish us to stay around?'

'No, we don't know what we are up against. I will re-order, don't want you sat here if something goes off, remember that 50-calibre in Belfast?'

'Roger that, sir, and I remember, we were lucky that day,' answered the lieutenant. The brigadier patted his shoulder.

Out the bird, the brigadier instantly bent over and ran to an awaiting quad bike.

'Put this on first, sir,' instructed the short man waiting. Charles raised his arms whilst the officer draped over the black bulletproof vest. It dropped and settled. A helmet was given to him next; this was placed on his head. He straddled the quad. The bike pulled away as several men ran carrying stuff to the centre. Charles watched as they surrounded the large letter "H", which was spray-painted in luminous paint on the world famous building's roof. In total there were ten Heras fence panels covered by chain mail and lead filled blankets. These heavy curtains were camouflaged by large photographs of the top of the building.

The quad bike roared across the 900 meters to the

external lift doors. Thirty seconds before the bike's arrival another operative pressed the green button.

The four wheeled bike drove straight into the large lift.

'Cut the engine, I've stopped smoking,' said the brigadier after the doors had kissed tight in the middle.

'Will do, sir, but I'd prefer you left the jacket on. I'm responsible for you whilst Operation Falling Bird is live, sir,' emphasised the man, wearing full black overalls, helmet and tinted goggles.

The brigadier, who had pulled open the Velcro on the side of the vest, replaced it, smoothing it over with his hand.

'Who put you in charge, soldier?' asked Charles.

'You did, sir, remember. No one in the building without personal protection equipment and you added at the brief, "even the pompous over-rated ministers and anyone else who tells you to shove it". Your words, sir, not mine.' he was desperate to smile but he knew better.

'We'll talk again later, Tiler, and a few more words will be added to that job description,' replied the brigadier.

'Look forward to the update on your policy, sir.' Tiler did smile this time. Charles wouldn't bring it up again: he was proud his men were carrying out his orders to the letter, and him attempting to remove the vest had been a test.

Ten minutes later in the minister's office

'Charles, you're early ... I suggested an hour to the PM, ... who agreed with me,' Clarence said, grinding his teeth and trying not to be obvious.

'Just observing, Clarence. Take your time please,

imagine I'm not here.' The brigadier went silent as he looked around, then spoke again.

'We've secured the full building, no one will be allowed in or out of Parliament without my immediate permission. Give my team a further twenty minutes and I'll give you a full building occupancy report.'

Charles spoke with confidence and natural authority, something that grated on Clarence. He did hate him, there was no doubt about that, but he also wanted to be him because of his calmness and his respect from his teams and being the right hand to the serving PM of the day.

Plus, the numerous connections he had across the globe, even a first name relationship with the head of the FBI. But what Clarence didn't grasp was that Charles had achieved all of this by respecting the men around him and the man he saw in the mirror each morning, not the false face some would put on in front of the TV cameras. Charles did what he had to, Allister did what he thought he had to! Usually what he was told.

'Thank you, Charles, for your consideration and I would appreciate that report when it's available and to be kept in the loop with any other developments,' he stated. But he knew nothing would come his way, well, maybe a generic couple of pages if he was lucky.

'Don't mention it, Clarence. I have total confidence in your abilities as ever.'

He didn't, he knew that the chief inspector was the offspring of the pre-top policeman. He'd been put on the beat for six months, then in subsequent positions, each going higher in rank and order! A judicial conveyer belt.

The members of the same gentlemen's club that Charles belonged to, made, and put Clarence where he was today.

So, as part of their continuous games even in retirement, they were still in power ruling the chess board remotely. This would also ensure that nothing malignant surfaced, or if it did, they were quickly in the loop.

The PM was also aware of this fact. A fact that was always uppermost in his mind when certain aspects of his complex job came into play.

18

THE TRUTH

'No, ma'am, he's still here, your ladyship, he's fast asleep in the Lake Room.'

'Do not allow him to leave. I don't care how he remains, but he is not to leave, am I clear on the matter?'

'Yes, my lady, very clear,' replied Caroline, replacing the old-fashioned phone, unaware of the true ramifications of Lady De Pen Court's request.

Sean wasn't asleep, as Caroline had reported to Emma, he was wide awake reading the file given to him the night before. Well over a hundred sheets of paper and to his surprise there were several photos and other documents included. There were two pictures which had grabbed his interest straight off.

Picture one was an old black and white family portrait of four people standing up straight and proud. "These can't be his parents", he thought, way too old a picture the photo had that purplish tint and was black and white plus the edges had started to corrode, which would date it to mid to late -19th century. A tall man over fifty and dressed in a black suit, clearly too small for his muscular physique he was wearing no tie or collar with a hat, some version of a bowler Doyle guessed, but fashion, let alone historical fashion, wasn't his strong suit. Although he did recognise the half hunter watch, dangling by a silver chain from the man's waistcoat pocket. Tony used to have one the same.

Standing next to him was a petite female she was also wearing a hat, which was tied tight under her chin. For some reason the word "bonnet" popped into his head. She wore a full-length dress also black, and the material was shiny with lots of frills. He struggled to guess the age of this female.

Next in the line was a young lad somewhere around 12-ish but given this was a teenager well over a century and a half ago, he could have been older. He wore long shorts which finished below his knees tied off with a lace. The rest of his legs were bound with cloth, which also covered the tops of the lad's highly polished boots; a white shirt finished it all off.

Last but definitely not least was a sweet little girl who can't have been more than five and very petite. Her dress which was way too big was of a similar design to the lady, matching also was the bonnet, this had been tied tight, so tight Sean could see the irritability captured in her facial features. She made him smile.

What was her name he wondered and who were these four people?

And why were they in a folder titled "Doyle"?

Laid on the bed he turned onto his back and continued to stare trying hard to capture not only the picture but the family, blotching had started to destroy some of the scene, but Sean could see the man had his hands in front of him on top off each other, he was wearing a hefty gold ring, but he could only see the side as another blotch cut into it. All four of them where stood in front of trees full of blossom, but these weren't real, they had been painted on a cloth back drop.

Picture two wasn't a family portrait and this one was in colour but still old, '70s, early in the decade Doyle guesstimated. His first thoughts were a surveillance shot, taken at a distance of at least twenty metres, or further with a decent lens attached. The photographer had captured an image of a man. A man of the cloth, Catholic, walking in front of a church. A small quaint church in a picturesque village.

This guy was tall and again he was somewhere in his fifties, the shot was a side view of the body, but the man's face was as plain as the day was long.

The man's head turned to face the camera just as if he was aware he had been tracked. Grey hair, lots of wrinkles, one old wide scar under his chin and nasty blue eyes full of self-importance. The type of eyes that tell you what they're going to do.

'Oh, you're awake, Mr Doyle. Sorry for bursting in. I have prepared some breakfast. Would you like to join us in the dining room?' asked a flustered Caroline.

'Yeah, sounds nice I'll be down, just give us ten minutes, thanks.' Sean nodded to Caroline as she backtracked to the door. She had burst in as she believed Doyle would have still been asleep, especially after the number of sleeping tablets she'd crushed then slipped in the cocoa.

The rest of the file's contents would have to wait.

Clasping the sheets together, he spotted an old birth certificate folded several times.

Name of child: Mary Doyle.

Mother of child: Mary Morag Doyle.

Father of child: this had been scribbled out.

Place of registration: Cork, Ireland.

Date of registration: 13 September 1943.

Everyone just imagined that Mary was Sean's grandmother; he didn't mind either. It was never contradicted by Mary or Sean, as it legalised their relationship. Especially given the fact that she had kidnapped him a few years earlier from the hospital and more permanently from that Magdalene Convent home.

The file was stuffed in his holdall, it sat next to a different file, the one that ended his investigation into Henry's death – and all that came with it.

He left the room and made his way down the stairs. Looking through the arched tall window it was made obvious to him why it was called the Lake Room.

The place was old and cluttered with interesting weaponry from every century and from every country in the world. Some of the weapons had also been used. The walls were home to way too many stuffed animal heads, well, too many for Sean's liking. Kill to eat and survive, not to gloat at the poor creature for an eternity.

'Would you like beans served with your breakfast, Mr Doyle? I know it's an English thing,' asked Caroline, as Sean entered the dining room.

'Put on whatever you would normally, and a little extra,' he said with his cheeky grin.

The room smelled clean but not clinically; the abundance of daylight was clearly a factor. Four others were already sitting at the collection of round tables, three on one, consisting of two adults and a child around six, maybe seven. A twitcher on the other, thought Sean, noticing the binoculars and bird figurine which was the mascot on the walking stick.

He parked himself on another with his back to the wall, a view of the doors and windows. A second female this one much younger approached his table.

'Orange juice, sir, freshly squeezed this morning.' She smiled, offering forward the glass jug.

'Please, don't mind if I do.' Sean held the bottom of the glass out of instinct - anticipating a spillage as the heavy jug rested on the rim of the glass.

The young waitress continued on with her job after successfully completing the orange pour. Placed on the table from her trolley next were the cutlery and condiments.

'Please ring this bell, sir, if you require any further assistance. I will be over as soon as possible.' She placed a small brass bell of a female Scottish dancer on the table, and she was off.

Doyle pushed away the bell to the far end of the table as he knew under no circumstances would he be ringing it.

Only a few minutes later. 'Enjoy, Mr Doyle.' Caroline placed the large oval plate in front of him. The time had come around to 11:10am as he tucked into the large breakfast, baked beans had arrived but as a side dish. The table of three had vacated, but it was soon full again replaced this time by an elderly couple with a young child of a similar age to the one who had just left, maybe a little older. Nice grandparents taking their grandson on holiday, presumed Sean.

The old lady glanced several times over to his table,

more than what he would have said was normal. But he knew he was a big guy and at the moment he was carrying a couple of fresh scars which had yet to blend in, so he put it down to glances of curiosity.

One sausage and half the fried bread left on the plate when a commotion began in the hallway. First out of the dining room was Caroline, he heard her voice, but the disturbance persisted. A larger than life man with no neck flew straight out of the kitchen the two-way door flapping in his wake. The commotion at first became louder but then eased off, in volume at least. The old lady started glancing over to Doyle even more. The old man stood and made his way to the hallway. The old lady's glancing became a permanent long stare. Sean couldn't ignore it any longer.

'Are you ok, luv?' he asked quietly.

'Don't let them take him, please don't...' She was silenced by the old man coming back into the dining room. It was then that Sean noticed behind the glasses and tight baseball cap, how subdued the young child was. He had never really moved, or spoke, not even touched his food. *Hard for a kid of that age to keep still, as a rule*, thought Doyle.

Caroline had returned to the dining room; the big man was yet to return. The old guy never re-sat.

Caroline came over to Doyle's table. 'I do apologise for all the noise, sir. I hope it has not spoiled your breakfast.' She poured more juice into his glass. Clear was the shaking of her hand. Sean smiled, still wondering what the old lady meant.

'What was it all about, the noise in the hall?' he asked her, throwing his head in that direction.

'A customer wasn't happy with the bill, that's all.

Nothing to worry about it's all sorted now.' As Caroline said that the man with no neck re-entered the dining area, no words or looks to anyone – straight back into the kitchen again, the doors wafting air as they flapped. The old lady had moved her chair next to the young lad, her arms went around him, the old man was leaning over, talking into her ear. Then his hands were on her trying to get her up.

Caroline joined them. She was trying to gently pull off the old lady's hands from the child. 'I know you have grown attached, Mrs Kell, but we mus...'

'Get off me!' demanded the old woman.

Enough is enough, thought Sean, not comfortable with the scene unfolding in front of him. 'Can I help?' he asked. The old lady stared at him again, she didn't say anything this time, but Doyle re-heard the words she spoke moments earlier. "Don't let them take him".

'We have everything under control, Mr Doyle, please go and finish your meal, there's no need for you to become involved.' Caroline spoke in her usual unprovoking soft manner, but the whole event wasn't right, not to Doyle.

'I've finished. Now I suggest that I have a word with the child and lady alone.'

The kitchen door opened. 'Everything out here alright, my love?' asked the man with no neck, his fingers twisting the tea towel tighter and tighter as he approached the table.

'Really?' asked Sean, up and walking to no neck.

'Is this a private party? Or can anyone join in?' asked Emma.

'Ma'am, you're back early,' said Caroline, with clear relief in her voice.

'My apologies for not calling ahead, Caroline, and you, ... Mr Doyle, were you going to ask to dance with Harold?'

'Something like that.' He grinned. 'And nice to see you on your feet, ma'am.' His grin now firmly in place, behind Emma stood three of her men, including Chalky.

'Sean,' Chalky said quietly, backed up with a nod.

'Well! Who is going to begin the explanation?' asked Emma, looking at the full room as only a posh woman could, her gaze ending on Sean.

His arms opened, palms out and his boy-like charm working through his face muscles. As his mouth opened Caroline jumped in and began the story.

'Mrs Kell got cold feet, ma'am. It appears she didn't want to return Maximillian to his parents at the moment. Mr Doyle wasn't sure what was happening and rightly so, he wanted to make sure the child was safe and well, that's all, like any decent person. Harold was just wondering if I was okay. Then you walked in, ma'am. That's it.'

Caroline was telling the truth. Behind Chalky appeared a very attractive woman, mid-thirties a rare type of woman.

'Alice is this the case?' asked the attractive short-haired lady.

'It is. I'm sorry, truly we are, but Max has told us so many horrific stories about the torture he has inflicted on him. This is not bad parenting or even neglect, its deliberate cruelty. He has cigarette burns under his arms and several of them. How can we...' Her eyes scanned the room... 'In all good conscience hand him over to them animals? Over my dead body.' Alice was no longer using a soft voice. Her maternal instincts had clearly kicked in, her arms again tight around Max.

243

The attractive lady asked the boy to come over to her. 'It's ok, go, Max,' said Alice.

Several step and Max stood in front of the attractive woman she took hold of the boy's hand. She knelt to achieve his eye level and began to speak to him softly.

'How would you like to stay a little longer with Alice and Roger, Max? ... ... Would you like that?' The boy's head went up and down fast before he ran back and into Alice's arms.

'Thank you.' The old woman whispered and lip-mimed to Sean. Roger also nodded to Sean as he hugged both Alice and the young lad.

'Now that all the fuss is over, I would like to see you in my office, Mr Doyle. We have business to discuss, I do believe.' Emma turned to her men. 'Lance, Chalky, you two, step down, and try and rest. Andrew, can you stay for a while longer, I believe Stewart is on his way to relieve you?'

'Of course, ma'am,' said Andrew.

Chalky and Lance looked towards Caroline.

'Yes, take a seat, I'll rustle something up.' She smiled after reading the lads' minds. Then her eyes went to Emma, 'Ma'am, could I prepare you a sandwich?' she asked.

'That would be divine. I have all the time in the world for our hospitals, but their food is not yours. If you would send it to my office.' She finished with a forehead raise and smile.

Sean lifted the sausage from his plate as he walked by. 'I'm all yours.' And he followed the short-haired woman and Emma as they vacated the dining room.

Andrew brought up the rear. They had only walked a few steps and no sausage left when they turned into the very large entrance hall. Two adults were waiting; one sitting slumped over with their head in their hands, the other frantically pacing from wall to wall.

The female was small in height, tiny in frame and dishevelled, her face held a good amount of guilt, and it was old before its time. Her once shiny blue eyes were unable to connect with anyone, so they remained locked onto the floor. Next to her the male stood tall – his neck stretched right out from the rest of his muscular body, but not over big, lean with veins popping everywhere. Eyes of a shark, clearly waiting to pounce on anyone who dared to make a challenge to his artificial, hard, persona.

'Mr and Mrs Piper, there has been a complication with the resettlement of Maximillian I am afraid. We will need to re-look at the paperwork. The interview with your son has been brought into question and as a result Max will not be going home with you today.' She paused for a moment. 'As we had previously planned upon, h...' The short-haired woman was cut short, her feet glued to the floor her upper torso shot backwards, she froze as the child's dad got in her face, his black eyes boring into her.

'He's coming home with me, now. Right now! You fucking bitch, I've had enough of this shit – he's mine, where is he? Max get ya cunting ass here, or you'll regret it.'

In the dining room the child began to cry.

Andrew moved in holding the man back from Roseanne. 'It's time to leave, sir.'

He pushed the man back. Going in for another push the man came forth and hit Andrew five times at speed, all around the head. The sharked eyed pro-am boxer was about to start the kicking, as Andrew had dropped to the ground – his face covered in blood.

Sean could hear Max, the crying had become screaming he was terrified, back in the dining room. Shouting no one can stop him,'

Emma looked to Sean.

He looked at the boxer.

'You want sum big boy, do yah? Cum on, cum on, yah fecking retard. Cum on.' said the man bouncing up and down.

'Now you've brought me into it, that's made it personal. Shall we dance?' Doyle looked to Emma on the word dance then passed the file to Roseanne.

Shark-eyes was ducking and diving while punching the air at speed, then beckoning Doyle more and more to come and get him.

'One question?' asked Doyle. The thug's head shook.

'Did you hurt the boy?' the short-haired woman stepped back.

'Wa, w … wat da fuck, wat's it to da-o wit' yah? He's mine, I can da what I want. A'll fucking hurt you.'

'Thank you.' Sean took a punch from the dancer and another, then the grin appeared.

'Is that it?' Sean hit him once. Down on his knees he went. He looked up. Sean smacked him again; he was out cold. Doyle picked up and dragged the piece of dirt outside of the castle dropping it at the short wall.

Doyle then snapped the fingers on both the hard man's hands after placing them on the stone steps, Rosanne cringed as she heard the snapping sound.

'Sean … enough!' shouted Emma. Doyle looked up at her. She watched as he as he snapped the man's wrist. He nodded and dropped him. 'No, it's not.' The other wrist was simultaneously snapped. 'That's enough now, Emma. I have a thing about bullies.

246

Every time he uses his hands in the future, he'll remember that he used them to hurt that kid,' said Sean, passing her on the way back in.

'No need for an apology, Mr Doyle, I understand... and a lot more than you would imagine.' She had just witnessed what she had prayed for, but she mustn't show the delight on her face.

Lance and Chalky came running out. Lance went over to help Andrew up.

Inside the foyer Roseanne had sat down next to Mrs Piper and was explaining to her the reasons why her son Maximillian wouldn't be allowed back home. Mrs Piper started crying, telling Rosanne how frightened she was of her husband and that he did hurt Max and she was glad that he was taken away from him, and it was right the child shouldn't come home. Roseanne placed her arm around Mrs Piper and started to explain that she could have her son back, but there would be a period of time in which she would, herself, receive a lot of help and support. Also, there are courses available. There really was a lot to look forward to, Roseanne reassured her.

'Will she get prosecuted?' asked Sean, as Roseanne left the mother.

'No, he's done a good job on her over the years. With our help we can reunite the son and mother and in the longer term this outcome will be much more of a benefit to both of them.'

'She allowed him to torture her son.' Doyle shook his head.

'It was also Mrs Piper who made the call to the school, telling them to get the police involved, and in no way allow the lad back home, but not to mention her name or he would kill her. She was petrified of him, she had only turned fifteen herself when she was pregnant with Max, so they didn't prosecute. If you saw her hospital admissions file, Mr Doyle, you may understand a little more. He has been abusing her since she was twelve years old; she is only twenty-two now. And he is thirty-one.'

'What about her parents? Where were they?' asked Doyle.

'They allowed him to have sex with her at twelve. The mother was an alcoholic and drug user and from what we believe was also having intermittent relations with Mr Piper. The dad shot himself, feeling worthless not being able to stop the abuse of his daughter.'

Roseanne told Sean all this, not pulling any punches then added. 'I know it isn't easy, but we have to look and tackle the big picture to stop the abuse cycle. It's the only way forward. If you haven't been abused or in an abusive environment, you may struggle to understand.'

Doyle's head shot round.

'Oh, sorry, I didn't know.' added Roseanne.

Sean nodded it was still a bit beyond him, but not everyone was strong in the same way. The child was safe and that's what mattered.

He spotted Emma talking to Chalky and Lance. 'There's some rubbish outside I would like it removed and it's never to resurface around these parts in the future.'

'Yes, ma'am, does it have a choice, or do you want it made permanent?' answered Lance.

'Give it a choice but make it clear if he returns it will then be made permanent.'

'Yes, ma'am.' Lance turned to Chalky. 'Can you bring the black van round to the front?'

The pair left.

'Come through to my office, Mr Doyle, I'm pretty

confident that you will have some questions.' Then she smiled at the young mother and then nodded to Roseanne. This was an indication that Emma gave her permission for the mother to enter the parenting program. Roseanne led the mother, who was in tears, into the dining room where she was allowed to see her son for the first time in three months.

Roseanne stopped at the door turned and called Sean over, 'Mr Doyle one more thing?'

Sean looked to Emma, who said nothing, he made his way to the dining room, she met him a couple steps away from the entrance, 'I believe everyone needs some love in their life. Please...' And she pointed to the dining room.

Sean moved quietly to the door and watched.

Although crying already, more tears came quicker from the mother, half now of joy. The lad ran as fast as he could into her arms. She smothered him, her hands running all over him, kissing his head, ruffling his hair. 'I love you, Max, I'm so sorry, I... l... love you so much,' she kept saying then she pulled away, one of her hands on each side of the boy's head, in she went and placed the biggest kiss on his forehead. 'Now listen,' she wiped her eyes, one at a time, and tried to stop sniffling, 'You stay with these nice people, you will be better off.' A second kiss was placed on Max's forehead. Sean was not sure what to say, he remembered the dream lady, his Mary, and every Sunday, she kissed him the same way. The emotion of what he felt tried to reappear. He walked away, to re-join Emma, saying not another word.

Roseanne entered the dining room, just as Alice spoke, 'If it is acceptable with Roseanne, now that your husband is out of the way we would like you, if you want to of course, to come and stay with us. We have a great big house in the country, and we think it would be better all round,' said the old lady.

Her husband added, 'Yes we have been thinking about getting some help with the cleaning and cooking, and there is a separate annex, we can't pay a lot, ... but we wouldn't expect you to pay any rent for the accommodation.' He looked to his wife and put his arm around her.

'Let's all sit down and discuss this very generous offer,' said Roseanne as her arm went around Mrs Piper.

Emma's office

'A few questions at least,' answered Sean, following Emma up the stairs along the corridor and into the office.

'Please, take a seat, Mr Doyle. Sean.'

'What the fuck, ... What's that?' asked Sean, looking into the ten-foot by ten-foot tank standing six feet high.

'That is my Nessie, a unique animal. Next year she will be released into a private lake. Two years after that, when she is 20 feet in length, we will sneak her in and out of Lock Ness. Could I offer you a drink, Mr Doyle? Tea or coffee?' asked Emma.

Sean's face was inches away from the glass staring, missing her question.

'Is it real? And why are you releasing it?' He kept staring through the glass, mesmerised.

'Drink,' she prompted, slightly louder than before.

'Yeah.' he answered absently, really just concentrating on the creature, not the tea or coffee.

'Think about it. For well over a century people have been seeing the Loch Ness monster and some of the top research centres from all over the world have checked out our loch from top to bottom. Numerous films made about her. Scotland will be put back on the map, we will be the size of Disneyland once pictures of her have been sent around the globe on social media.' She passed him a glass containing frothy coffee.

'Good idea. So, what was happening in the kitchen? What's with the kids and scum like that coming here?' He made his way to the chairs.

'We run a charity for abused children and those who are in care for a variety of reasons. The hotel is the meeting place for the family mediation and all that goes with that. Roseanne, whom you just met, is a qualified social worker. My charity pays her salary and other expenses. We have a couple of administration staff and an activity coordinator employed as well, our legal work and other specialists do pro-bono for us.

We try to intervene when the council are not able to reach a conclusion. Basically, they won't admit sufficient funds are available. If we can prevent a child being lost in the bureaucratic system, we will. And the top and bottom of all the "shit" that is going on, is the poor children. They have no autonomy over their own lives. We are also working on this in the European courts, allowing the child to have their own protection law, no matter what the age or intelligence of the child. We believe they have the right to be safe. This can be the real cruelty to them. You've seen an example of the parents we deal with.' Emma placed a second cup under the coffee machine and continued 'Chain-Link tries to intervene with children between the ages of four and nine.'

'Why them ages? Is Chain-Link the name of your charity?' asked Sean,

'Chain-Link is actually a very, very old charity. It was

instigated originally by one of my ancestors in the 15th century.

Its main aim has always been to prevent the misuse of children for industrial, sexual and financial profit. Which sadly has been occurring on a great scale for hundreds of years.'

'You're a very intriguing woman, Emma, you come across as a bloody hard case, yet there's something in you that's humanitarian, yet you h.'

'Big words, Mr Doyle. And I have an image to maintain, remember. The world I operate in does not allow for me to display any weakness and being a beautiful female in a male dominated society, means I may sometimes give off the wrong first impression. Forgive my self-flattery.' She tipped the porcelain cup,

'I know a few more big words, but don't be asking for any spellings, and the description of yourself is correct so don't be bashful about that.'

Emma heard the complement but it didn't land as it was a daily occurrence for her.

'Thank you. And to answer your question, we chose children in that age range as we have discovered we still have a chance to alter their lives. Under-fours usually have no problems being adopted; children over nine and unfortunately, we are, sadly in most cases, too late as too much damage has been inflicted on them. It is so sad we have to operate in age brackets, but we are fighting a forest fire with buckets, Mr Doyle.'

She sipped her drink before continuing. 'Talking about families, did you read the file I put together for yourself?' The room was quiet even with the conversation on the go. She asked him if he would like a second drink.

'Not for me, thanks, I read through some of the file but

wanted to check mine before giving you it. It's my findings on Henry; sadly, it's not the best news. I've yet to summarise the findings and it's not easy reading as it stands.' Sean was reluctant to share any information right now.

'It has been a truly sad affair has all of this, a very sad affair, and believe me, it has been intriguing as well.' She sat down on one of the comfy chairs, lacking energy as her mind thought of her son, her beautiful Henry. For a moment she allowed herself to be off guard, strangely feeling safe in Doyle's company.

She started to pass over her feelings in verbal form.

'It has been my fault on more than one occasion, my bloody mindedness regarding Henry's father is what caused him to flee the family home in the first place. I should have told Humphry to leave, he was selfish, worthless, an... ..., but love did not allow me to see clearly, not until it was too late.' Her stare was to the floor, she continued but in a awkward tone.

'I imagined I would never get another man. You see,' Sean sat down opposite her, his expression changed but he remained quiet. Looking at her – how could this lady believe or think that way, she was a ten in anyone's eyes? Male or female. And a lady with a title to boot.

'Mr Doyle, you're looking purely at the outside shell, relationships are different in my world.' Emma placed the cup down and walked to the decanter.

'Hindsight is a wonderful tool, but it's never around when we create the issues, and that's when we need it. Don't beat yourself up, And the shell is stunning, but you have depth as well, people see that.' he offered.

'It is easy for you to say, yo... oh forgive me, Mr Doyle, I'm whining to you and that is not acceptable, forgive my self-indulgence.' She looked to the fire the cup had swapped for a glass.

'Well, you were going on a little. I was about to ask if you wanted some cheese.'

Emma turned at speed from the flames and stared at him. 'A bit of cheese?' she enquired, looking perplexed.

'To go with your whine,' explained Sean as he grinned.

'Thank you for that, Mr Doyle, I needed a reality check. Funny... you are funny.' She laughed genuinely but it was still an effort and didn't last.

'Here is the file. I'll be honest, and I've struggled with a lot of the connections. But after finally deciphering a crazy girl's words and sketches - I'm confident I'm ninety percent there. Feel free to call me at any time if you need any further explanation. I'll have the complete report for you in a few days.' Sean passed over the large sealed envelope, bulked out to the max. 'Yeh, there's just one further thing,'

'Yes,' she replied.

'The attempt to assassinate you. I couldn't make any headway with that, dead end. At first it did link to another name, but it didn't sit right. Just not enough motive there.'

'You will not find a connection to that, Mr Doyle, as it was I ... who instigated the whole show. I discovered that Alaskin was abusing his adopted daughter. I didn't, however, anticipate being shot myself. I can assure you of that much, it bloody hurts.' She laughed and moved her shoulder before continuing. 'So, you can leave that segment out of the final report. Let's not complicate matters. The names you mentioned regards Henry, would you tell me the names of these individuals?' Eyes of diamond connected with him; he was unable to leave the capture.

'I can tell you one of the men is no longer with us, but the other, I need to chat with him first. A few more loose ends Emma, and like I said, a few details to tie up. If a man is to be found guilty on my watch, I like to be thorough!'

'I admire your grit, Mr Doyle. Keep the file. I would prefer the complete version all together.' She released him from the entrapment, seeing sense in what he said.

19

FREE SPARRING

'14 days left, are you ready? From the numbers I've been given today there'll be ten fights during the evening. Apparently, it's been a great turnout this year.' Danny finished talking to Sean and walked up to the ring.

'COME ON, WORK HIM, YA LAZY SHIT, WORK HIM. WORK HIM HARDER!'

A few more seconds passed, and he rang the bell. The fighters didn't break and then one of them head-butted the other. Danny frantically rang the bell again; still the now full-on scrap continued.

Sean ran over and climbed through the centre ropes. In-between the pair, he at once realised it was a set-up.

Both the fighters smiled at each other before flying in to attack him. First punch came, he stood back, one hit the other; a kick came his way.

Danny and another were clambering into the ring. 'Get out, I need a bit more sparring, and this is free,' shouted Sean.

'I'm not insured for more than two in the ring.' Danny panicked.

Doyle nodded then elbowed the one who had thrown the kick.

'That better?' asked Doyle.

Danny and the other guy grabbed a foot each and dragged the unconscious man from the ring, whilst Doyle and the other waited in the corners.

'You wanna carry on?' calmly asked Doyle.

He ran at Doyle, milling. Doyle threw his arms up and took the onslaught.

Danny looked at the man next to him who had woken up. 'What was you two thinking of doing?'

No reply at first but all of a sudden he sang like a canary as he had become surrounded by a group of fighters all waiting for the same answer.

'Got paid 500 quid each off Ahmid, it was to test this Sean Doyle bloke and hurt him enough, so he doesn't show up on fight night.' At that moment his partner gave up the onslaught and pulled away, panting.

Sean came to the ropes. 'Danny! Now, I'll show you the in five properly.'

His opponent was still panting.

'When you're ready, son,' said Doyle, beckoning him to come again.

'Cunt, yah going down.' And he spun around his leg up in the air – his foot came towards Doyle. Sean's arm stopped the muscular leg dead in its tracks. His right and left hands flew at speed into the head of his opponent. Still at speed his right elbow struck the centre of the Adam's apple and from nowhere Doyle was off his feet putting all his power into a second right hand travelling down from above. His opponent was no longer an opponent. The crowd began clapping – shouting – banging – a gladiators salute.

Water was tossed over the one out cold. He was lying face down on the canvas next to his mouth was blood, saliva and two of his teeth. Both were escorted out the gym.

'Make sure you go back and report to your boss, and you earnt your purse tonight,' said Danny tossing the teeth out the door.

'Ahmid?' asked Doyle.

'Yeah, that's who got them to come in. He paid them a monkey each. He must be worried about you.' Danny patted Sean on the back before the rest of the lads joined in.

The questions started.

'Where did you learn to fight like that?'

'Can you show me how to use my elbows as good as that?'

The questions kept on coming, but Sean answered none of them. He'd seen this before dozens of times and knew that it was all bravado the same thing that whipped up crowds at football matches and other big events. He was the peacock of the moment, that's all. A part of evolution, and like it or not it would be a few more years before the alpha male was extinct.

Plus, the only question he was interested in still hadn't been answered. It still eluded him. All the excitement and noise around him was of no consequence.

He thought back to when he'd been attached to the intel boys in Northern Ireland, and they had taught him a lot on the investigative side: profiling, case formatting, information de-clutter and reassessment, timeline extensions and how to fill the empty blocks. Yet he had still to decipher fully the crazy girl's notebook – yet this young, tortured soul's notes didn't fit into anything he'd learned so far, but his gut told him the answers were there to be found. Yes, he had resolved enough to finish his report, and just like the Egyptologist he believed working out the individual icons was the way forward, anything less could mislead.

Doyle was thinking about the case he was working, whilst all the people around him were talking about changing their bets for the big fight after witnessing the annihilation.

An hour or so later that evening.

Sean stepped out of the shower to be faced by Sophie. Immediately he knew she wasn't here to practise breeding again.

He saw her face was in moving torment.

'They' ... ve ... pu ... put Kev in hospital, he' ... s ... in a right mess.' The sobbing came. 'The doctor said they're not su ... sure ... if he'll pull through.' The full burst of tears came through.

'WHO? Who has?' He demanded as she fell onto his chest.

'Ahmid's men, that' ... that's who, ... they came to our flat about forty minutes ago, one ... ... looked pretty beat up – teeth missing ... the other had a broken nose. They beat him with baseball bats, I couldn't stop them.' She spoke through the upset as the tears rolled, yet some anger had begun rising.

'Get back to the hospital be with Kev, I'll join you later.'

'What are you going to do? Sean? SEAN? I don't want you getting hurt as well.'

'Stop with the fucking worrying. I'm going to sort him and his fucking gang, including your brother.'

'How... whe...?' she asked.

'I'll call you a cab back to the hospital and keep me informed.' He dialled 45 – 45 – 45. A couple of minutes later he received a text: "Your car has arrived outside, a red Ford Mondeo".

'Cab's here, Soph.'

She came out of the toilet.

'I'll take you around the front.'

She kissed him as she went to get in the car. Watching from the Mondeo's window she witnessed him talking straight into his mobile phone.

'Tanya.'

'It's late, Sean.'

'Yeah, guess it is, sorry. I need yo...'

'My help, I know, that's the only time you call.' She wanted to be nice, but the late hour and lack of communication won her over.

'Have you heard of a Ahmid Basheer? A London gangster, he has some sort of protection from one of your, lot, I think a government minister.'

'The name doesn't ring a bell, why? And I don't have the level of clearance to search ministers' informants,' she said, yawning with a second glance to the clock.

'Some of his men have just put a friend of mine in hospital, an innocent, genuine, guy who wouldn't hurt a fucking fly. And it's not clear if he'll survive the night.' Doyle spoke with a formidable strength. To many people, strength wasn't an emotion but to him it was and a very real one, one that had always reassured him. He continued as Tanya listened.

'Ahmid was a bully at school, he still is, but now he's also getting away with murder and everything else. What's wrong with you lot, providing cover for scum like him?'

'I'll call you back in two minutes.' Phone off, she called her father.

'Sir, can you give me today's code for high level clearance of informants please?'

'Petty, I will send a text containing the other half.' He didn't question her why, he never did.

The text arrived.

Your favourite colour - then my full name and rank

She switched on the computer as she re-dialled Sean.

'Give me his full name and age and any other information you have.' The laptop's screen illuminated. Doyle passed over all that he knew about his target.

'That's all I know. Is it enough?'

'We'll soon see,' she replied, as thousands of names and numbers appeared on the screen, then it began rolling becoming a thousand times faster than the credits at the end of a movie. Colours changed and merged into one mixture, the screen started to roll even faster, now at a phenomenal speed. The screen became one block of purple; seconds later only a dozen names remained, and the screen slowed down and stopped.

Tanya entered some further information. The tension on Sean's side was growing; one name now remained.

'Well, well, that is very interesting – It looks like you assumed correctly, he has been under the protection of ...'

'Who?' demanded Doyle.

'Minister Shoebridge.' She kept reading.

'Why is it interesting?'

'Shoebridge has just recently died. Murdered to be precise.'

'I know that, hang on, what? So, Ahmid's no longer under anyone's protection?'

'It appears that way. If a supporter dies, protection ends until another willing person takes over. However, ... reading through his files he has a big operation going on and that would slow the pass-over down significantly. What are your intentions, Sean?' She waited to analyse his reply.

'I'll do what I was trained to do, take him out as an undesirable. Do you have any objections to this?'

'On your own?' She kept on reading from the screen. 'I think you may need to read this file and yes you were trained to eliminate, but by using planning and teamwork is how you operated, was it not?' She could hear him thinking.

He knew she was right, and he had a personal attachment to this kill which was never good for timings.

'What do you suggest, Tanya?' Was his attempt to rationalise the situation.

'Carry out the operation and treat it just like any other you have executed. His file states three main kingpins, and an unknown, are part of the leadership. Over thirty operatives are under his command, of which ten are known killers and all recruited from prison and very loyal to Ahmid himself. There are three main premises that we have listed, and they also own lots of other property. Looking at the list it really is a substantial portfolio. Sixty-eight houses, nineteen shops and four storage places.

And a five percent share in the new Waterfront, I think that's the new homeless hostel. However, it says here that his headquarters are based at an old fish shop located in Brockenhurst Avenue.' She finished reading.

'That's the first property he owned, he killed his uncle, aunt and two cousins to acquire it. That shouldn't be too difficult to find.'

'Wait, Sean, there are special notes attached, an eyewitness report from an undercover Met operative. The inside of the place is reinforced with steel doors, bars, locks, cameras, the works and you're correct, they even call it the "Fish Shop".'

'Does it give us any specifics about what we'd be up against on entry?'

'No, ... there's nothing apart from one comment from the operative.' Tanya scrolled down the screen deciphering the speech. 'It says when I left the shop, four doors were opened by electronic locks, two of these made from steel and the last one had three locks on both sides. There's an amendment here ...' She scrolled a little further her voice dropped.

'The operative was discovered on wasteland, two days later, he was naked, dead. His arms broken in several places and dragged behind his back, then tied to his ankles, his head blown off with a shot gun. Nothing left above the man's jaw.' Tanya closed her eyes for a few seconds.

'That's the hallmark of the IRA, it's what they do to informants.'

'Sean, ... promise me that you won't go Rambo tonight, and I'll call you in the morning with a report. Let's do this properly. Not all of us in Whitehall like protecting scum, that I can promise you.'

'Deal, and thanks, Tan, sorry for the late call.' His conversation ended with Tanya. Sean rang another number. He agreed that he shouldn't do this alone, he needed people he could trust and who did it his way. 'Tonight, I'll need you to ensure I'm left alone.' A few more words were said. That was it, no come back.

A second cab pulled up in front of Barchards and Ward funeral parlour.

'The hospital, please, mate.' Sean had to be prompted by the driver to put on his seat belt. There was no conversation during the journey. He kept his promise to Sophie and went to see her and Kev.

'Cheers, mate, keep the change.' Sean closed the door and walked to the reception desk to locate Kev.

'Are you family?' asked the female, smiling just enough to be polite.

'His brother,' replied Doyle.

'Yes, sir, we have him with us, he's currently in ITU, and at the moment that is limited to only two visitors at one time. I'll page a nurse for you.'

Sean remained at the desk, quiet as the receptionist spoke into the bit of sponge attached to the hands-free headset. Behind him walked a tall guy.

It didn't take long before a slim female turned up wearing green scrubs, her long hair tied back rolled up and tied up again, no make-up.

'Hello, I'm Tina, one of the ITU nurses, your brother at the moment is still heavily sedated. He has had a bleed on the brain and has also sustained some damage to his liver and left kidney.' She was still explaining to Doyle, as the tall man crossed in the foyer and exited the building.

'The surgical team have managed to relieve a lot of the pressure from the cranium, and at the moment we are all very optimistic, and he should pull through. However, I have to explain to you that percentage wise he has a fifty percent chance of surviving the next twelve hours.' She wasn't cold the way it was put across, emotional protection on her part. 'I'll take you through to see him now – but prepare yourself because he has a lot of tubes and instruments attached to him.'

Sean followed her without talking. The facts that he had just heard were still entering his head. He, over the years, had lost friends and seen horrific injuries, but somehow this was different. Kev didn't belong in "that" world.

'Your brother already has a couple of visitors with him,' announced the nurse.

'I know one, it'll be Sophie, who's the other? Kev's mother,' asked Sean.

'Sophie? No, it's your mum, Christine, I believe her name is, well of course you know her name and a man he's tall with a tattoo on his forehead, his friend.'

At this point they reached the door. It took several seconds for Doyle to catch up with what she had said.

The tall man started the car and drove out of the hospital car park.

'Sean, thank you for coming. Kevin has been so much happier since you have been back home and giving him that job, thank you for that. He'll be up and better in a couple of days – you'll see. Back to building your house, he won't let you down.' She rambled on, only half the words making any sense, but she kept talking to prevent the tears taking over.

Sean stared at Kev. Clearly his mam was in denial he wasn't going to be up and about in weeks, never mind a couple of days.

The tall man parked up the car no more than a quarter of a mile away from the hospital. He switched on his phone. 'He's in there now, I passed him as I left,' the tall man said into the Bluetooth device.

'Do it,' replied the female voice at the other end.

The nurse asked Kev's mam what the box was on the side as gifts weren't allowed in the ICU.

'I don't know, a man from the oil rigs brought it, not long ago.' she answered.

'Sean Doyle has signed in at the reception. Was it him?' asked the nurse.

'No, he's Sean Doyle, I didn't know the other guy,' replied Kev's mum, pointing.

'I thought he was Kevin's bro...' muttered the nurse.

'Get down now, get down!' demanded Doyle. He opened the lid on the box. The digital clock displayed.

2 minutes 59 seconds.

He smelt marzipan

A tiny antenna flicked up and was sticking out the top of the box; Sean snapped it off. He was off, sprinting towards the roof. Three flights of stairs, he crashed into every wall on the turn and pushed off again up the next flight, his eyes caught the numbers.

1 minute 19 seconds.

Another two flights and he was out in the fresh air, his eyes went down.

29 seconds.

In front of Doyle was a six-inch by six-inch square device. Four wires, a basic clock to the left and three small clear glass bottles on the right.

He knew from experience that he was dealing with an incendiary device. But this one was the Rolls Royce of firebombs. Underneath all this what he'd described lay a thin slab of C4, the cause of the smell of marzipan. The green illuminated digits throbbed.

19 seconds.

The four wires were soldered to copper nibs, a red, a blue and an orange and another orange with a thin black stripe.

12 seconds.

Again, his experience told him he had to cut the orange, one of them, but which one as the other would be a dummy – but it could have a back feed to the ignition switch or a loop to the C 4.

9 seconds.

He removed the bottles. At least it would now only kill him as the fire wouldn't start.

2 seconds.

Snip, using his teeth he cut the orange with a black thin line running down the side. He closed his eyes.

1 second.

"Shit..."

BOOM!

The nurse and Kev's mam remained in the ITU room unaware of the stress hormones being injected inside Doyle's body.

Both heard and felt the rumble. They looked at each other as the security guards ran by the room. The elevator doors on the roof opened. The scene that was waiting for them was horrific.

Sean had been correct regarding the flames: there weren't any. The chubby security guard couldn't look at the body against the wall.

HE thought he could after watching all of them action films, He froze, sweating like a dog, as his eyes focused on the blood rolling from the left ear and nose of Sean Doyle. As he lay against the bricks. Sixteen minutes it took the medics to get to the top floor via the stairwell.

'He's dead, I didn't know what to do, what could I do?' said the guard standing there next to his own vomit.

The medics didn't respond to him – too busy setting up next to the limp body – back against the wall – hands on his stretched-out legs – head down.

§▲

The phone was answered in the old fish shop. 'You owe me, I've taken care of him.' The phone call was ended.

'Thank you and I'll return the favour by taking you out,' said Ahmid out loud.

'That won't be easy boss, no one really knows who the Bitch is.' The man's fingers and thumbs moving at speed.

'That's why I'm the boss. I know who she is, I've always known,' Ahmid replied, then walked off; his lacky continued playing the Xbox.

§▲

Doyle was rushed to a secure clinical room with armed police officers placed outside, plain clothed detectives impatiently waiting in the hall to interview him, the powers that be alerted with the fear of this being a terrorist attack.

'So, you're telling me, that the gentleman...' Her eyebrows levelled in a line, pen tapping her notebook, 'Ran to the roof with a box that was already in this room,' stated the female detective.

'Yes, and for the third time, his name is Sean Doyle, and he is a friend of my son!' Her hand touched Kev's wrist, 'And a bloody hero, like that Jack Reacher in the

Tom Cruise films, but in real life of course,' said Kev's mum stroking her son's hand.

'Why are you questioning us? Why aren't you out there looking for the tall guy with the tattoo on his head? He brought the bomb in,' asked the nurse.

'Are you certain this man brought the box in with him?' asked the female detective for the fourth time.

'That's enough, I've had it! Get out, GET OUT NOW!' And the nurse pushed the copper towards the door as Kev's mum started crying from the interrogation.

'Tan, Tan, Tan, Tanya, Tanya.' Sean was talking in his sleep as he tossed and turned.

Inside his room sat quietly in the corner was a young WPC who had recently been attached to anti-terrorism.

Kathy O'Conner called her friend and mentor.

'Hi, Tanya, sorry for the call at this late hour.'

'I was up, Kathy. How are you?'

'Have you got any of your team over at the hospital tonight?' she enquired, unsure if she'd get a reply to a delicate question. She did.

'Not that I'm aware of. Why do you ask this?'

'We have an ex-soldier here. He picked up a bomb and ran to the roof with it. He saved a lot of lives but injured himself … and pretty badly. I'm in his room right now, he's a big man with a couple of scars on his face. Left side.'

'I'm on my way, do not let anyone talk to him, even near him and that includes your colleagues. Clear?' Tanya finished the call – grabbed her bag and coat then rushed for the underground car park.

She knew it was Doyle, and he was doing what came natural to him, saving others, over himself, a hero: The Oxford Dictionary meaning of the word.

During the drive she contemplated what was going on.

269

Lady De Pen Court and her houseman being shot, explosions at the old pumping station, thirty UK residents die on a flight to the USA, a high positioned minister rips out his own throat like something out of a horror movie. Several of her own team killed – lost and injured and this fresh intelligence.

She started to rationalise. This Bitch character, Ahmid and his crew protected by one of the most influential ministers in the government today. And now Doyle was back in the hospital. It wasn't long before she'd parked up and was entering the hospital.

'Kathy, thanks for calling! How is he?' asked Tanya entering the room, putting her ID away she removed her coat.

'Stable, I've been informed, but he looks much worse than he is. He could awake at any moment or that's what the doctor told me.' Kathy rose from the chair, not sure whether to sit or stand.

'Do we know what has occurred here, and where did this IED originate?' Tanya was close to Sean, touching his hand, she sat on the side bed.

'Can I see him, how is he?' asked Sophie pushing her way through the door.

'Who are you?' demanded Tanya, half officially, half personally.

'I'm his friend, Louise King I was visiting Kev, our other friend and I was told about the bomb.'

Sean was tossing and turning, sweating profusely. 'Is everything okay?' asked Tanya.

'I'll call for the nurse.' Kathy pulled at the red cord. He arrived quickly and saw for himself Doyle's restlessness. 'Can you all vacate the room, please, there's too much talking, it's agitating the patient.'

'Kathy, keep me informed,' instructed Tanya, leaving the room.

'Will do, every hour.' She showed a soft smile with the intention of relieving her friend's anxiety.

Sophie followed Tanya from the room. She turned left going back to the ITU. Tanya headed for the elevator. Her destination was her own office, things were not right. A rat is what she smelt, and an opportunity had presented itself to repay Sean. On the drive back she contemplated contacting her father. This wasn't a job for a lone wolf, even though Sean Doyle was probably the best lone wolf you could come across and look where he was right now.

She called him. 'Sir, my apologies for the hour and the subject matter!'

'I was awake, lass, you require less sleep at my age. What's the tenuous subject matter?' He had a glass in hand and his shoeless feet up and crossed in front of the roaring flames. A rare moment of peace for a powerful man.

'I am aware he is not your favourite person, but it looks like he needs our help. And I fear it's related to Shoebridge. Also, it may be an idea to brief the PM, as some dirt will rise from all this, of that, I am positive.'

'Your hesitation to mention a name implies that our Mr Doyle is the topic, I take it.'

His feet fell from the stool as he sat upright.

The rare moment was over.

'Yes, sir, it does and he's in the hospital as we speak. He was visiting a friend and we are not sure of the reason as yet, but an explosive device was placed in this same friend's room, presumably to kill his friend, but that is only speculation on my part. Doyle, true to character ran with the device all the way to the roof. He managed to separate the incendiary aspect of the IED, but the ignition source exploded.'

'What's his condition?' The powerful man was on his feet.

'Stable, a few superficial wounds, but a deep puncture to his lower abdominals, and that's what the medics are concerned about, sir. We all know how belly bleeding turns nasty.'

'A real hero that one is – it's in his blood.'

'Sir! You've changed your opinion.'

'I believe the time may have arrived to have a chat with you about our Sergeant Doyle. And a...bout you going behind my back regarding extra security.' Charles was now walking into the kitchen. Feet no longer shoeless, he wore Tanya's last Christmas present to him.

'You know? When, how, who?' She gasped.

'It was me who instigated it. I had the anonymous tip-off sent, knowing you would feel strong enough to contact him. Sergeant Doyle was already in my employ two weeks prior to his first visit to Whitehall. I met with him in a greasy spoon, named Joe's, nice spot. You would have had kittens if you had seen the fried breakfast we had.' Charles laughed.

'I don't know what to say. Why all the cloak and dagger sir? And am I not trusted enough to be informed of a ghost operating in our own section?' Her voice was unusually off-tone.

'Calm down, lass, only Sergeant Doyle, Dave and myself were privy to his contract and the operation he was carrying out. It was a must as too much information was getting to Allister.'

'What was the operation he was carrying out?'

'Bring yourself over to mine. I'll speak no more of it over the air.'

Phones were switched off.

Tanya had to pull over from driving as she felt a little betrayed, but that didn't last. She, without a doubt, knew that there must have been a bloody good reason for her not to have been informed, and Dave was in the loop because he'd have been what in their world was called a "curator".

The keeper of hidden knowledge, *the curator would come forward in the event of the operative's handler dying. Someone would need to establish contact and show evidence of the clandestine operation.*

Back driving she made her way to Kensington. *What was going on?* swirled around in her head. She soon arrived at the mini mansion. She was bending in the boot to retrieve her case; Charles opened the door the exterior light came on.

'Father!'

'Come in, lass, and before I get a telling off, give me a chance to explain why you weren't informed.'

Tanya gave him – her father, a look, and placed her case on the side.

He closed the door behind the most important thing in his life and started the tale.

'Do you remember the last check-up you underwent for the lupus?' He showed her a bottle of whisky.

She shook her head and opened the fridge. 'You should be drinking this.' And she tipped the fresh orange into a glass. 'What about my last check up, it came back all clear? I showed you the results to stop you worrying, remember.'

'The results you showed me ... had been fabricated.' He waited for the backlash as the whisky entered the mouth.

'WHAT ELSE DON'T I KNOW?'

The backlash had begun.

'I understand that you're upset, I will explain if y...'

'Upset, what am I, a child?'

'Tom was concerned after reading the test results, so he approached me worried the real results would have caused you more stress, and this by proxy could have brought the attack on prematurely, resulting in more damage to your organs. We decided to keep quiet thus giving your body valuable healing time.'

'S...' Tanya went quiet, the one person in the world she trusted with her life, seemed to have turned.

'That's also why you weren't informed regarding the ghost, Sergeant Doyle. I just couldn't take the risk of too much pressure being placed on your shoulders. And that's the only reason, and a selfish one on my part. Nothing to do with your capability or trust. Like I said, I was selfish. I put your health first without your permission. But I would again Tanya, sorry but you will always come first.' The glass was emptied and refilled.

'I understand, I do; however, there's nothing wrong with me now so fill me in,' she demanded, in an official manner.

Charles gave a small smile for himself. She was back to Tanya.

'Take a seat, and you may need one of these.' He shook the bottle again. Her head shook.

'Doyle was forced on leave from the regiment, that bit

wasn't fabricated he wasn't happy about it at all and about to quit the army. I had a phone call from David that same evening, you remember David, and you also knew that bit about him being forced on leave. It was in the brief?'

'Yes, of course I know him, he's my Godfather, carry on,' prompted Tanya, raising her eyebrows.

Charles smiled yet again he was so proud of her he continued.

'I already had my eye on him. But with his grandmother being shot we didn't want him going rogue and playing Rambo on the streets of London. And to be honest, when you brought that Thames case to my attention, it was then I brought him on-board fully.

'I knew Shoebridge was dabbling in supplies, just didn't figure on body parts, I edged on weapons. Doyle was straight in there and you passing his details over to Emma, well that was the icing on the cake. We couldn't have planned an entry better, Shoebridge found Doyle, he did the work for us – we were in and Shoebridge wouldn't suspect a thing believing sergeant Doyle was just an ex-soldier dabbling in detective work.

'He has been collating intelligence ever since. In fact, we were aware that the African connection was going to end Shoebridge's life three weeks before the day.'

'You could have prevented his death?' asked Tanya, only just beginning to absorb the information her father was coming out with.

'Well, I guess we could have, but it saved us a job. Shoebridge had been placed on the guardian's watchlist months ago, he was a dead man walking, we were only waiting for an opportunity.'

'I see, well clearly some of Shoebridge's operations are still in motion,' added Tanya.

'We had discovered that Shoebridge had a clandestine partner, we believe a female, named on the streets as the "Bitch". She reigns with fear equal to that of the twins, a formidable person. However, we, including Doyle, couldn't get as much as a breadcrumb on her identity or whereabouts and she has been operating for years around here, slowly growing and growing.'

'Was Doyle in on this, as well?' asked Tanya, gently sipping her whisky.

'He was, lass, and I fear that it may have been her who wanted Doyle killed, not Shoebridge. Shoebridge was a nasty, selfish, narcissistic shit, but his motivation was greed, plus an IED wouldn't be his style and he'd had to have arranged the hit before his departure. Doesn't add up?'

'So, where do we go from here, sir? Clearly, we are not dealing with an idiot gangster,' she asked, back on track.

'Well, your old bedroom is made up. Off you go its late, tomorrow we'll put our heads together,' said Charles.

Tanya leaned in and gave her dad a sweet kiss on the cheek, treasuring the memories of him. 'I thought I would have to prove myself to you to earn more trust.'

'You proved yourself to me when you were a little scrawny whip of a lass coming across China, and every day since. You will never have to increase that level of trust, ever. But sometimes we need to be able to rest, hard as that maybe. Go and get a good night's sleep, it looks like tomorrow the battle starts.'

She passed the glass over to Charles, still half full. She hated the stuff.

20

BLINDING NOSTALGIA

O810 hours, a late start for Tanya
'Morning father ... is this fresh?' she asked, lifting the glass coffee pot.

'Made ten minutes ago, lass.' Charles never moved a muscle in his well-worn face, yet he wanted to hold her. Seeing Tanya back at home was as good as the medicine he'd just been prescribed by the hospital.

'I received a text during the night from Kathy. She informed me that Sean came around just before midnight. He's still very tired and in and out of consciousness. I gave orders to her that no one speaks to him about the IED event until we have a chance to get to the hospital. However, she was worried about her chief inspector. He wanted to know the moment Doyle was awake and he was to be interviewed. I hope you don't mind, but I assured her that you would supersede those orders.'

'Not a problem, it's SOPs in fact. There's cream in the fridge for the coffee.'

Tanya smiled as she made her way to the fridge.

'Allow me fifteen minutes and I'll be with you. We'll go

straight over to the hospital. Like I said... the battle will start today and if you really want to win a fight then you take the scrap to the enemy and before they have chance to think.'

Charles walked off. In the bedroom he stood looking in the mirror, alone he was allowed to show the pain, but never in front of his daughter.

'Dave, you're up early.' Charles answered his mobile.

'Very funny, Charles. I see the tablets haven't sedated your sense of humour. I'm just calling to see how you're feeling.'

'I'm doing fine, Tanya stopped over last night.'

'So, you've told her. Good, you'll need some support. And she would want to know.'

'No, not told her, we had a different subject to discuss. She's been through enough; I can't burden her with this.' Charles remained staring into the vanity mirror; an old man who he didn't recognise looked back at him.

'Charles, I want to tell you to stop being fucking stubborn, but I said a few years ago when a lot of shit really hit the fan, I would never turn away from any request you put my way, I'm here, mate, and that promise still stands. But think about telling her, please, and keep in touch. I don't care if it's when you're pissed and looking at the bottom of the glass and need to talk, I'm here, anytime, day or night.' Dave had no choice but to end the call he couldn't allow Charles to hear how upset he'd become. And for a man as hard as Sissons to well-up, it took a serious amount of emotion.

Phone down Dave leaned on the big desk – knuckles face down feeling helpless as he looked out of the vast window in his office, located twelve miles outside of Bradford. England.

'Dave, you alright?'

'Don't you fucking knock, get out!' shouted Dave, who was one of the hardest bastards walking. He had sat behind his desk in his mansion, crying like a small child at the thought of a true friend, colleague, mentor, and great all-round guy dying.

Outside the door Dean was gobsmacked, not at being shouted at, that was water off a duck's back, but his boss crying! That he'd never known.

'What's up with you?' asked Bash.

Dean shook his head.

'What?' Bash came again.

'The boss is crying,' whispered Dean.

'Fuck off, you're winding me up! You on drugs? You're not in London now!'

'No, listen.' Dean knocked on the door.

'I said fuck off. What don't you understand?'

'Disappear,' suggested Bash, who then knocked again.

'F...' Bash opened the door. 'I'll k...' Dave was cut short.

'You don't have to kill me, I'd die for you, you know that, and without a second thought,' said Bash, locking the door after him.

'It's Charles, Bash, he's ...'

London. Hospital ITU Room

'Morning, Sergeant Doyle, I hear you have taken up sprinting.'

'Good morning, sir. Felt the need to stretch my legs.'

279

Doyle looked at him and then at Tanya then back to Charles then back to Tanya.

'She knows, sergeant, she has been brought up to speed,' added the brigadier.

'You're not going to hit me, are you?' Sean pushed himself away in gesture, as he asked Tanya, with that glint in his eye and grin worn all over his face.

'An Oscar is more in line. If you want a change in career, I suggest the theatre.' She laughed turning away from Sean.

'Thank you for covering for us, Kathy. You can inform your inspector now.'

'She already has, Charles, this is a new low even for you, instructing serving police officers to neglect their duty.' Clarence spoke whilst walking through the door.

'Good morning, Clarence, how are you?'

'Slightly put out, Charles, if I'm to be honest with you.'

'Quite frankly, Clarence, I supersede you every time you open your fucking mouth. And if I decide to show interest in a case, that means I have twelve hours to take it over or not. You have zero say in what I do or when I do it, do I make myself clear!' loudly replied the brigadier.

Mouths fell open in the room.

'Where do you get off talking to me like that, and in front of these lesser people, an... and ... in that tone? Let's see what the Prime Minister has to say on the matter, shall we?' defended Clarence.

Charles had his mobile phone out and began tapping the screen.

'Which number would you prefer to contact him on? – his work mobile, office, personal mobile or his weekend holiday home?' The brigadier waited for a response keeping his stare on the inspector.

'You have not heard the last of this, Howlett, and you're suspended WPC O'Conner for disobeying a direct order, come with me.' He turned to vacate the room.

'She is not suspended; she's seconded – to me. Sit down WPC O'Conner.' counter-ordered the brigadier.

Kathy didn't know what to do, Tanya pressed on her shoulder, she remained sitting.

'Under what allocation?' flustered out the inspector, in a desperate attempt to save face.

'She is an essential witness, listening to this baboon all night rambling on in his sleep. Lord knows what he has said. She goes nowhere – 'til she has been briefed by one of my staff, and I am satisfied she has heard nothing classified.

Goodbye Clarence, and have a nice day.' Charles wasn't normally like this. Rude and bullying were his pet hates, however, Clarence was a despicable man.

'Fucking prick!' mumbled the inspector under his breath, as he left the room.

No one said anything.

'Right, sergeant, a debrief is our next step. Tanya, can you do the honours.'

She opened the silver box that had come in the room with her. The next five minutes she was everywhere with the pen-shaped detector, stopping on a shelf.

'Well, well, it is warm in here, sir,' she said, pulling out the small round marble and placing it in the stat machine.

'It is, I agree, feel free to turn up the air conditioning,' Charles played along.

She picked up the marble and placed into a cloth insulated bag which also went into the silver case.

'The room is now clear, sir.'

'Right, first things first, how are you feeling, sergeant? In fact, more to the point, how long before we have you back out on the street?'

'Sir, ... he's just been blown up,' interrupted Tanya.

'Two or three days, boss, tops, it was only the detonator, Tanya.' He answered her stare.

'Good, good. Right, WPC O'Conner, now – what to do with you.'

'She can assist with admin and liaise with all our calls, sir. I will ensure her training. Even if she could run the point to point, that will be a great help,' answered Tanya.

'Do you believe you have what it takes to operate at our level?'

'Yes, sir, I do sir. I won't let you down, sir.' Kathy had sprung to life, flying out of the chair.

They all laughed. Sean tried to stop himself due to the pain in his ribs. Charles turned to the bed.

'Tanya informs me that you're about to declare war on this Ahmid character, is this correct, sergeant?' asked the brigadier, with a small nod.

'He has beaten the shit out of a good man, an old school friend of mine and for no reason apart from to get at me. In my world that requires a response and the more I discover about him and his gang, the more I want to eradicate them all from the planet.'

'Kill him?' perplexed Kathy. 'Like dead, dead – for real?' she continued. Nobody answered her innocent and naive question.

'Well, sergeant, whilst I have the upmost respect for your friend, you still work for my department, and I do not have rogue employees. Add to that, even if he is removed today, his role will be replaced before the week is out, there is another ...'

'The Bitch, sir,' interrupted Doyle.

'Yes, and that's to be the priority. We need ASAP her identity. Let's close this loop and end at least the terror for a while.'

'There was another turn up I didn't expect, sir, and she may be able to shed some light on the Bitch's ID for us. Molly Malone is a police inspector.' Inputed Doyle

'Molly, ... from Cardboard City?'

'Do you know this Molly?' asked Tanya, bringing Kathy back into the conversation.

'Yes, really well, I've, well shall we say, we've escorted her to and from the city on more than one occasion, in fact I used to carry some air freshener in the duty bag on nights for that sole purpose.'

'I can vouch for the air freshener being needed,' added Sean.

The room became quiet as a knock came on the door.

'Sean, how are you? They called and said you were awake.' Sophie entered.

'I'm fine, bit of a misunderstanding. How's Kev?'

'We'll get going, leave you two to catch up,' said Tanya.

Charles tipped his hat to Sophie.

Out in the corridor, he spoke. 'Twenty-two-hundred hours your office. I expect this Molly to be brought along if she is indeed what Doyle tells us. She is most likely in danger.'

'Roger that, sir.'

'On second thoughts we'll make it at my place, the house not the apartment. That shouldn't be on anyone's radar.' He then left.

'Are you alright with working in this world? It's not all excitement and posh dinners. And you need to be very adaptable.' Tanya asked Kathy, her hand on her shoulder.

'Are you kidding, I love it already, did you see the way the brigadier spoke to my inspector?'

'Calm down we need to focus; this role is all about the long game.'

'Sorry, yes, of course, sorry, Tanya,' she added.

Tanya was silently having second thoughts about her coming on-board but only as a live operative – she would make a great admin line assistant to a handler and even a handler one day with some assistance.

But for now she was stuck, as it was Kathy who would get through to this Molly.

Because like the brigadier had said, if indeed she was an undercover officer then she must be deep under and would not show her true identity lightly, as in the clandestine world – no one trusted anyone.

'So, Sophie, what's new? I thought you were coming over to see Kev last night?'

'I got scared and went home,' she replied, pulling fruit out of her bag placing it on the side.

'No problem, glad you weren't here, that bomb and all.'

'I can't stay, Sean, I have a museum opening to attend, but I'll return tomorrow.' She leaned in and kissed his forehead.

He watched her leave then his thoughts turned to his friend. He blamed himself. He had returned home and unwillingly let his guard down as emotion flooded in from his past. He allowed people in and now they suffered. The past was repeating and repeating, something had to be done.

The room hadn't been empty, for long.

'Doyley, Doyley, Doyleyyy.'

Sean looked to the door.

'Ahmid, nice of you to visit, long time no see,' Sean replied, then he wondered how Ahmid had got past the armed officers. Through the glass he witnessed an envelope being passed from someone to the silhouette of the armed officer holding the machine, gun. 'It's a shame you've ended up in here, I was looking forward to our rematch at the fight night.'

'Don't write me off just yet, you were no match at school, I can't see that anything would have changed.' Sean smiled, genuinely believing the words he spoke.

'Look at me. What do you see?'

Sean remained silent not wishing to engage with the idiot in front of him.

'You, Doyle, to me are nothing but an obstacle. Since you arrived back people have remembered our little tussle outside the school gates, but they don't remember when I whipped your ass.' Ahmid looked at Doyle trying to intimidate him.

'You and Gary and a couple of others who held my arms, while you slapped me like a little girl,' added Sean, with his grin in place.

'We all remember the past differently. I just came by to let you know that me and you, it's nothing personal – just business, you understand. But you have to go, one way or another, you have to go. And to show you I'm a fair man I'll give you ten thousand pounds if you leave the city before Friday night.'

'I have an alternative solution you donate hundred grand to the homeless fund, and I'll pull out the fight. This will save you the humiliation of getting slapped in front of the city.' Sean reached for a few grapes tossed one up catching it in his mouth.

'You have developed a sense of humour, I see.' Ahmid laughed and turned.

'Before you go there's one thing I need to ask.'

'Feel free as you won't be around for much longer,' replied Ahmid.

'What do you see in me?' Doyle finished the question and stared at Ahmid. He said nothing else but didn't remove his look.

Ahmid said nothing and left. In a couple of seconds, the silhouette of the armed officer was alone again. Sean pulled off the sheet. He was bruised and there were a couple of cuts amongst the powder burns. Then there was the main laceration, a couple of inches below his left pec caused by the tin flying into his abdomen.

A flashback to all his days in the regiment and the operations he'd carried out, then the thought of Kev laying in a hospital on the floor above. 'Here, mate, could you get me a can of Coke, I'm parched?' asked Sean.

'I can't leave my post,' replied the armed officer.

'No problem. Oh, how much was in the envelope?' asked Sean.

'Diet or regular?' replied the officer.

'Diet will do.'

With the officer gone, Sean was up and dressed in what clothes remained, and gone from his room before his so-called protector returned.

More than a handful of people of all shapes and sizes gave Doyle a good look as he tried to leave the hospital without being noticed.

A cleaner challenged him. 'You're bleeding, sir, are you aware, have you seen a nurse? Let me get you a nurse, there's blood dripping everywhere.' Sean just smiled politely and carried on walking. He'd caught the bandages whilst dressing in a hurry and the fact he'd been pumped with fluids all night made his blood like water. It may have looked bad but Sean knew it superficial, made worse by the concussion caused by the detonator.

'Hey! Stop! ... You! Stop!' The armed officer raised his weapon. The cleaner was knocked clean off his feet by the copper running at speed to detain Doyle.

The droplets of blood increased in distance as Sean's pace quickened. The sliding automatic doors opened and Sean was out and free; left and right he looked.

'Thank you, gods,' he said as a courier pulled up on a motorcycle, stupidly leaving it running.

The armed officer threw his arms in the air. 'Shit, fucking shit, how do I explain this?' And his hand patted the envelope.

'What, no, no, no! That's my fucking bike! Just got it, my bike?' cried the courier.

Sean had travelled a mile if that. Turning the corner at speed he hit the front of an old Transit van that was cutting across the lanes.

'Sorry, sorry, you okay, mate, you, yo...' He went silent as he saw the blood all over Sean's shirt. He ran to him lying on the ground. Sean didn't move. The man struggled but managed to pull the bike off him. Sean was up and running to the van, in and off.

The overweight builder was left standing, bewildered at the sight of this miracle and also relieved as he thought he'd killed someone.

'PC Loftuss to central, over.'

'Central, receiving, over.'

'The terrorist suspect at the Royal has done a runner.

Currently travelling west on a stolen motorcycle.' He leaned into the courier. Then back to the radio.

'Ducati 250, silver and pale blue,' said the courier.

'The suspect is covered in blood, over.'

'I've only had the bike two weeks?' rattled the courier.

'Received, await further orders, central out.'

An APB was sent out meaning a full description of both the bike and of Sean was circulated across the patch.

Doyle ditched the van a mile later on the other side of the canal. The engine off, in it went, it sank quickly for the first few seconds, then seemed to float but then the bubbles came. A short walk and a difficult swim with only one of his arms, the other wasn't fully cooperating. He stripped off in his container. Thirty minutes later, he called Sophie for help.

'I'll be right over, Sean. Don't you move. You're hurt. I will be quick.'

Doyle dialled another number; the conversation lasted ten minutes.'

'I knew it when I heard Sean call her Sophie the penny dropped. She has changed her name and is doing very well for herself, but this is where it becomes interesting, sir, S...' Tanya was cut short.

'Come on Stephen King get to the point, less of the drama, more of the story,' added Charles.

'On Shoebridge's file it stated he had ordered a paternity test on a young girl, age of six at the time and named as X on all the paperwork. Since then, all the files have been updated and certain information has been scanned in. Well, on the bottom of the results page, in

Shoebridge's own flamboyant writing for all to see is the name, Sophie Cellest. It's scribbled out, yes, to depersonalize it but the scan acts like an x-ray revealing the original words.'

'Excellent work we need to get in contact with the sergeant immediately. We both know he's going to sort this issue out himself, and that means he will call on the people he trusts,' said Charles.

'Sophie! If she is involved, then we may need help and quickly. Did you hear back from Dave?' she asked.

'No, he's gone on an Evolve op, so no communication. What about Emma, isn't one of Doyle's friends in her employ now?'

'Yes, and I think she has taken a shine to Sean. I will make the call right away.' Tanya switched off and turned. 'Kathy, we need to find this Molly, and quickly. Where else might she be? Think?'

'Maybe the meat market or that restaurant on the High Street ... ...' her head going side to side slowly, searching her brain, 'The Bistro.' recalled Kathy with a sense of achievement.

'Ken's?' added Tanya.

'Yes. Do you know the place?'

'Get in the car.'

'You went through a red light, Tanya, and again,' Kathy remarked swinging her head around. She wasn't answered and she said no more, somehow the realisation of being in the different word had suddenly dawned upon her. The Audi screeched to a halt she was out at speed Kathy followed.

'It's the lovely Tanya. Have you come to eat, darling? On the house and your friend,' said Ken.

'No, maybe another time. I urgently need to speak

with Molly Malone, and I believe she frequents your place?' she asked with urgency, scanning the dining area.

'She does, I'm her biggest fan but she won't visit 'til way after seven this evening,' said Ken as Green Mile came from the kitchen. The man mountain dried his gigantic hands on a white and blue tea towel as he walked. 'Miza Howett, ar ya well?' he asked her in his newly learned, but broken English, proud of his language skills.

'Excellent, and you are a fast learner.' She smiled.

Green Mile hugged her, picking her up, she became invisible in his arms. Kathy remained quiet.

'Tanya is looking for our Molly,' added Ken.

'You not try my food?' added Green Mile.

'Next time, I promise. We really have to locate this Molly, it's urgent. Doyle is missing.' Green Mile glanced at Ken.

'Oh! Okay,' he unwittingly said, then gave her an order. 'Wait here!'

Ken returned behind the bar and disappeared through an open door. Five, maybe six minutes had passed. 'Tanya!' was heard. Ken re-appeared, waving dramatically for her to come through. She was up to the open door and standing there on the other side, was who she presumed to be Molly.

'Ken here tells me you require to speak with me, and urgently. What could be so important that a homeless woman could help you?'

Tanya turned and kicked away the cast iron cat; the door closed under its own weight.

'First off, can we cut the pretence of you being a homeless person?' asked and demanded Tanya. Molly looked at Ken, who put his hands up to deny saying anything.

'I work for a Whitehall department. One of our operatives discovered your true identity; however, he is now missing and in danger.'

'Why was one of your operatives carrying out surveillance on me?' Molly had swivelled completely around in the captains' chair to face Tanya.

'It's a long story, Doyle was investigating another ca...'

'Doyle? Sean Doyle?' Molly asked quickly.

'Yes, why, do you know him?'

'Met him, but I knew his mother very well. What sort of trouble is he in?'

'Can I speak in front of Ken regarding your true position? I really don't have the luxury of time.'

'Yes, Ken allows me to use this office for my "work" work. He knows all about it, come in.'

'I'll come straight to the point. We believe Doyle has unknowingly got himself taken by the bitch, so we're hoping that you know her name and whereabouts.' Tanya looked at Molly, hopeful of an answer containing if nothing else, an address.

'Sophie Cellest, AKA Louise King, AKA the BITCH. We don't have a location as such, there are a few offices she uses, but all above board and she never settles in one place. Her clandestine work is all virtual, she is very clever. We've never managed to find a footprint of her under takings.'

'I knew it was her. Sean knew her from school, and they have become very close friends since his return, so I'm told. However, we believe she has just tried to kill another close friend, and Sean with a bomb at the hospital.'

'Why? And at the hospital as well? Is that what that bang was?' Molly was shocked and forced to take a breath before continuing. 'She really is a clever bitch, a full-blown psychopath with incredibly high intelligence. This whole operation has been set up around catching her out, yet she's never slipped up once. She has grown in business and the fear she wields on the streets is terrifying.' Molly had stood but sat back sat down.

'Are you aware that she is also Shoebridge's biological daughter?' added Tanya.

Molly raised her stare quickly, as did Ken.

'Sir, Shoebridge, the minister, are you certain?'

'The very same and he was killed, murdered in his office yesterday.'

'I thought he died from a heart attack. Well, according to the news reports that was the cause.' It was clear Molly was still amazed with the bloodline connection and the other intelligence Tanya was in possession of. 'Well, my dear, your department is good, I'll give you that. I would put money on it if she has gone to the lengths of kidnapping our Mr Doyle, then Ahmid will be involved. She uses him and her brother for muscle. She does run a few lads of her own; none of them have ever seen or spoken with her. They're paid weekly into a bank account, each getting a couple of hundred pounds as a retainer then they receive a text with the details of a job and the amount they will be paid extra if completed to her satisfaction.'

'The fish shop then, is that where they will be taking Sean?' asked Tanya.

'No, no, too central. Yes, it's his office, but he's not stupid enough to take people there. He has a pig farm a few miles past Blackheath on the road going out to Abbey Wood, my money is on that's where they will have taken him. The shit doesn't know we are aware he has the place.

Its front is a city farm. By day, people get to meet the animals, and by night the pigs are fed people by "animals".

Shoebridge opened it officially a year ago. We have pictures of him shaking Ahmid's hand, and on the wrist for all to see: a £50,000 Paris Rolex.' Molly was out of the chair and grabbed her long coat 'What we waiting for?'

Molly was out of the door, Ken followed and then Tanya trying to hold her breath. In the bar Kathy had been telling Green Mile that Sean Doyle was missing, that was the urgency that had brought them to the restaurant.

'I come, my friend in trouble.' His finger pointing to his own chest, emphasising "me".

Outside Tanya called the brigadier. 'Sir, I have Molly. She is what Doyle said and more than happy to help us, we have a possible location of Doyle's whereabouts.'

'Bring her to the estate. I have a couple more operatives coming over, we have to be prepared for this, we don't know how far these roots go?' stated the brigadier.

'En route, sir.' She pressed the red "end call" button on the screen.

'We'll follow you in Ken's car,' said Molly.

Tanya nodded in relief.

Sean's phone sent a text. It was received on the brigadier's phone.

I need six hours, boss!

The brigadier blinked and gave a half smile.

His phone used again. 'Thank you, Emma, I really appreciate your gesture and it will be remembered.'

'Think nothing more of it, Charles. In fact, I'm looking after my own invested interests. I have more work allotted for our Mr Doyle, as there aren't many like him around. I will have Lance and Chalky booked on the next flight to Heathrow.

They should be landing in a couple of hours. The flight details will be emailed to you in the next ten minutes.' The phone conversation ended.

Within four hours ten people had gathered at the estate. A room with only skylights, and hidden behind a bookcase, is where the venue was to take place.

Thirty minutes into the briefing Tanya looked at her phone, after feeling the vibration on her leg. Up and out with no words spoken the panel behind her, closing on its own.

'Sean?' she said.

'You sound surprised to be talking to me,' his laughing clearly heard, well aware there would have been some sort of mission set in place, even after his text, but he trusted the brigadier to honour his request.

As he was chatting with Tanya he sent the second message.

Done early, boss.

'Are you alright, where are you?' she asked again. Relief had taken the place of surprise in her tone.

'I'm fine. Not sure exactly where I am, though. At a guess, I'd say in the countryside somewhere.'

'Are you on a farm?'

'Yeah, how did you know?'

'You're only a few miles away, close to Abbey Wood. Is Ahmid with you?' she asked.

There was a short silence.

'Sort of, he'll show up again in about four hours, give or take,' said Sean looking at the pigs chomping their way through the last few remnants of the Asian gangster.

'I'll need you to send a few of your colleagues in blue, and a couple of vans.'

Outside the steel pen lying on the dirty floor were six of Ahmid's men, two awake and tied to the gate. One of them screaming as the large boar was about to tear off his fingers. The others lay unconscious their hands and feet secured with bailing wire.

'Is there anyone else there with you?' asked Tanya, unable to say the actual name.

'A few of Ahmid's crew.' He sensed that she was querying the involvement of Sophie. He said nothing relating to her.

'Wait there, we're on the road now, thirty minutes maximum do not leave are you listening to me.' She went silent, 'Sean???'

The rest of Tanya's words came out the phone and made it vibrate on the tin; on Doyle's mind was one person.

Everything had fallen into place.

Right from the beginning she had not quite added up, but all this came with the wonderful benefit of hindsight and even he admitted he had been blinded with nostalgia mist, and a touch of love, maybe. She was always asking some odd questions, as if to see where his loyalties lied. Or picking up little bits of information by pushing himself and Kev, regarding his fighting skills and the history of him in the army.

Then there was the conversation with that minister at the auction that day, ten minutes down the corridor. What could that have been about, surely not the auction, and why do it in private? Sophie persuaded Sean to leave seventy percent of the proceeds from the sale in her personal account until he had registered all the charities, better for tax, so she persuaded him, two weeks that's all.

Then there's the fact she knew about the explosion and the location of a disused cellar. When it had been reported in the media as a building collapse and there was, NO mention of an underground cellar in the papers. It was her who had told him to go to the hospital at the same time the IED was delivered, and she felt tired, going home, not going back herself, even though she had displayed so much concern for Kev?

The shock on her face when she saw the crime scene pictures of Mary. Obviously, at the time Sean put this down to the gruesome display of the content and anyone would have reacted the same way. It was, in hindsight – the object in Mary's hand, that had truly freaked Sophie out, she had realised that if Sean put two and two together – It would lead to her. As it was the one photo she looked at on the floor.

A small blue tube made from paper and stiffened by painting it with glue. This was Sophie's hobby as a child, she would make paper jewellery and give it to people she liked. She had given Mary one, years ago when they were all kids. Mary must have kept it with her other jewellery on the dressing table and she had been able to get a hold of this tube knowing that Sean would know why she held it or be able to work it out. And finally, when she left the hospital room, turning left, Ahmid came from the left, they would have had to have passed, yet she was supposed to be petrified of him.

So, the night he had left hospital, he had intentionally called Sophie to come over and help. But he had called Lady De Pen Court first. And like Chalky had told him outside the posh hotel, she had a lot of contacts and in every walk of life.

Emma told Sean about the pig farm and confirmed the Bitch's name, just like that as if it was an everyday occurrence. Sean had made another call shortly after and heard the answering machine.

Earlier phone call

"The Cock and Pussy. We don't do weddings or bat mitzva's. If you're still listening? Leave a message.'

'It's Doyl…'

'Sean.' The voice said.

'Tank, I'm in a bit of shit, mate, could do with my back being watched. And maybe a few heads slapped.'

'What's the trouble and where are yah?' asked the biker and former soldier. The conversation lasted several more minutes. What people didn't realise was all of the members of the Fallen Angels once served in the British army and all were good assets. Sean's unit had saved Tank and two of his mates in Bosnia and this had never been forgotten. Seven Harley Davidson motorcycles set off from the back of the old railway arch heading over towards Abbey Wood.

Sean remained in his container that he called home, he looked through the drawings Kevin had left for him, patiently awaiting the arrival of his female friend. If she was the Bitch, no harm done, he was covered. If she wasn't she would never know what had been arranged? The worst outcome was he'd owe the bikers some beers.

'Soph, thanks for coming.'

Six men walked in behind her. 'They followed me, Sean.' She was acting… still.

'Cut the crap, Louisa Shoebridge. Sorry, I didn't ask, do you prefer The Bitch?'

She raised her hand.

Two of the men ran at Sean.

They were floored in seconds, like something out of a Bruce Lee scene.

The other four pulled out gats. Sean wasn't stupid, or bulletproof. He placed his hands behind his back and produced that grin.

'Make sure that's tight, I don't want him getting free,' ordered Sophie, as Sean's hands were secured behind his back, the cable ties tugged on.

'He won't get out of that.' Laughed the thug.

Sean tensed his arms and shoulders, pumping them up, his grin grew. 'Make it a bit stronger, if you twist the ties, it releases the zip.'

'Shut up, stupid.' He pushed Doyle forward.

He revealed his free hands to the short guy, then placed them again behind his back. 'Told ya. You just can't help some people.'

'Use that rope over there.' Sophie pointed to the far corner.

'Where's Ahmid? I was looking forward to our rematch.' His grin still present.

His face was punched from the side, his grin remained.

His face was punched again, blood came from his mouth. His grin still present, he spat out the blood.

'You'll get your fight,' said one of the men, seconds before he pistol-whipped Doyle.

More blood came from Sean's mouth, and now a cut above the left eye, but the grin was still there. Next came the baseball bat from the rear.

'Take him to the van while he's out.' ordered Sophie. She remained in the container for at least another half an hour, searching through all the information Doyle had gathered on the case.

Two hours later Sean had, had his rematch.

One minute he was tied to a chair, laughing at the cardboard gangster in front of him, the next he heard ...

'Can anyone come in?' eight bikers asked.

Eighteen people were instantly caught in a Mexican stand-off. The only two heads that didn't have guns pointed at them were Ahmid and Doyle.

'I have a solution,' offered Doyle. 'Ahmid and I fight, winning side walks out.'

Ahmid had no choice but to agree, unless he wanted to lose face. Slowly he peeled off his expensive jacket and held this out at arm's length. 'Go on boss, kill the fucker,' said his lackey taking the Armani coat.

'Do yah wanna pick a couple of lackeys to hold my arms behind me, back like at school?' Sean pulled off his T-shirt.

'Don't fucking need anyone to slap you Doyleewoyllee.' Ahmid interlocked his fingers and bent them backwards, several audible cracks were heard.

Doyle laughed. 'You ready?'

Ahmid sprinted at Doyle, rugby tackling his waist the pair went back into the wall together. Doyle's knee came up - Ahmid staggered backward then wiped the blood from his mouth. He ran again, head down, arms wide for another tackle, his arms locked behind Doyle. No movement backwards, Doyle stood fast like Gibraltar.

His knee shot up again at a phenomenal speed, Ahmid's arms flew outwards, Doyle hit his head three maybe four times, too fast to count. The jellified gangster flopped to the floor. Doyle was instantly over him, his eyes turned black.

'That's enough, Sean. DOYLE! Enough!' shouted Tank.

Sean didn't listen, his fist pounding into the head of his old school bully.

Tank and another pulled Doyle off.

Doyle took out his Magnum. 'Gary!' shouted Sean. *CRACK!* The shot was perfect, the body collapsed with the hole between its eyes. 'Anyone else still working for Ahmid?' asked Sean, his pistol pivoting around the room.

One guy fired.

Tank went down.

Doyle shot the gangster twice.

10 minutes later.

'Thanks lads, and sorry about your leg, Tank.'

'Hey, we did good tonight, an injured leg is a small price to pay.'

Eight bikers left, two of them supporting Tank, taking him to an underground doctor. Doyle acknowledged their parting and started talking into his phone.

The mobile was then placed on top of the BMW on the tin roof, and it began vibrating. Taking a few steps, he tried the door on the white Range Rover and just as he guessed, it was open with the keys under the visor. *Gangsters*, he laughed, *they believed no one would dare to steal their cars.*

He drove off, now visible in the mirror were the blue flashing lights travelling at speed from the direction of the big city. He was out of sight as the six vans, two Range

Rovers and four cars pulled into, and around, the perimeter of the inner-city farm.

Present moment - outside the farm

'Sergeant Howlett!' shouted one of the armed officers.

Tanya turned to face the formidable figure dressed fully in black, including a balaclava. 'Yes,' she replied, still anxious that Doyle hadn't been located.

'I found this mobile phone it was just lying on the top of the car. It has a picture of you on the screen,' he stated only the whites of his eyes visible.

'Thank you.' Tanya relieved the officer of the mobile. Straightaway, she knew it was Doyle's, all the cracks on the screen. Something made her enter Doyle's name in the password box. It came to life. She pressed the small triangular shape then put the phone to her ear.

'Well done for figuring out the password, and by now I'm guessing that you are well aware that Sophie is responsible for the bomb at the hospital, and from what Ahmid squealed a lot more...

Tanya continued listening to the recording with the phone pressed close to her ear, as shouting was all around her.

14TH November

Two days before Mary was shot and killed

'Sophie, nice to see you,' Ann placed the papers on the desk, 'What brings you around?'

'It's the anniversary of when Mary took me in. If she's free, I would like to take her out for a surprise lunch, to the new Italian that's opened up on Clough Road. It's been receiving a lot of good reviews.'

'I'll make sure she's free, she could do with a treat,' Ann was out of her seat and off through to the back. She pushed up the sash window.

'Mary, you have someone here to see you, they're up here.' Ann shouted, as loud as any old docker's wife.

It wasn't long before Mary had reached the office. 'Sophie, what a nice surprise, but to what do I owe this honour?' asked Mary, a bit flustered and out of breath.

'I would like to take you out for lunch, it's the twelfth anniversary of you ta...'

'I keep telling you, please, you don't have to keep doing this it was nothing, a pleasure having you here. My reward is seeing how you have turned out.'

'It was a very big deal to me, Mary. Lord knows where or what would have happened to me if you hadn't come to the rescue.' Sophie was not taking no for an answer. 'Ann has already said you can be free.'

Mary looked at Ann.

'It will do you good. Go, go, she's taking you to that new Italian place.' Ann was already shooing Mary from the office.

'I will need to change.'

'Away wi' yah. You look fine as you are.' Ann placed Mary's coat in her hand.

Sophie was laughing and sort of apologising for the fuss she had caused, even though with good intention.

Half an hour into the meal

'Thank you, Sophie, I needed this break and Ann was right it is a lovely restaurant, bit pricy though.' Mary's last comment was whispered as she leaned forward, and her eyebrows rose.

'You let me worry about that, now let's have one of those ice cream sundaes.' Sophie's eyes turned to the far table.

Mary joined her gaze and gave in. 'Go on then.'

Sophie raised her hand, finger out and pointing to catch the attention of the waiter. She really didn't have to try hard as both the male waiters hadn't stopped looking in her direction since her arrival.

'Would you like 'a tha strawberryeea, the chocoolart, da minta or freshly made 'a vanilla... But for beutaafula ladies,' he looked both ways, 'I can do all da flavours in one, with a touch of da ruma. You-like-a...no?' He smiled scoring a ten on the cringe flirting scale. Sophie looked to Mary for her choice.

'The rum one sounds really nice,' said Mary.

'We will have two with all the colours, and don't be stingy with the rum, please.' She smiled at Mary.

'This has been a wonderful afternoon, thank you so...' Mary was stopped from finishing her sentence.

'Mary is that you?' loudly shouted a small female, as round as she was tall, with locks of copper Irish hair.

'Maddie! How are you? Where have you been? It must be six months,' replied Mary.

Maddie approached the table, full of joy at seeing her old friend.

'My son had to move away. I've been to help him settle in.' Maddie moved in, to kiss Mary.

'This is Sophie, she is m...'

Mary was cut short as Maddie turned to see Sophie and flustered, 'Is that the time? I'll catch up with you later.' Maddie was off at a speed faster than what her body naturally allowed.

'She seemed nice,' stated Sophie.

'Yes, she is, and my bingo partner. Not like her to not to stay and talk, you can't usually shut her up.' Mary stared at the ice cream.

The following day Ann passed Mary her coat again. 'I shouldn't be long,' said Mary.

'Take your time and give my love to Maddie,' replied Ann.

It took three attempts of hard knuckle knocking before the curtain to her right moved.

'Go away, Mary,' said Maddie.

Mary's knuckles knocked again and again; they hurt but she knocked again, shocked by the hostile greeting. The door opened to a gap of no more than three inches and then held strong with the four chains and Maddie's bodyweight. 'I'm leaving again in the morning and for good this time, go and tell her that. Tell the bitch that?' The three inches narrowed to two. Mary's shoe shot in.

'Who, tell me who? What do you mean the bitch? And why are you leaving tomorrow?' Mary demanded as she turned. 'What you looking at? On your way,' she shouted at a couple of women watching.

'Come in, but I can't believe you're working for her.' The door opened to eighteen inches, then closed sharply after Mary was in. Seven locks, top to bottom were manually closed and the chains re-fixed. 'What the hell is going on, Maddie? I don't see you for months, you re-appear and now you're living in Fort Knox.' Mary pointed out the locks.

Maddie remained silent peering through the curtains.

'Tell me what's wrong?' begged Mary; still no answer.

Maddie ran out the room and up the stairs to twitch the bedroom curtains.

Mary remained quiet and stationary in the front room. Maddie was back down in minutes. Her first action was to look out of the window again.

'You're scaring me. Maddie. What's going on? What have I done?'

'I never thought you would have been involved with the likes of her. Did you have a hand in this?' Maddie shoved over a couple of photos.

'My God, who's that, what's happened to him?'

'That's my beautiful Terry, as if you didn't know.' Maddie was still showing all the signs of severe agitation. Unable to settle she started rambling again. 'Why do you think I took Jonny away? She said she'd do the same to him.' Maddie collapsed onto the sofa her tears no longer contained.

Mary had only just allowed herself to stare fully at the gruesome picture. It was Terry, he was topless and sliced open from his Adam's apple to his groin. A shiver travelled through Mary, her fingers and thumbs sweating at the touch of the paper. She gulped looked at her friend of some twenty years.

'Maddie, please, I truly don't know what to say and you keep saying she did this. Who did this? Tell me! And why would I have anything to do with this,' she shook the pictures in her hand, 'I loved your Terry, you know that,' She pushed the photos back towards her friend.

Maddie couldn't stop from crying even though she tried. Her real tears rolled and rolled.

'Just tell her not to hurt me, please. Please, I'll go away, back to Jonny.' The words gave away again to more tears and jerked breathing.

'I don't know who this woman is. Let me help you.'

The stare that came back from Maddie would have terrified the hardest of the hard.

'Her picture is in the photo. She's holding the knife whilst laughing at my son dying in front of her eyes.' Maddie stood and snatched the photos back. 'Here, here!' Her finger tapping hard and fast on the glossy paper. Mary could only see the mutilated body of poor Terry.

Then, coming into focus, reflected in the laptop's screen was the image of Sophie, her Sophie. The pretty face spotted with blood all over it. Sophie's smile was in Mary's words, pure evil.

The two friends were silent. Mary's legs gave way, she felt sick to the stomach, then she was sick. She looked again at the photo telling herself it was a trick of the light it wasn't her sweet Sophie. How could it be the caring girl she knew? There was a loud banging on the door. Mary looked at her friend; the banging came again. Maddie wasn't going to answer. She ran to the old sideboard her hands grabbing at the handle the top drawer pulled open. Before Mary could rationalise the moment, her friend Maddie had an old pistol to her head. 'Maddie! No, Maddie!'

Mary saw for a split second the smile, then her eyes closed. The mess was everywhere. Her eyes remained closed.

The banging came again much harder and faster this time.

'Hello,' spoke Mary, not shouting but loud enough to be heard through the door.

'The police, Detective Lund.'

'How can I help? What do you want?' replied Mary. *How could they have heard the shot and got here so quickly,* she thought, her head spinning. She hadn't even looked at her friend, she'd kept her eyes closed until her hand touched the living room door. Was she dead? Was it a dream?

'We have a warrant to search this address,' was the detective's comeback.

'She's not well, and unable to come to the door.' The heavy knocking came again.

Mary opened the door. Instantly she was pushed aside by the three officers rushing in, the chains didn't stand a chance. 'You two upstairs. I'll do down here,' said Lund.

'What are you looking for? Tell me,' asked Mary. He ignored her and entered the living room. Mary rolled up the photo and shoved it down her trousers. She followed the officer into the living room.

'Can we see your warrant?' she asked in a stern manner.

He was trashing the place. He saw Maddie on the floor with half her head missing, but for some reason, she didn't appear in his sight. He found the folder housing several other pictures of Terry being tortured, it was grabbed. He barged past Mary. 'Come on, lads let's go. I have what I came for.' They were out the door.

Four loud size elevens came bouncing down the stairs. The door slammed but bounced back open. Mary closed it and returned to the room. She hadn't imagined it: her bingo buddy lay in a pool of her own blood. The police had ignored a dead body! She left the house and subconsciously walked a good few hundred yards before calling over a taxi.

'Right you are, ma'am.' And the car was moving. Mary was out in 20 minutes; she paid seven pounds eighty pence to cover the journey.

At first unable to enter the parlour, she tried, but a strange feeling held her fast to the ground. Her thoughts for a moment to her friend. She turned and walked to the train station a mile away.

'Can you put them sim cards in any phone?' she asked the stallholder.

'What phone 'ave ya, luv?'

Mary showed him the old brick. He laughed. 'Don't think it will work in that. How old is it?'

'Ten years, I think. Okay, ta.' And she turned to leave.

'I have these on sale. Do yer a good deal, if yer don't want a box...'

'How much?' she asked.

He made funny shapes with his mouth, imitating Delboy. 'Fifty, and I'll put one of the sims in with a fiver credit.'

'I'll take it.' She took out her card.

'Woooo, what yer trying to do, lady, burn me hands. Johnny Cash is king round here, dear. Unless you want me to add VAT?'

She managed to scrape the amount together and left. It was a long way home and after the distance the new phone found its way to the bottom of the canal after she had called the police and reported Maddie's suicide.

'Ann, you're still here, it's late... Come on, let's have you away, your John will be getting worried.' responded Mary to her surprise.

'I wanted to get the bouquets designed for the child's send off,' replied Ann, drawing away on paper.

'Let's take a look then.' Mary hung her coat up in its regular place, right next to where the old Mac lived, they would hang together like an old couple.

'They're beautiful, really done yourself and the family

proud. Now off with yah, before your other half comes a looking.'

'I'll drop the latch on my way out. Night,' replied Ann.

'Thanks. Ohhh, Ann, have you heard of a Bitch?'

'Plenty,' she laughed, 'Why do you ask?' replied Ann surprised at the question.

'Oh, no real reason several people were talking about her over at Maddie's. I hadn't a clue who she was, that's all.' Mary wasn't sure if she should continue, but she needed to know.

Ann responded. 'Apparently she's been taking over a lot of the criminal enterprises around here, and I mean taking over with a violence not seen since the days of the Krays,' Ann told her.

'So, she's real then. Have you seen her in person or know who it is?' asked Mary.

'No, and apparently no one knows her identity, the two so far that did were killed and mutilated, I guess to terrify others into not speaking. See you in the morning. And don't be worrying about people like that.'

Mary heard the latch drop she took a deep breath and dialled Sophie's number.

'Hello.'

'It's only me. You busy tomorrow?' asked Mary.

'I have an hour in the afternoon around three, why?'

'That is just perfect. Can you come over to my flat?'

'Yes, of course is everything okay?'

'I have something for you, a gift, that's all.'

'You sound quiet,' summarised Sophie.

'A little under the weather, a daft cold. See you tomorrow.' Mary replaced the receiver and felt cold.

She slowly rose from the chair then pulled the photo out of her trousers. Staring at the picture was hard enough for any decent person, but to see the culprit as a close friend, virtually family, was ripping Mary apart. She knew that it was her, she just didn't want to believe it. Yet somehow, she knew, and tomorrow she would ask Sophie outright, and then shoot her if it was confirmed. Maddie's death had yet to register with her.

Mary's next job was to remove the old German Luger from the safe and clean it. It may be an antique from the Second World War, but it would kill the Bitch.

The tiredness was clear in Mary after the restless night's sleep. 'Ann, we need more milk?'

'I'll send Kerry.'

'No, will you go please,' Mary didn't look at her.

Ann thought it strange but obliged without question. Her hand reached for the jacket, 'I'll get biscuits as well.'

'Take the money out of the petty cash.' Anxious, Mary checked her watch Mary noted two-forty-five.

The hands showed her three ten just as Sophie entered the hallway.

'Only me,' she tapped softly on the open door, 'Mary, you home?' she asked sweetly.

'In my bedroom,' Mary replied staring at the shape of the Luger on the dressing table. The pistol was covered with a white lace gypsy handkerchief.

'Is that you? Did you do that? Are you the Bitch?' asked Mary passing over the photo. There was to be no pretence from Sophie, she had seen the handle of the Luger in the mirror. She remained silent and sat on the edge of the bed. Her hand slipped inside her handbag; she was up at speed.

'Is that me? Yes, it's me.' And she fired a round in the centre of Mary's chest. Mary spun around her hands fell on the dressing table, her fingers clasped tight as she fell to her knees.

'Did I do that? YES!' And she shot Mary top left of her back.

'And I am who they call the "BITCH". Yes, I am.' And she released another shot in the centre of Mary's back.

Next, as calm as the night sun Sophie picked up the handkerchief and removed the blood splatter from her face.

'Mary, is everything okay? I heard shots,' shouted Ann running into the flat, then the bedroom, her heart virtually stopping when she saw her boss and best friend lying on the floor covered in her own blood. The milk was dropped and splashed everywhere.

Sophie straightened her arm out, the one-off handmade Cartier .22 pistol now pointing straight at Ann's head.

'Now then little Ann, what are we to do with you?' Sophie was wearing the same sick smile that Mary had seen in the photo.

Ann tried to swallow, but the gulp was too big, she wanted to beg for her life, but words wouldn't come out, her best friend, her everything lay dead on the floor.

Sophie moved to Ann the diamond encrusted barrel was pushed against her temple. The bitch took hold of Ann's hand wrapping her fingers around the carter's grip, the gun straight into her bag.

'Tidy up the mess, Ann. I will be back in an hour.'

Sophie left. Ann began to shake and was sick. Sophie was back an hour later with two men Ann had passed out and lay on the bed. Mary was placed in a coffin.

The pig farm, Black Heath Wood. The present

The phone's recording finished with, 'Heads up, Tanya, her brother Gary is dead. At the end of this recording there is also a list naming police officers, local councillors, and others in positions of power on the payroll of the Bitch and Shoebridge. Make sure you're sitting down when you listen to this bit, I was surprised.

'Tell the brigadier that I will resurface at some point, but I have a little house cleaning to do. Take care. Oh, Tan, do me a favour will you, keep an eye on the parlour for a few months, would yah, and Kevin. Make sure he doesn't want for anything. There should be a substantial injection of funds being placed into the Barchards and Wards account.'

Next, she heard, 'PC Fell,' the list had begun. She switched off the phone, turned and looking at her was her own brigadier. She smiled; he slightly moved his mouth. He already knew Sean was okay and responsible for the clean-up. He ensured Doyle had his six hours. He had sent the text and stalled Tanya's interference. But this wasn't anything to do with Whitehall or the government or even the law. So, Tanya didn't need to know. It was the regiment.

Two weeks later, Sean had visited Kev a few times, only at night. Not once had his friend been conscious or showed any signs of change; his 50 / 50 chance of survival had drastically reduced due to infection and his mum had been informed that her son may never leave the hospital, not alive. No one had seen Sean for two days, the warrant out for his arrest was no longer active. A friend of the brigadier had seen to that.

Ahmid's crew were all sat on remand in prison.

2334 hours, Sean attempted to see his friend again 'Mr

Doyle can I have a word,' asked the nurse, Sean stopped, hands in his pockets and his hood up.

'I have some bad news I'm afraid?'

A week later, Sean was leaning against a giant oak tree, his Mac open at the front and blowing gently in the wind. It was a crude attempt to misshape his figure, camouflaging himself against the ancient oak.

He was on the boundary of an old cemetery, one that was full today. Completely full of the living – over six hundred people of all ages and backgrounds had gathered to send-off this young, loveable, kind, and hardworking young person.

The service was over in thirty-five minutes. It took nearly double that time for everyone to leave the graveyard.

Sean waited – not keen for anyone to see him, he quietly watched as the two men tidied up around the hump of fresh soil. He could see they were talking happily to each other, not laughing, but jovial.

A lot he guessed would have taken offence, given they had just filled in the four-foot deep hole. But he knew that anyone who worked around death had to develop a sense of gallows humour, with its limits, of course.

The pair had left and apart from the kneeling old lady changing the flowers on another's final resting place Sean was the only one there. His strides were wide and in three minutes he was reading the freshly chiselled words made permanent in the polished granite.

Put to rest too early before she fully blossomed
Sophie Cellest.

The police report stated she had been shot three times in the upper torso; her arms had been arranged in a cross shape; one of her hands grasped a small object.

The coroner described it as a pendant made by a child from card and painted blue. Sean walked away from the grave, hands in the big pockets, the right one came out holding a bit of paper. He read the receipt from the craft shop: £4.57 for paint, glue, and a brush.

Several days later, under the cover of darkness, and his face partially covered with stubble he stared through the misted glass of the French doors, wet through and hungry.

The key turned on the inside of the doors.

'Come in, you'll catch your death. I wondered when you would make a show,' said Lady De Pen Court, closing the French doors behind him.

'Had some thinking to do.'

'And what was the outcome of this self-torture?' She showed Sean the decanter of whisky.

'You have a way with words, Lady De P...'

'Please, Emma, tonight, please, just Emma, Sean.' She passed the glass over as she turned and walked to the window. 'I could have a room made up for you, if you're staying. Or you could ...' she was looking at the rain.

Sean joined her and removed the glass from her hand.

'Could what?'

Her lips touched his.

A spare room wasn't made up for him.

The following morning both were awake, but neither of them left the covers.

Two hours later in the kitchen

'Nice of you to visit us again, Mr Doyle,' said Caroline.

'I'm looking forward to another one of your breakfasts.'

The meal was over, it was time to bring Lady De Pen Court up to date.

He had completed the file for Henry, which led him to Dr Moe and the work he was doing in the Waterfront hostel. And again, with that wonderful hindsight, the penny dropped regarding the explosion at the old mill: the girl didn't want to leave the cellar because she was looking straight at the BIG man from her nightmares, the minister, Shoebridge. He was the devil that had caged her and her friends, both mentally and physically as he sucked the blood out of them for re-sale. Sean had been correct with his recollection at the auction: the man talking to Sophie had been the minister or as he knew him then, the dog walker who helped him out the cellar.

But how would he have ever guessed that Sophie was the minister's daughter, the biological spawn of a high functioning psychopathic narcissist. This is how she had got the positions she was in. There were more than Christies and the museum.

Yet the world would remember both her and Sir Shoebridge as great people doing lots for the lesser off.

Shoebridge even had a state funeral, attended by the royals. The truth also emerged from Dr Moe. He confessed to shooting Henry on the discovery of hepatitis, and to using Henry's girlfriend and unborn child to produce a new heir for the De Pen Courts. Ironically in doing so he was killing a true heir and Frankensteining the next generation.

'This was unwittingly orchestrated by yourself, Emma. Shoebridge became involved once he discovered that Dr

Moe was sharing his DNA expertise with you, and on all accounts Shoebridge didn't like to share.

Located in the minister's office was the paperwork for a scheduled hit, and with your name at the top of it, Emma. He had falsely documented that you had involvement with Al Qaeda. Ironically, the assassination you arranged yourself, well that ensured Shoebridge shelved his attempt for a while, given the fact the plod would be investigating and you would have increased your own security. This saved your life as he was then killed a few days later.' Sean looked directly into Emma's beautiful eyes.

'Whether it was murder is not yet clear, some still say it was a demon or some powerful witchcraft, and as far as I'm concerned Mulder and Scully can have that one.'

Doyle had discovered all the people involved were in the notebook. The crazy girl had it all in there, as plain as day, once you knew what you were looking at. Pictures of shoes, bridges, sheets of paper with images of medical bags and stethoscopes, all being stapled, images of a bar serving human blood, with the names of the drafts, "A" "AB" and so on.

Others were guns, knives and mannequins licking the shoes and having sex on the bridges. Fire came from the shoes when they touched the bridge. The pages became darker as they were turned.

On the twelfth page was a demon-like figure full of human organs and pound signs floating, mating with dollar signs.

The demon's eyes were shoes and the nose, a bridge. One page at first glance looked out of place. It was a colourful pleasant drawing a vegetable plot, but on closer observation you could see that the sprouting vegetables had different human body parts instead of fruit: arms, and eyes, and legs, and hearts.

The last page of this modern day Ann Frank diary was a portrait of a man. Yet the very talented artist had created a diptych ... the man was Shoebridge – turn the image to the left slightly and there for all to see was Lucifer.

Sean continued debriefing for another hour, answering all Emma's questions. Explaining the complexities of the charity set up by Shoebridge.

'Emma, this charity of yours...'

'Yes.'

'If I got a name of a young girl, could you... uhmm... maybe name something after her? I would also give a donation.'

'You mean as a memorial, to give remembrance?'

'Yeh, yeh ... would it be possible?'

'The artist that the notebook belonged to?'

Sean's grin made an appearance, his head slightly nodding.

'She was clearly someone special to you and of course. Tell me her name and a little bit about her, and we will see what is possible.

'All I know is Lucy.' He threw back the whisky. 'I'll get more information.' Sean stood and placed the glass on the desk and went to leave, door open, his big hands holding it steady, he turned; a sad version of his grin in place.

Emma was about to speak, to ask him to stay, but she stopped herself knowing full well what the answer would be.

The door closed as he left.

At first she sat behind the desk contemplating all that had been talked about for the past couple of hours. In front of her sat the file Sean had compiled. It was in her hand and then in the drawer and locked away. The rage grew inside her. She contemplated the execution of Moe, yet her own guilt made her think. She believed that she instigated Henry leaving in the first place. And had she really done enough to locate him before she commissioned Moe to create a child!

A knock came on the office door.

'Will Mr Doyle be staying for dinner, ma'am?'

'I don't think we will be seeing Mr Doyle for a good while, Caroline.'

Emma knew this because her parting gift to him had been a ferry ticket to Ireland and she had left the credit card open.

TWICE WOUNDED

THANK YOU FOR READING ONE OF MY BOOKS.

Grab your passport and join Sean Doyle in Dublin
Twice Wounded is his next adventure.

Printed in Great Britain
by Amazon